WAKING UP DEAD

THE LIFE AFTER SERIES

WAKING UP DEAD

AMANDA FASCIANO

4 Horsemen
Publications, Inc.

4 Horsemen Publications, Inc.
1497 Main St. Suite 169
Dunedin, FL 34698
4horsemenpublications.com
info@4horsemenpublications.com

Cover and Typeset by S. Wilder
Editor Kristine Cotter

Library of Congress Control Number: 2022945573

Print ISBN: 979-8-8232-0057-8
Hardcover ISBN: 979-8-8232-0141-4
Audio ISBN: 979-8-8232-0055-4
E-Book ISBN: 979-8-8232-0056-1

Table of Contents

CHAPTER 1

The Ghost of Detectives Past

When Detective Cadence Riley awoke, she had no idea where she was or how she had gotten there.

She found herself in some kind of waiting room. Disoriented and mildly panicked, she realized she didn't recognize the room and could not recall how or why she was there. She tried to find something familiar to lock on to, but the décor and the room's inhabitants were strange. Subconsciously, she reached for her belt—for her badge. Her unease grew when she discovered it was not there, and as she moved, she couldn't feel the weight of her gun or its shoulder holster.

As she leaped to her feet, the chair wobbled, threatening to topple over. She focused on those around her, attempting to find a common thread; the act calmed her. The others in the room were all different shapes and sizes, all different ages and ethnicities. There was a middle-aged black man clad in a utility worker's uniform. Beside him sat a young woman in a grocery store uniform. An older man wearing a hunting outfit occupied the corner, humming some random tune. They all seemed to wear the same expression on their face; their eyes glassy and their muscles relaxed. None of them seemed to notice her.

I am a cop, she reminded herself. She was not going to let panic rule her. Someone had to know where they were, right? She moved a couple of chairs down and took a seat next to the utility worker. Getting a solid grip on her emotions, she tried to sound congenial as she greeted him.

"Hey, how's it going?" she asked. He didn't respond. He didn't even twitch. The man gave no sign that he had heard her.

"Hello?" she asked, waving her hand in front of his face.

She looked around to see if anyone looked as if they had heard her. She waved her hands at them. No one acknowledged her. They all just kept staring straight ahead, their eyes glazed over and vacant. The older man in the corner just kept humming his tune.

She got up and crossed the room, running her hands through her dark blonde hair as she went. This had to be a dream, right? A place she didn't recognize, no memory of how she got there, and nothing with her other than the clothes she wore. It absolutely had to be a dream.

She leaned against the wall, refusing to sit back down with the vacant people; they gave her the creeps. This had to be the most ridiculous, pointless dream she had ever had; nothing was happening in it. She crossed her arms over her chest and sighed, leaning her head back against the wall. She broke that pose only to see if she had her cell phone with her. Stranger things had happened in dreams before. Keeping her nerves in check, she reached into her pockets, one by one. She would be damned if she was going to appear as frantic as she felt. Alas, she did not have her phone, and so she went back to fuming at her subconscious for keeping her here.

A door suddenly opened in the wall, which was remarkable because there hadn't been a door before. Cadence straightened, eager to see what would happen. A somewhat harried-looking man emerged. He was one of those people who seemed ageless. He had graying hair and some lines to his face, and his blue-gray eyes seemed to exude both youthful energy and wisdom. Cadence wasn't sure if he was thirty, fifty, or somewhere in between. A file folder was open in his hands.

Osmund Snow was intently reading the description of the person he was there to retrieve; a 30-year-old woman of average height with an athletic build. The latter made sense, given that she had been an officer. Blonde hair and green eyes completed the list of things he needed to search out. He closed the file and examined those waiting. He then spotted her standing by the wall.

"You wouldn't happen to be Detective Cadence Riley by any chance, would you?" he asked, his accent marking him as an Englishman.

At last, her subconscious had decided to do something. She took a step toward him. "I am."

"Oh good," he said with a sigh of relief. "You woke up earlier than expected. I was afraid I'd lost you. That wouldn't do now, would it?"

"Um, I guess not." She shrugged. He beckoned for her to follow him, and she did. Once the door closed behind them, it again disappeared into the wall. She looked him over, trying to figure out his age, or anything else other than his obvious heritage. While not as physically imposing as some, he seemed to be someone who kept fit. "Who are you? How do you know my name?"

"Oh, I'm Osmund Snow. Pleasure to meet you," he replied, offering his hand to shake.

She took the offered hand and shook it. "Nice to meet you, but you didn't answer my second question. And where are we?"

"Ah, yes. Well, why don't you come with me? I'll answer all your questions in my office."

Cadence arched a skeptical eyebrow but followed. Through rows of desks they went, passing by people who sat with headphones on and computer screens in front of them. She could see different things on the screens but couldn't really make out what was being done on them. She held her questions, though, following Osmund Snow through the area to one of the many doors on the far side of the room. He opened the door, which let them into a room that felt oddly familiar.

The walls were a kind of pale cream or beige, the usual color office designers choose when trying to stay neutral, but not go with white. There were two desks facing each other. One was obviously his, with files and papers on it. The other was clear and didn't seem to belong to anyone.

He gestured toward the empty desk as he closed the door. "Have a seat." As he settled into his, he looked up at her. "Has anyone ever told you your eyes are the most beautiful shade of jade?"

Cadence looked off, slightly embarrassed at his random compliment. "Yeah, uh … thanks. So … where is this place?" At this point, Cadence assumed that she was dreaming. *But hey*, she thought, *I might as well find out what my subconscious has cooked up for me this time.*

"I suppose limbo might be the most proper term," he said and shrugged, looking slightly embarrassed.

"Limbo? So, I'm what? Waiting to come out of a coma or something?" That made sense as to why she was dreaming at any rate, though she didn't recall being injured. Her brows furrowed as she realized that the more she thought about it, the harder it seemed for her to recall anything specific about recent days.

"Not quite," he said and leaned forward, his icy eyes searching her jade ones. "Detective Riley, I'm sorry to have to be the one to tell you, but you're dead."

Cadence sat there for a moment in stunned silence, then shook her head and laughed. "Nice joke. Is this some kind of trick the guys put together?" She momentarily forgot that this was supposed to be a dream and began looking around for cameras or people peeking in and getting their laugh out of it. She was a bit discomfited to find no evidence of any of that.

"No, no joke, I'm afraid," Snow said. "You've died. This is a place for processing, of sorts."

"Processing? For what? Heaven? Hell?"

"Well, neither, to be honest. I don't want to get into theological discussions about the existence of Heaven or Hell or what they are. All I can do is present you with the choice you now have. You can end—go into whatever kind of heaven or hell your own personal ideology and conscience creates for you, or you can stay here and help out."

Once again, she tried looking for cameras or snickering cops. This had to be a joke. She started opening drawers, in the vain hopes of finding some kind of recording device. The closing of the drawers became successively harder until she was yanking them open and slamming them shut.

"This is a dream. This is a joke," she kept muttering to herself, over and over again.

"Detective Riley, I can understand you're upset, but really..."

"You can understand?" she yelled, jumping up to loom over him as he sat in his chair. "Well, I'm so happy that you can understand. That makes me feel so much better."

"Neither sarcasm nor temper tantrums will help or change the situation."

"I don't care. I'm not dead." She crossed her arms over her chest and glared down at him as she remained standing, her expression daring him to gainsay her.

Snow opened the top file on his desk. "You were kicked..." He began.

"I am not dead! I don't care what that damned file says!" she protested, interrupting him.

"... and the impact of the kick threw you over the rail of the fire escape. You plunged seven stories to your death."

"I didn't die!" she yelled. "This is just a dream, some stupid dream I'm having while I wait to wake up in the hospital with probably a few broken bones and a wicked headache."

Snow was on his feet in an instant, his icy eyes hardening, going arctic. His voice, when he spoke, lost all of the softness and compassion that had given her the first impression of an English librarian. "Do you want me to tell you that your head hit the pavement first? That it cracked open like a melon under that fellow Gallagher's mallet? That your legs broke in so many places that they made a half circle out and away from your body? That, between the force of the kick and the impact of your landing, your ribs simply became bits of bone matter that lodged in your lungs like pebbles on the bottom of a stream? Because I could tell you all of that and more, but I really don't see how it is going to help the situation. I know it is difficult to come to grips with, but come to grips with it, you must, in order to make the decision that is now before you."

Snow caught himself and straightened up, taking a deep breath. After a moment, he sat back down, leaving a stunned Cadence to slump back into her seat, as well. "I'm sorry," he said after a moment, his voice softening once again.

She nodded in silence, her mind spinning as she tried to get a handle on her thoughts and emotions. "Okay… assuming you're telling the truth, why am I dressed in my normal clothes? Aren't dead people supposed to wear robes or something?"

Snow relaxed back into himself and shook his head with a bit of a smile. "No, you appear as you would normally." He gestured to her clothing. "Your clothes are a mental image. A projection of your former physical self."

"Well, I'm glad that I can, at least, remember enough to project. Why am I having such a hard time remembering other things?" she asked.

"That's a common side effect of dying. You'll get your memories back in time, I promise. Though some you may wish had stayed lost."

"What was with the people out in that waiting room? And what was with that waiting room, anyway?" she asked.

"The waiting room is a place we put souls who are waiting to be processed. Most of the time, we have enough people here that not many end up in there, but if everyone is occupied, then the excess souls will wait there."

"So, you are one of these processors?"

"Not exactly," Snow said with a vague smile.

"What are you then?" Cadence asked.

"I am what you have been given the option to be; a police officer of sorts."

"So…you're telling me there are cops in the afterlife?" she asked, looking at him in disbelief.

"Yes," he said. He nodded and closed the file, now that she was talking a bit more sensibly.

"For what? Ghosts stealing other ghosts' chains and sheets?"

Snow gave Cadence a sour look, obviously not amused with her sarcasm. "No. We more or less police the interaction between haunting spirits and what your generation terms ghost hunters."

"Why?" That was all Cadence could think to ask.

"Well, back before science got interested in ghosts and haunted locations, there really wasn't much for us to do, except to police interactions with non-human spirits. However, given the influx of interest in the so-called 'paranormal' in the last century or so, we have all sorts of work to do now."

"And again, I ask why?" She reiterated.

"Well, we can't let on too much now, can we? The afterlife is supposed to be this great mystery, and it needs to remain so. Our job is to make sure that the haunting spirits don't sit down to a cup of tea with the psychics and ghost hunters to spill the beans, so to speak."

"So, you have a force that polices hauntings?"

"Yes," Snow replied with a shrug.

"Well, why let any communications happen at all, then? If you want to keep things so secretive, why not just disallow it completely?"

"It's not so simple," he said. Sighing and leaning forward on his desk and folding his hands together. "There have always been interactions between the living and the dead. The veil between the two planes of existence is too thin to stop communication. Think about it; stories of ghosts and demons and hauntings have been around for centuries. Millennia, perhaps. Back before such things were even written down. Given the scientific developments of the last few decades and human nature's drive to explain the unexplained, we've had to become a bit more proactive in making sure not too much proof gets out there. It still has to be a question of belief among people. It still needs to be something of a mystery."

Cadence nodded, taking in that information. She pressed her lips together in a thin line as she tried to figure out what to ask next. She took a deep breath, trying to wrap her mind around it all. A million things were going through her head—ways to protest that this was actually happening, ways to accept it, attempting to recall her life and what had happened or what she had left undone.

"Oh, God," she blurted out suddenly. "My cat ... he'll starve." In trying to remember, she had managed to get a glimpse of something. She had seen her cat, a riot of black fur. He was rubbing himself up against her legs as she got home from work, meowing at her.

Snow shook his head. "Your partner has claimed him; he's well looked after."

"How do you know?"

"We tend to know a lot around here, especially when processing the new arrivals. Now look, I can give you a night to say goodbye to loved ones or see special places once more, but that's all. I'll need a decision by morning."

"A decision on what?" Cadence asked.

"On whether or not you want to continue making a difference, being an officer of the law. A different kind of law. Or whether you would simply prefer to go on to whatever personal heaven or hell awaits you."

"Well, that's a hell of a choice," she said as she grumbled. "No pun intended."

"It is, yes," he agreed, "but a necessary one. I know thrusting this decision on you is asking a lot, but you have to move on, in one capacity or another."

"So, if it is all so important that I move on, and I can barely remember my past, why do I need a night to say goodbye?"

"Because as your memories come back, it will be important that you know you had one last chance to go home, to say goodbye to a friend. It helps ease your soul."

"Who or what do I get to say goodbye to?"

"Well, you can say goodbye to your partner, your cat, the precinct—anyplace or anyone you wish to, but be careful, time is limited."

Cadence nodded and took a moment to think. Where should she have Snow take her? To her home? Maybe, that might jog some memories loose, at least. To her precinct? Yes, it would be nice to say goodbye to her fellow detectives. She couldn't recall many specifics of her partner other than the knowledge that they had been good friends and his name, but she definitely wanted to say goodbye to him. What about family? She searched for a moment and then came up with at least one piece of knowledge, if not a memory, per se. Her family was no more. They were all dead.

She paused, brow furrowed. "Are any of my family ghosts? Haunting spirits?"

"I …" he faltered, "I don't have their files. I'm sorry." He looked down at the desk for a moment, moving her file aside.

Cadence lifted a brow as Snow's body language and tone suggested he was lying, but she let it go for now. "It sucks to say goodbye to people. Especially if they can't hear me or answer me."

"I can help with that, at least for some of the living. The cat will be able to see and hear you."

"He will?" she asked, clearly surprised.

"Yes. You didn't really think that they looked so steadily at nothing, did you?"

"No shit. He was looking at ghosts?"

"Very likely," Snow said.

"Huh, go figure. So, how can you help with the people?"

"I can let you talk to them through a dream."

"Really? How?" Cadence asked, surprised.

"I'll show you when the time comes. I'm assuming you'll want to speak with your partner. Anyone else?"

"No, no one else," she said and shook her head. "At least, I don't think so. I can't remember anyone else. But I'd like to stop by my home and the precinct."

"That won't be a problem at all." He watched her as she thought, and knew that she was trying to stretch her mind, to force herself to remember. Part of him wanted to help her, to open her file and let her go over it, let the memories come rushing back. But he knew that it was better to let her deal with this incrementally. It was an organic process and rushing things often resulted in damage to the spirit.

"Well, I guess we should get a move on then, right?" she asked, cutting into his thoughts. She had given up on trying to remember, trying to force her mind to recall what it could not.

He saw the change in her face and recognized it for what it was. It was the resolution to get on with things, no matter what. It was something he was guilty of at times. He nodded. "Right," he said as he rose. "Let's go."

CHAPTER 2

The Hardest Part of Goodbye is Saying it

Cadence lugged two heavy suitcases up the stairs toward her new apartment. She was very thankful that this was the last load of things from the truck.

"You had to get the third-floor walk-up, didn't you?" Andy asked as he carried two boxes in his arms, climbing the stairs behind her.

"Quit your bitching," she said with a grimace as she hoisted the roller suitcases over the last step to the third-floor landing. "At least I didn't get the one on the fifth floor." She looked behind her and grinned at her partner before moving down the hallway to her door.

"Yeah, yeah," he grumbled.

Once inside the apartment, they put down what they had been carrying and flopped on the black microfiber-covered couch. They had spent the morning bringing up all of the furniture and putting it all together before they started to bring up the boxes and bags. This meant that they had the couch and television in place so they could relax after it was all done.

Andy looked down as Cadence's phone landed in his lap. "Why is your phone visiting me?" he asked, looking over at her.

"You call, I pay," she replied. "But no weird stuff on the pizza this time."

"Pineapple is not weird stuff," he said and protested with a roll of his eyes. He got up, his muscular frame topping six feet tall, and glowered at her for a moment before moving to the kitchen counter where they had tossed all of the "new resident" papers, which included coupons for the local pizza place.

"Fruit is for dessert or a snack; it is not a pizza topping," she said. Even though her muscles were protesting movement, she got up as well and headed for the fridge. She out two beers from the case she had put in there when they first arrived. They were now blissfully cold. Grabbing her keychain, she used the bottle opener she had on it to remove the caps. She handed Andy his beer when he hung up the phone.

"I knew there was a reason I agreed to help you move in here," he said, taking the beer and downing a swig of it.

"Yes, pizza and beer. I know how to bribe well." They clinked the necks of their bottles together and drank.

"I'm honestly surprised you didn't stay at your old place," Andy said as they sat back down on the couch.

"Nah," she said, shaking her head. "I couldn't. After Mom had died, once I was able to start donating her *things, the place just felt, I don't know, alien," she said as she shrugged. "Once the stuff that made the place our home started going, it just wasn't home anymore. You know?"*

"I get it," he said. He looked around the sparse apartment. "Are they going to let you paint the place?" he asked, noting the walls were all white, and he knew how much she hated white walls.

"Yeah, I have to repaint them white before I leave, though. I was thinking a light blue or pale gray or something."

"I don't know," Andy said, looking around. "I see it more in a kind of pink color."

"Pink?" she asked, looking at him in disbelief.

"Yeah." He grinned, knowing he was getting her goat. "I mean, you're a girl and all. Aren't you supposed to be all pinks and purples and lace and..." He was cut off by a couch cushion hitting him in the face.

"Sexist asshole," Cadence said, though she was laughing as she said it. They both laughed, and he tossed the pillow back at her.

After taking another drink of his beer, he leaned back and eyed her for a moment. "You sure you're going to be okay here?"

"Why wouldn't I be?" she asked, a little surprised at his concern.

"Eh, never mind. I know you can take care of yourself."

Cadence nodded, more gratified by his knowledge of her abilities than his concern for her. A knock sounded on the door, and she rose with a groan. "Man, I haven't been this sore in ages."

"You're getting old, lady," Andy called over his shoulder, and he didn't even have to turn to know she was flipping him off for the comment.

The memories of who Andy was and how close they had been came flooding back. A few months after they had been partnered, she and Andy had traded keys to each other's homes. Just in case. That had been six and a half years ago. They had been partners, best friends, and confidants but had always managed to stay just this side of the line that led to them being something more.

As Cadence stood in her apartment, looking around the living room, she thought it seemed a little strange. Somehow, her death had made it seem more foreign to her. She was looking at the place now, not as her home, but as if she was visiting someone else's. She knew that Andy had been here to collect her cat. Snow had told her that much. The lack of the little fur ball in the apartment was very obvious to Cadence.

She looked around at the books she would never get around to finishing. The movies she wished she could watch one more time. She paused by the bookshelf and frowned at an empty shelf. The lines that lacked dust in some places were a stark contrast to the light layer of dust on the rest of the shelf, outlining that some things were missing. "My pictures are gone," she said as she reached out to touch a dust-free line where a frame had been on the shelf.

"Sorry?" Snow asked as he turned from looking at her movie collection.

"I remember, I had pictures on this shelf. Family pictures, my folks, my brother. They're gone."

"Perhaps your partner claimed them when he claimed your cat? Given how long the two of you knew each other, it's very likely he knew what your family meant to you."

Cadence nodded, acknowledging that Snow was right. Andy had probably taken them. She doubted anyone else would have come to her apartment to remove things. Andy was the only one with a key, and she doubted the building manager would be so swift to start taking things out of her apartment since she was paid until the end of the month.

As she looked around, she realized how true Snow's words had been when he said she barely spent any time at home. Other than the memory of moving in, with Andy's help, she didn't really have any fond memories of this place, even though she had lived here for five years. On work days, she really only came home to sleep, shower, and change. On days off, she was at home a little longer, but even then, it wasn't by much. She would take her time with breakfast and coffee, but then fill her days with things to do and activities that took her out of the house.

The apartment reflected that, too. Dishes were in the sink from that morning's breakfast. But that was really the only sign the place was lived in. Otherwise, it could have just been an unoccupied, furnished apartment. Without her cat and her family photos, there was little to no personalization. Her brow furrowed as she looked around again and realized just how sparse the place was.

"Is something wrong?" Snow asked as he watched her.

"No, just..." she said, trying to find the words.

"Saying goodbye?" he suggested.

"More like realizing there is nothing here to really say goodbye to," she said.

Snow nodded and crossed the room to her, holding out his hand. "Then perhaps we should head over to your precinct building?" he offered. She nodded and took his hand so he could teleport them.

The colors of her apartment seemed to blend and streak like a watercolor painting someone left in the wind and rain, and the room felt like it was spinning. Then, in an instant, everything solidified once more and she was standing beside her desk at work. The windows reflected the inside of the precinct as the night beyond them rendered them into mirrors. Despite the late hour, there were still a few detectives in the office, but it didn't look like Andy was one of them.

It was a tradition in the station that when someone died, you wrote them a goodbye message and put it on their desk or in their mailbox. Her desk had been covered in sticky notes. It made her smile a little as she saw it. She moved around her desk as she read them.

"That's a nice gesture," Snow said as he read some of them as well.

"It is. I can remember when I started here; the Captain said that it helped us have closure when we lost someone. I know I've written them a few times. I never thought I would be reading ones for me."

"No one ever does," Snow said solemnly.

As they stood there reading the notes, a plainclothes detective with a name badge stating "Keller" came up to the desk, a note in his hand. He was larger than she remembered Andy being, with a barrel chest and some mid-life weight to his middle. He looked drawn, and his eyes were red. She had noticed him at his desk when they arrived and an officer had congratulated him for having gotten the arrest of the year. Yet for such an accomplishment, he looked far from happy. Of course, no one was ever happy when one of their own died.

"Wish I'd known you better, Riley," Keller said, his voice rough. "I wish today had gone differently." He frowned deeply and then placed the sticky note on her desk lamp. There were only two words written in black ink on the orange square of paper: "I'm sorry."

Cadence turned to Snow. "What does he mean by that?"

"That he wishes he'd gotten to know you better?" Snow asked, acting deliberately obtuse.

"That he wished today had gone differently," she said, crossing her arms in front of her chest.

"I would imagine everyone wishes the day had gone a different way when one of their own dies."

"You are a terrible liar, Snow. Was he involved in what happened?"

"He was." Snow nodded. "But that is something that you will remember in your own time."

Another detective, one who must have been new to the precinct, came up to Keller looking puzzled. "What's with all the notes on the desk? Is it some kind of prank?" He hadn't been there long enough to know.

"I wish it was, kid," Keller, who called anyone under 45 a kid, said.

The new detective leaned forward and read some of the notes. "Woah, wait. She died?"

"In the line of duty," Keller said. "So, if you have anything you wanted to say to her, write a note and put it on the desk."

The new detective looked a little shaken that someone he had just seen that morning could be dead a few hours later. Being slapped in the face with your own mortality has a tendency to provoke that kind of reaction. Cadence wandered away from her paper-covered desk toward the office of her Captain. Snow followed at a discreet distance.

The Captain was hunched over his desk, entrenched in paperwork. A cup of coffee sat on one side, which had long since gone cold. His door was open, so Cadence drifted into his office, feeling somewhat odd because of entering without pausing to knock. Captain Rodriguez was a man in his fifties who usually looked very good for his age. Tonight, he looked tired, haggard, and overworked. She had seen that look on his face a few times before. Each time had been when an officer had gone down in the line of duty.

"I've always hated seeing him like this," she said, whispering to Snow.

"You don't have to whisper. They're not going to hear you," Snow said.

"Oh, right." She frowned. Out in the bullpen, there was a constant murmur of noise from voices and phones and such. Due to the noise, she hadn't bothered to try to be quiet. In Rodriguez's office, however, there was no such background noise, and she had given in to the desire to not break the quiet solitude in which he worked. She stood there for a few minutes, just watching Captain Rodriguez as he filled out paperwork.

"Are you saying goodbye, Cadence? Or putting off our final stop?" Snow asked. Cadence opened her mouth to protest, but then closed it when she realized he was right. She wasn't lingering at the precinct because she was going to miss it. To her, the station represented the part of her job she detested: the paperwork. There was some camaraderie and such to be had there, but the majority of time spent here was spent doing just what her Captain was currently saddled with. She wasn't going to miss it, and there was no pretending she was saying goodbye to it. He was right. She was putting off their final stop.

"Fine, you're right. Let's go," she sighed, reaching over to put her hand in his so he could transport them once again.

Cadence stepped off the treadmill, uncapping her water and taking a big drink from the bottle. The gym at the Police Academy was a popular place, and there were several other recruits working out. It was noisy with clanging weights and music, and the smell of sweat seemed embedded in the walls, but she enjoyed it. The treadmill was the last part of her workout routine, so as she recapped her water, she began to make her way to the door. Just a short walk across the campus separated her from a gloriously hot shower.

Going from the musty, sweaty gym to the fresh air of the night was a small luxury in and of itself. The light breeze helped cool and dry the perspiration on her skin. Cade enjoyed her walks, enjoying the silence of the night.

It was a nice change from the noise of her classmates. She was halfway across the quad when she saw them. Three guys from her class who had apparently elected themselves class assholes. They picked on the guys in their class that were smaller than them, and they treated the few women that were in class even worse. She was determined to ignore them as both she and their group approached the fountain in the center of the quad. She hoped they would be too busy or entertained with their own conversation to notice her.

"Well, if it isn't little Riley," said Petrucci, who was the ringleader of the group. His greeting was followed by snickers from the other two. Cade rolled her eyes and continued on; her eyes fixed on her dorm building. "Hey, I'm talking to you," he said in a growling voice.

"How lovely for you," she said, sounding bored. "Now, excuse me, I have a burning desire to be anywhere else but here." She hadn't slowed or turned, but the two others with Petrucci sprinted up to block her path. "Really?" she asked, looking between the two grinning fools.

Petrucci's massive hand came down on her shoulder, and she spun around, knocking his hand off of her in the process. She was of normal height for a woman, but he still towered a good foot above her. The buzz cut of his hair made his head look huge, almost comical. "What's the problem, Riley?" he asked, smiling. "Got a rug to munch?" He had made it known in classes that he thought any woman in this line of work had to be a lesbian.

"What's the problem, Petrucci," she echoed his words, "the circle jerk end early?"

For a big guy, he could sometimes move fast. Her head snapped suddenly to the side, and she saw stars a second or two before she felt the sting of his hand-print on the side of her face. She hadn't anticipated he would actually hit her, but the slap only served to anger her, not make her cower. As she turned her head back to him, she noticed the stillness of his partners, who were definitely not smiling anymore. She wasn't sure if they were surprised that he had hit her as well, or if they were simply preparing for a fight.

"Wow! Guess I hit a nerve," she said. He moved to strike her again, but she was ready for it this time. "But you made a big mistake," she continued, catching his hand with hers.

"Let me guess." He sneered, not dropping his hand. "Thinking I could get away with hitting a woman?"

"Nope. Thinking I wouldn't fight back." With that, she threw his hand aside and punched him hard in the gut.

He doubled over as his friends grabbed her arms and pulled her back away from Petrucci. She kicked high as they pulled her and landed a kick on Petrucci's jaw. He howled in pain and anger. Cadence managed to get one of her arms away from the guy on her left. Still, the guy on the right was quick, and he kicked her legs out from under her and then let her go. She fell unceremoniously to the ground. Petrucci quickly straddled her, kneeling over her waist.

"You'll pay for that," he growled.

"Hey," another male voice cut in, trying to break up the fight.

"How unoriginal of you," she quipped back to Petrucci as she threw another punch, but this time, he caught her hand in his. He pulled his free hand back, aiming squarely for her face, and brought it down with the full *force of his strength and anger. Cade twisted violently to one side as his sledgehammer-like hand came down. The sound of the impact of Petrucci's fist on the concrete was punctuated by pops and cracks as bones broke and was quickly followed by the sound of his scream. He fell over to one side, and Cade scrambled to her feet, as Petrucci's goons were now occupied with trying to get their leader on his feet.*

A hand on her arm made her rear back, ready to punch until she recognized the face as someone else from her class. "Easy," he said. "I'm on your side. Let's get out of here, though."

She nodded, and as Petrucci's friends got him back up and began leading him off toward the clinic, Cade and her new friend began heading toward the dorms. "You're Riley, right?" he asked.

"Yeah, and you?"

"Andrew Halleran, but call me Andy."

Andy sat on the brown leather couch in his apartment. The television was on, but he wasn't really paying attention to the show. His eyes were red, the only evidence of his tears. He had never lost a partner before. Hell, she had been practically the only partner he'd had.

Going back to the precinct alone after the arrest had been awful. Being there had been worse. The silence of the officers at the precinct when he came in with Keller and Saddiq to process Scott Sage was deafening. They all knew. When an officer was injured in the line of duty, word spread fast. When an officer lost their life, it spread like wildfire. He had somehow managed to wait until he was home to rage and cry.

When the Captain told him to take some time off and make an appointment with the police shrink, he took it in stride and didn't argue. He needed the time off, needed to adjust, and he couldn't handle the silence and looks that followed him around like a cloud. A few of the other detectives had come to him at the station, offering their condolences. Most had not been able to brave the awkwardness of the situation or the cloud of anger he had cloaked himself in to get through the remainder of his duties that day. Many others couldn't bring themselves to talk to him. They didn't know what to say in the face of a situation every single one of them prayed to never find themselves in.

Once off the clock, he had gone to Cadence's apartment and gotten her cat, Darwin. He wasn't about to leave that black ball of fuzz she had raised from a kitten all alone. He had also grabbed a few pictures of hers that he knew meant the world to her, mostly pictures of her family, since she had lost them all so young. The pictures were in a box in his room. Darwin sat next to him on the couch, having not left his side since being let out of the cat carrier.

The cat turned sharply, looking at Cadence as she and Snow materialized in the room. It meowed and began purring, looking off to the right where she was. Andy looked down at the sudden meow and petted the cat.

"What's up, Darwin?" he asked. Cade noticed that when he spoke, his voice was rough, as if he had been screaming earlier. The cat didn't answer, but it kept its yellow eyes glued to where Cadence stood.

Cadence wrapped her arms around her middle as she looked at Darwin and Andy. She wanted to hold her cat; draw comfort from snuggling him as she usually did. It also left her raw inside to see the pain and grief so very visible on Andy's face. Snow put a hand on her shoulder.

"Are you okay?" he asked, his voice gentle.

"I'm dead. What do you think?" she replied dryly.

"I think seeing the grief you leave behind can just about kill you again if you let it." Snow meant that in a very real way, not that Cadence would know.

"I'm fine," she replied, her voice harsher in its insistence than perhaps she meant it to be.

Osmund nodded and took his hand from her shoulder, taking a step back to let her have space. Cadence moved forward toward the couch. Darwin's eyes steadily followed her as she moved. He purred a little louder as she neared. Andy, however, thought that had to do with his petting of the cat. Cadence smiled at Darwin and reached out but paused as she remembered she couldn't touch him. She frowned at the reminder that she would never again feel the soft velvet of his thick black fur. She took a deep, if unsteady, breath and tried to clamp down on her emotions.

"Take care of him for me, Dar. He needs you now."

The cat meowed in response and turned, padding onto Andy's lap, curling up there. Snow inched forward, following Cadence toward the couch. "We'll have to wait for him to go to sleep for you to talk to him. Judging by the beer cans on the coffee table, it won't be long."

"He's blaming himself," she said quietly.

"He lost a partner in the line of duty. Not to mention a friend and someone he loved," said Osmund.

"He's been crying … He never cries."

"He's never really lost anyone like this; I would venture."

"No, he hasn't. His family is still alive. His grandparents died when he was a kid, but he was still in elementary school. He lost a couple of friends in high school to a drunk-driving accident. But …"

"But you are the first person he has loved as an adult to die. And to die when he believes he had the power to stop it."

"I know what he's thinking. That he should have been faster getting in there. That he should have taken the fire escape instead of me. It's what I would be doing if the situation was reversed. He's blaming himself."

"Should he be?" Snow asked, curious to find out if she blamed her former partner for her demise.

"No." She turned to look angrily at Snow, incredulous that he could even suggest such a thing. "Shit happens. It's the risk you take when you sign up for the badge."

Snow nodded and crossed his arms over his chest as Andy rose from the couch and headed into his bedroom, Darwin tucked under his arm. He gestured for Cadence to lead, and the two ghosts followed the officer unseen into his bedroom.

When he began undressing for bed, Cadence turned to face Snow to give Andy his privacy. "So how come you could touch me?" she asked suddenly. "That's something I meant to ask. We walk through walls and furniture here, yet the floor holds us up. You can touch me, and the things in your office seemed solid enough."

Snow chuckled lightly. "It's something of a trick of the mind. The floor here holds us up because we think it should. Because this is where we want to be. As for things being solid, we're solid to each other because we exist on the same plane. We're both ghosts. He's alive, so his plane of existence is just ever so slightly removed from ours. And because of that, we pass through the things here if we wish to."

Cadence gave him a skeptical look, but shrugged. "I suppose that's what I get for asking. Were you always a ghost? Is that how you are such an expert on this crap?"

Snow drew himself up to his full height. "This crap, as you call it, is the very fiber of our existence. Understanding it can be very fundamental, especially when your job entails dealing very heavily with haunting spirits."

"And processing newbie ghosts who need to make afterlife decisions?"

"Yes, that too, as they do tend to have more questions than a toddler."

Cadence took that in stride and calmly stuck her tongue out at him. "You didn't answer my question."

"Sometimes I hate dealing with detectives," he sighed. "No, I have not always been a ghost. I was an inspector for Scotland Yard. I died in 1968. And when I died, I was given the same choice you have been presented with."

"So, you're a cop? And here I thought you were some kind of ghostly guidance counselor." Osmund graced her with an irritated look, which only provoked a grin from her.

"Oh yes, get your laughs in now. This isn't going to be as easy as you want it to be." He moved forward, and Cadence looked to see that more time had passed than she had thought. Andy was fast asleep in bed. Darwin had curled up at his feet, but the cat was watching her intently.

Cadence followed Snow to the bed and sat down beside Andy at Snow's behest. "Now take his hand in one of yours," he coached her. "Then take my hand in your other one." She did so, following his instructions without a word. "Now close your eyes," Snow said. "I'll do the rest." Cadence closed her eyes.

The sun was high in the sky as Cadence climbed the creaking metal stairs of the building's fire escape. The breeze brought the not-so-pleasant scent of the garbage dumpster to her nose, despite being almost seven floors up. The bulletproof vest felt bulky, as always, but was necessary. She climbed to the seventh-floor landing and stopped by the window there as she unholstered her gun.

The room beyond the glass was devoid of people and very spartan in its furnishings. A twin bed and a dresser were all it housed. The room could have been mistaken for vacant if it weren't for the clothes sticking out of a dresser drawer and the cell phone charging on the dresser top. Cade made note of where the closet door and the door into the room were. She then pulled the radio that was velcroed to the shoulder of her vest from its resting place.

"Riley, clear," she said into it, whispering.

She ducked back by the wall to keep out of sight as a towel-clad man walked into the room. She could feel the adrenaline pumping through her as she strained to hear noises in the room, to tell where he was, but over the noise of the city, in general, it was almost impossible to make out individual footsteps in the next room.

A thudding sound and muffled voices were heard from inside the apartment, and a second later, Cade saw the window beside her lift open. Scott Sage, the man who all evidence was pointing to as the Sommerset Strangler, began to climb out onto the landing of the fire escape but stopped halfway out of his bedroom when he saw Detective Riley there with her gun leveled at him. He had managed to dress quickly in jeans and a T-shirt, although he was barefooted.

"Freeze," she barked at him. He glanced back into the room, and the sounds of the other officers starting to break down the door could be heard. He put his hands up and moved fully out onto the staircase landing. Cadence moved to him, pulling cuffs from the side of her belt. As she opened her mouth to start reading him his Miranda rights, he lunged into her, using the weight of his body to try to knock her down.

The fire escape protested with a metallic scream as Sage landed on top of Cadence, knocking them both to the metal-grate landing outside his window. Her hand released as it hit the landing awkwardly, and her gun fell from her grasp to the ground seven stories below. Despite that setback, she did manage to get a cuff on one of his wrists as he picked himself up off of her, and she followed him right up, getting back on her feet. She reached for his other hand as he tried to pull the cuffed one away from her. He twisted, and with his free hand, he punched her, his fist impacting her cheek. He tore his cuffed hand away from her in the brief moment she was stunned, but she moved her leg in a well-trained strike, sweeping his legs out from under him. Flecks of rust fell like snow from the fire escape as the entire thing shuddered under the impact of Sage's hard fall back to the landing.

Her cheek and jaw would be black and blue later, she knew, but it didn't matter. What mattered was getting this psychopath contained and under arrest. She bent down to wrench his arm up to continue cuffing him, but he twisted himself around, putting his arm out of reach.

All the while, they could both hear the thudding of the door being broken down within the apartment. The sound of wood splintering echoed through the apartment and open window as the door broke and Keller and Saddiq, with Cade's partner Andy hot on their heels, ran into the apartment.

Sage knew that if he didn't get her off of him that he would never be able to get away. He swung his legs around and kicked up with all of his might. His feet connected squarely with her chest, and he threw all of his strength, heightened by his adrenaline, into the kick.

The forceful kick was stronger than she anticipated, and it threw her back. She grabbed for the railing, trying to steady herself and maybe use the momentum to propel herself back into the fight with Sage. However, the sun, rain, and years of exposure, as well as wear and tear, had worn the strength of the metal away. The railing was rusted and the metal was brittle. It gave way under the force of her weight. As she grabbed the railing, it snapped off, doing nothing to keep her from falling. She fell backward in an arc away from the fire escape, watching as the window of the apartment, and Sage himself, grew smaller and further away.

Entering Andy's dream, Cadence found herself outside Scott Sage's bedroom. The setting of the dream had triggered the memory of how she died, and now she didn't think she would ever forget the place. Apparently, it weighed heavily on Andy's mind, too, since it was his dream. She had materialized on the landing of the fire escape, where she had last been wrestling with Sage. Andrew was just walking into the room. When he saw her, he ran forward and grabbed her arm, pulling her into the room through the open window and into a hug. She hugged him back fiercely, fighting back tears.

"I'm so sorry," Andrew finally said after a few moments of silence between them. "I'm so sorry. I should never have let you take the fire escape."

"It was a solid plan, Andy," she said and found her voice as gruff with raw emotions as his was. "It's not your fault. It's no one's fault but Sage's."

"We got him, though. He's in jail. If there is any justice in the world, he'll get death." He finally let her go, and his brown eyes roamed her face as if searching it for answers. "I'm dreaming, aren't I?"

"Yeah," she said. "You are. I had to come and say goodbye, though. Make sure you knew it wasn't your fault."

"But it was." He ran a hand through his brown hair, something he did when he was upset, and turned away.

"No, Andy, it wasn't. Come on now, don't be an idiot." She moved forward and caught his arm, turning him around to face her once more. "You know as well as I do that when you sign up for the badge, risk of injury or death goes with it. And at least you guys got the bastard. No one else will be hurt because of him. Just please, stop blaming yourself. You all need to stop blaming yourselves. You, Keller, Saddiq, all of you. It sucks, but that goes with the job."

He searched her eyes for a long moment, then lowered his gaze. "I loved you, you know."

"We were partners and best friends for years, of course ..."

"No." He interrupted her. "Not like that. Not as partners, not as friends. The timing just never worked out, and I never got up the courage to say it. I kept telling myself that I didn't want to ruin the partnership or the friendship. I came up with a thousand different excuses over the years, and it boils down to me never having the balls to tell you. I loved you. Hell, before we got the call to run back up on the Sage arrest, I was about to ask you out. I'd finally worked up the courage for that. Too little too late, I guess."

She rocked back on her heels as if she had been slapped. She had never known. What was even more shocking was the sudden realization that she had loved him as well. She had spent eight years with him as her best friend. The person she had spent the majority of her time with, even when not on the job. When she did date someone else, she always compared that person to Andy and the relationship she had with him. That was when the tears did fall.

"I love you, too," she said and forgot that she should probably use the past tense. They stood looking at each other, just letting the words sit there for a moment. It was as if, for just that moment, time stood still. Cadence forcefully shook herself out of it. He had been right in saying it was too little too late now. "But you still have a life, Andy. Live it. Please. And don't ever be afraid to tell someone how you feel again. Take it from me, life is too short," she said and managed an ironic grin through her tears.

He slid his arms around her again, holding her close and nuzzling into her hair. "Don't go. Please. Let me wake up and find this was all just a nightmare, and you're still here. Please…" his voice broke, and a fresh wash of tears rained from his eyes as his body shuddered against hers.

His tears brought fresh sobs from her. It wasn't fair, damn it. She didn't want to go. Hell, she didn't want to be dead. But to realize now that love had been at her fingertips, all this time, tore at her. The time they had wasted being too blind or too cowardly to own up to their feelings was sickening. And now it was all too late.

"We need to go," she could hear Osmund's voice in her head, even though it seemed that Andy couldn't hear him. She did have to go. She had already been told she couldn't stay and haunt, and honestly, she didn't want to haunt Andy. That would only keep him from moving on with his life. Reluctantly, she pushed away from him, breaking their embrace. She lifted her tear-stained face to regard his, and she took a deep breath.

"Grieve for me, Andy, but move on, please. I don't want you to spend the rest of your life beating yourself up over what happened. I don't want you hanging on to some romanticized notion of me and not living your life and loving someone else." He opened his mouth to protest, but she lifted a hand to stop him. "No. You will find love with someone else. Only next time, don't be so afraid to say something. I know it sounds trite and cliché, but time really is precious. Live and move on, Andy, please."

Andy frowned but nodded, tears spilling over his cheeks again, choking him up to where he couldn't say anything in reply. Cadence fought down the urge to hug him again, knowing if she held him again that her resolve would crumble. She had to go. If she didn't, she likely never would. She climbed back out the window and stood once more on the fire escape landing. She looked back over her shoulder and offered him a sad smile as fresh tears spilled down her cheeks.

"Goodbye, Andy," she said. Then she was gone.

Cadence staggered out of the bedroom, sobbing. Snow followed behind and was, for the first time, seriously concerned about her. It was normal for the newly dead to grieve over their lost lives, but it was always diffi-cult to see. He wasn't generally involved in processing the newly deceased. He had gone through the process a handful of times but always with someone else as he had been learning how to do it. He had been so hopeful for her since she had been taking things so well once she had gotten past the initial shock of it. She had been focusing more on figuring out her new situation instead of focusing on what she had lost.

However, when they had reached the apartment, he had known the score. He saw what her former partner had looked like, how grief-wracked he was. He had known then that the man had loved her as more than just friends, more than just partners. He had even tried to hint at the fact in order to prepare her. She had remained oblivious to her own feelings until Andy had finally made the confession. Now things were going to be harder for her. It might have been best if Mr. Halleran had remained quiet about his love. Then perhaps she might have remained oblivious to her own feelings. But now it was out in the open, and she stood in the living room, crying.

"We can't stay," he said gently. He knew she needed to deal with her grief, but he was afraid that if he let her dwell on it too long, he would lose her to desolation. That emotion had the potential to twist, corrupt, or even obliterate spirits. He didn't want that to happen, so he was gently trying to refocus her.

"I know," she said and angrily tried to get herself under control. Then, more calmly, she repeated herself. "I know." She wasn't angry at Snow. She was angry at being seen as vulnerable. She hated crying and detested being seen doing so by others.

"I was married, you know," he said and hoped to ease her nerves by letting her know he had been there, too. "We had been married for fifteen years. We had five children. No doubt there'd have been more if I hadn't died."

"How did you do it?" she asked as she wiped her cheeks and dried her eyes. "How were you able to turn around after saying goodbye and leave them?" she asked and tried to focus on the mechanics of the situation, the how-to, anything but her feelings.

He regarded her for just a moment, glad that he had once more been able to get her mind into questions instead of drowning in sorrow. But it still cost him a little to think about his own past. "I had a mentor who reminded me that I could still make a difference and help people. He also reminded me that we all leave loved ones behind. That it's best just to make the cut and go so everyone can heal."

"Rip the band-aid off fast; because the slower you do it, the more it hurts," she said.

"Yes, exactly. I know how much you want to stay right now. Believe me, I do. But it's not what's best for either you or for him. Neither of you can act on your love anymore, and neither of you would be able to move on if you stayed; however strong the temptation is to do so. I'm sorry, but it's best we go." He could simply remove her from the apartment and take her back to the office in the blink of an eye. He wanted it to be her decision.

She sighed, wiping the last of her tears away. It hurt far more than she had thought it would, but she knew Osmund was right. She needed to just rip the band-aid off and let things heal. Andy would be okay. And somehow, if she could keep moving and doing and thinking, she would be okay eventually, too. It's how she had gotten through her family's deaths before. Just because she was on the other side of death's coin didn't mean she had to approach things any differently. She nodded and moved over to Snow. "Alright, let's go."

He smiled softly at her and offered her his arm to escort her out.

CHAPTER 3

Decisions, Decisions

"So, what happens now?" Cadence asked as she settled back into the chair in Osmund's office.

"Now you get a little time to think about your decision," Snow said as he sat down in his chair as well.

"What decision?"

"Your decision about whether you want to stay on as a kind of ghostly police officer or not." Snow leaned back in his chair and crossed one leg over the other.

"That's not a decision," Cadence said with a scoff. "It's a foregone conclusion. I'm a cop; it's what I do. Alive or dead, apparently."

"You're sure?" He regarded her with interest. "It's not like you haven't earned your rest. For someone only thirty, you've dealt with quite a lot."

Cadence shrugged, trying to appear unemotional. She still hurt from the encounter with Andy, but she preferred to ignore it for now. Ignoring her emotions was something she did very well, and she had gotten a lot of practice over the years. She would do well to take the advice that she had given to Andy and move on. For her, the best way to do that was to stay busy. "Everyone has a lot that they go through," she said as she dismissed Snow's concern. "One way or another, we all have baggage. But this is what I want to do. I became a cop because I wanted to help. If there is a way I can still help, despite being dead, that's the way I'll choose to go."

"Well, I'd be the last person to want to stand in your way, that's for sure," Snow said, and smiled. "You were a hell of a detective from what I've seen," he said and tapped her file. "I'm sure you'll make a hell of an officer here, too."

"Thanks. So, how does this work? Do I have to go meet with someone? Attend some kind of police academy for ghosts? Do I need to check the ghost paper for ethereal apartment listings?" She added the last as a way to try to make a joke to lighten up the mood.

Snow laughed and shook his head. He was feeling a bit better about this now. She had a certain amount of spunk and determination to get through things. He admired that. "You'll be set up with something of an apartment. There's no academy, per se, but you will be partnered with a mentor who shows you the ropes of the job on this side of the grave. They also help you adjust to existing here."

"Lucky you, you finally get to shove me off onto someone else," she said and chuckled. Then she paused, seeing him shift uncomfortably in his seat. "Wait, you mean … You're my new partner?"

"I am," he said. "Is that alright?" Not that it would really make much of a difference if it wasn't alright with her, but he tried to be polite.

"I … I guess. I mean, nothing personal, it's just … the idea of a new partner …" She shifted a little in her chair as she rolled the idea of him as her new partner around in her mind.

"I know," he said with a nod. "Especially after Mr. Halleran, I can see how the idea of someone new wouldn't sit too well. Nor, knowing how private a person you were, does the idea of partnering with someone who has seen you at your most vulnerable. Grieving and lost. You should know I've been there, too. That's why they partner us together from the moment someone crosses over. That way, you have one person who has been through it, so they can understand what the other is going through. My mentor was my partner from the moment I died in the late sixties until just a few weeks ago. So, don't worry about my having seen you in an emotional moment. I'm not going to use it against you or think any less of you for it. Besides, we're ghosts. Transparency goes with the territory," he smiled, trying to add a bit of lightness to the situation with his own attempt at a joke.

He was rewarded by a returned smile, and she nodded. "Yeah, I guess that makes sense. But, just so you know, I'm staying away from fire escapes from now on."

"Agreed," he said and chuckled.

"So, you spent almost fifty years with your mentor? Does it take that long to learn the ropes here? Did your mentor move on to mentoring someone else, or … can we die again or something? Move on to heaven or hell or whatever is waiting?"

He decided to leave the more existential question alone for now. Answering it would likely just bring more questions, and that line of thought wasn't as important right this moment. "My mentor was Alistair Croft. He decided that he was no longer going to take on any more trainees. I was his last, and I suppose no one saw any need to move us on to other partners until he was promoted a few weeks ago. He's spent a very long time mentoring and training officers during his time."

"So, he's been doing this for a while?" she asked.

Snow nodded. "Yes, he was an officer back in the White Chapel days."

"The what?" Cadence asked.

"Sorry, Jack the Ripper."

"Oh. Did he die during that investigation?"

"Oh no, he died some years after. That was his heyday, though, to hear him tell it. But yes, he has been training officers for some time."

"Did you get a little downtime between being let go and getting me, or did you work the entire time on your own?" Cadence was finding that the answer to one question only led to more.

"Well, there was some downtime, as you say. Regions had to be assigned and shared out. I had a partner for a little while, but it was a temporary situation for us both. We were both waiting for new recruits."

"Regions?"

"Yes, as you would say, the area where we have jurisdiction. We have a particular region that falls under us to protect and police. But we can discuss more of that tomorrow. For now, we should get you settled into your lodgings. It's not quite an apartment like you're used to. You'll not have a bathroom or a kitchen, as you have no need of them. But you will have a living room and a bedroom."

Cadence nodded and rose as he did. She was ready to follow her new partner as he showed her to her new home, but the door had opened before they reached it and a woman who looked to be in her sixties walked in.

"Oh, I'm sorry," she said, backing up a step so as not to be right in Snow's face. "You asked me to get you if there was a call."

"Oh, wonderful, thank you, we'll be right there," Snow said.

"A call?" Cade asked as the woman left the office.

"Yes, this will be a good chance to give you some training. That is, if you are up to it, of course."

"Sure, what the hell," she said as her shoulders lifted in a shrug and the corners of her mouth upturned a bit into a smile.

"Wonderful." He led her out into the wide-open space full of desks, computers, and people. They crossed the room and stopped by the desk of the woman who had gotten them.

"It's a sleepover," the woman explained, pointing to the monitor where a handful of young teenaged girls could be seen huddled around a Ouija board. "Six girls, twelve to fourteen years old."

Cadence watched, confused about what kids at a sleepover had to do with anything. They finished setting up their game, and then they each put a hand on the planchette. As they did, the phone on the desk began to ring. Snow motioned for Cadence to watch as he picked up the phone but stayed silent, his eyes on the monitor. The planchette made slow circles on the board, and the woman sitting at the desk turned the volume up on her computer.

"Is there anyone here who would like to communicate?" one of the girls asked.

"Yes," Snow said, and on the monitor, Cade watched as the planchette slid to that word on the board. The girls all seemed spooked by this.

"Are you serious?" Cade asked. "This is what we do?" Snow shook his head in reply and put a finger to his lips, indicating she should be quiet for now.

"You're moving it, Brittany." One of the girls accused another as the planchette went back to idly circling around the board.

"No, I'm not!" the one named Brittany said loudly in protest.

"Stop it," another girl said and then asked another question. "Did you die in this house?"

"No," Snow said, and the planchette obediently slid to that word on the board.

"What is your name?" the same girl asked as the giggles of the other girls started to abate.

"B – O – B," Snow spoke into the phone, and sure enough, the letters spelled out on the board.

"Let me, let me," one of the girls said. "Bob, do you know everything?"

At that, Snow handed the receiver over to the woman. "Thank you, Betty. I just wanted to show Cadence here a little of what you do." Betty smiled, took the receiver, and began spelling out another answer for the teens as Snow led Cadence away from her desk.

"So that's what you do? Party tricks?"

"No, that's not what you and I do," he answered. "But things that are used to make contact with spirits, like those boards, do call in to that area, and they are the ones who answer."

Cadence laughed. "You're telling me this area is a Ouija board call center?"

Snow paused a moment, thinking it over, then nodded. "In a way, yes. They also monitor haunted locations for signs of trouble. They have a lot of responsibilities, but I thought you might find that bit interesting."

"So, if a kid pulls out a board, they're talking to someone here?"

"Most of the time." Snow nodded. "There are times when something or someone else takes the call before us."

"Like demons?"

"We prefer to call them Non-Human Spirits. Now, shall I show you to your new home?"

"Lead the way." She smiled and gestured for him to lead the way.

They stood outside of a door in a fairly unremarkable hallway. The door, however, was unique in that it did not have a doorknob. Snow gestured to the door. "Your touch is the key to open it."

Cadence reached forward, hesitating only for a moment before laying her hand on the cool, smooth wood of the door. The door swung open and Cadence stepped inside, followed by her new partner. She let out a low whistle as she looked around. "This is mine?"

The main room was very nicely appointed, with rich blues and creams and soft fabrics and rich woods. The couch was pale blue suede with darker blue and cream-colored pillows in silk and velvet neatly placed on it. The carpet appeared to be made of a very thick, very soft pile. The coffee table was a dark wood that seemed to have been polished to a high shine. One item in the living room stood out tremendously to Cadence, and her jaw dropped in surprise. "We get TV?"

"Not like what you are thinking, no. This is a way you can check in on those you love and watch over them. There is the usual two-week ban for the newly arrived, so the screen is useless to you now. When they send me word of your activation, I'll be happy to show you how to use it."

"Two weeks? Who decided that?"

"It's generally the time it takes for us to begin to let go and move on. Some go through it faster, others slower, but generally two weeks is the time frame we use before we let spirits look back in on what they've left behind."

"Do you ever have any who never let go?"

"Those like that, who never want to let go, are haunting spirits. But that pertains more to work than to home, so we'll discuss that tomorrow."

"Does your place look like this?" she asked as she ran her hand over the soft fabric of the couch.

"No, it's different. Our homes tend to cater to our personalities."

Cadence looked around at the soft, plush fabrics and colors with an arched eyebrow. "I'm a cop. I hardly think soft and frilly fits me."

"Cadence, you're dead," he said plainly. "No more façades are necessary. There is no need to keep up the tough appearance. There's no harm or shame in enjoying the feel of velvet or soft cushions. No need to be ashamed of having a softer side."

Cadence looked back at him and narrowed her eyes a moment. "Why is it I get the feeling you know a whole lot more about me than you have said?"

Snow merely smiled and lifted his shoulders in a shrug without saying a word.

"How much do you know?" she asked.

"How much do you wish me to know?"

"Wow, that is so very much not an answer."

"Forgive me. I know a great deal about you. I did have to read your file after all, and it did not simply keep to details about your work performance. This is the after-life. It had details about everything, so I can best help you adjust." Cadence frowned and shifted her weight from foot to foot. "You would prefer me to have lied?" Osmund asked.

"No, it's just … I don't know. It's not normal for me to open up to anyone. I know so little about you, and yet you seem to know a whole hell of a lot about me. I just feel flat-footed and at a little bit of a disadvantage," she explained. She didn't like people knowing things about her that she hadn't told them. It made her feel exposed, naked.

"I'm not trying to make you feel like that. I just have to know about you. It helps me to assist you through this transition."

Cadence nodded. "I get it. I do. It's just weird for me. I'm the kind of person that just doesn't open up to others. Which I'm sure you know, since you seem to know so much about me. It's just not something I'm used to. And it's been a hell of a day."

"Yes, well, it's not every day that you die, get a new job, and a new home. In that order." He added the last with an understanding smile. He pointed to a darkened archway. "Your bedroom is through there. And yes, you will need to sleep to recharge your energy. Clothing is something of a mental-image matter, as I explained to you earlier. I'm not sure how it will work for you, but I, personally, have drawers of clothes and change on a daily basis."

"Really?"

"Yes. They try to keep things somewhat normal, especially for those making the transition. And I'd hazard a guess you're not absorbing information anymore." She looked tired and her eyes seemed to be glazed over. He reached out and took her arm. "Come on." He led her through the darkened archway; the room beyond lit up as they entered.

There was a chest of drawers against one wall and a wardrobe, both of the same rich, dark wood that the coffee table was made from. The bed was easily a king size and had a maroon velvet comforter on it. Snow pulled down the covers, and Cadence eased down into the bed.

"My apartment is just across the hall. I'll pick you up in the morning, but if you need me in the meantime, I'll be there, okay?"

Cadence nodded, feeling the wash of fatigue all through her. It had indeed been a hell of a day, and she was feeling every second of it. Her head hurt, her muscles felt like lead, and all she wanted was to just curl up and sleep. She laid back, enjoying the feeling of the soft mattress, fluffy pillows, the cool sheets, and a warm blanket.

"I would say sweet dreams, but I think you would be happier if you didn't dream at all." He let her lie down and then tucked her in before he turned to leave.

"Osmund?"

"Yes, Cadence?"

"Can I call you Ozzie?"

"Absolutely not."

They smiled at each other, then Snow turned and left, and Cadence drifted off to sleep.

CHAPTER 4

First Day on the Job

A plaque on one side of the office door now read "Snow and Riley."

"You kept saying yesterday that 'they try to make things easy,' and 'they decide' this or that. Who is 'they'?" Cadence had been peppering Snow with questions since he had picked her up at her apartment.

Snow opened their office door and gestured for her to enter as he replied. "Let's get you past the things you have to know before we start venturing into the world of things that are nice to know, shall we?"

Cadence arched an eyebrow and shook her head, chuckling. "Sometimes I almost forget you're English. Then you go and say something that just smacks me right upside the head with your Englishness."

"I'll take that as a compliment, actually," he said as he sat down and gestured for her to do the same.

"Okay, Ozzie, so what is it I have to know?"

He held a disapproving brow aloft at the nickname she seemed so determined to foist upon him. He shook his head and sighed. "A lot, actually."

"Should I take notes?" she asked in a teasing tone.

"Only if you think they'll be helpful," he said, annoyance creeping into his tone. He was glad she seemed to have gotten her emotions in check and that she was bouncing back as quick as she seemed to be, but the banter at times just grated on his nerves. He wanted to get her up and running and ready for the job, but every jibe she made was just wasted time.

"Wow, someone put on their cranky pants today. Okay, okay," she said with a sigh of resignation as she threw up her hands in surrender. "Teach away."

He paused for just a moment, giving her a reproachful look, then pulled a folded map out of his desk drawer and some push pins. "Help me hang this on the wall between both desks." He unfolded it and put it against the wall, sliding it over to her a little. "Yes, that's it. Now make sure it's straight."

They pinned it up, then they both stepped back. "Right. Now what you see there, colored in light blue, is our area. We monitor all haunting spirits there." He watched her closely as she took in the area, and he saw what he was looking for. Those jade-colored eyes of hers lingered on a specific area on the map.

"Is this?" she asked as she pointed to a specific spot.

"Yes, it is the college both you and your brother attended, and no," he said and headed off the question before it was voiced, "you are not allowed to go there."

"But it's in our jurisdiction," she said.

"True, but you are still adjusting to your life … or death; however you wish to phrase it. Going there … I wouldn't recommend it unless we have to. Not yet."

Cadence frowned, but nodded. She understood. Just because a fresh wound is starting to heal doesn't mean you should pick off old scabs to see if they still bleed. "Is there a reason we got the area around my old neighborhood? And doesn't our area seem kind of small?"

"We're just starting out. This is my first time as the senior partner, and you're one day dead. Once we get traction, get our footing, and have proven we can adequately handle this, then we'll likely be granted a larger area."

"So, we're starting off in the kiddie pool, then?"

"Something like that, yes."

"And we monitor haunting spirits, which means what exactly?" she asked and sat back down at what was apparently now her desk.

Osmund sat back down as well and sighed, searching for the best way to put it. "Well, we make sure that they aren't giving away too much, for one thing."

"Too much what?" she asked, confused as to what he meant.

"Too much evidence of their existence. Apparently, interest in the paranormal has skyrocketed, and science is trying to catch up with the interest by making all sorts of gadgets that can detect and record evidence of our existence."

"Oh, you mean like the stuff they use on those ghost hunters shows on TV?"

"I've heard of those. Have you seen any of them?" he asked, his interest piqued.

"I've caught a few. It wasn't really something I spent a lot of time on, but around Halloween, I would catch a few episodes of one of those shows. Believe me, there are tons of them out there now."

"What equipment do you recall them using?"

"Well, night vision cameras, of course." She began ticking things off on her fingers. "They also use audio recorders for electronic voice phenomenon, or EVP as they call it, thermal cameras, things that measure temperature or electromagnetic fields or EMF readings. There were also some weird things, too." She paused in remembering and chuckled. "One of them had some stuffed teddy bear they would bring out for child spirits to play with, and it would supposedly light up if a ghost touched it. Oh, and some really annoying radio thing that flips stations all the time, really fast, and they think ghosts talk through it."

"You say that as if you don't believe it."

"I'm a cop. Skepticism is like air to me," she said.

"Says the woman no longer breathing."

"Rub it in, Ozzie, rub it in."

He smiled a little, glad she seemed to be taking it all in stride so far. "So, with all this new equipment those gents use, we have to make sure that the haunting spirits are more careful with their communications."

"What I don't get is why you let them communicate at all, if you don't want them communicating."

"Oh, we want them to communicate, Detective Riley."

"We're partners, Ozzie; you can call me Cadence. Or Cade for short, if you want."

He nodded. "We do want them communicating. We want the interest, the hope of life after death out there. What we're concerned with is how much they give out and how they interact with the living. We can't have someone giving out all the information on how the afterlife works. It needs to be a mystery. It needs to remain unknown. We can allow a haunting spirit to answer a few questions to affirm their existence. Or to at least cast a shadow of a doubt for those that don't believe. However, something like appearing to them in full color as a solid human is strictly forbidden."

"What about the supposed demonic spirits that attack people or possess people?"

"Well, for one, we frown on calling them demonic. Evil, chaotic, non-human in most cases, those terms are fine, but demonic indicates theology, and we tend to shy away from that here since there are so many religions and differing views out there."

"Hey, good question; which one is right?"

"Which one is right, what?"

"Which religion is right? Every single one of them says that they are the right one and all the others are wrong. Even the offshoots within Christianity, the Catholics saying the Baptists are going to hell, the Methodists calling the Mormons out as wrong. Then you have Islam, Buddhism, Judaism, and Paganism. Who is right?"

"There really is no 'right' or 'wrong.'"

That took her a moment, as she wasn't expecting it. "Of course, there is right and wrong."

"Let me rephrase. No religion has it all right or all wrong. Most of them have the same basic foundation, not that any of them would admit it. It's just in the particulars that they begin to disagree. So, while we may encounter non-human spirits, spirits that have never had a human incarnation, or evil spirits, or chaotic spirits, we don't classify them as demons, since that has religious overtones."

"Separation of church and state, so to speak, gotcha."

Osmund nodded, somewhat amused at her ability to jump from topic to topic like this. It was like this with all of the newly dead, but it never ceased to amaze him. "Tell me, Cadence, are there any other large looming questions you have?"

"Probably a ton, and I'm sure we'll get to them. It's weird. It's like my mind is fluid. I can't seem to just ignore the off-topic stuff and focus on what I need to. It's all just there, flowing along like a river."

"Ah yes, stream of consciousness thinking. You'll get better at controlling it. Being newly dead can be a bit like being a child. You have to learn to control your mind once more, now that it has been freed from the flesh. You have less input for it to deal with, so in return, it has opened the floodgates."

"Well, here's hoping my brain-to-mouth filter is still somewhat functional. Not that it was ever all that great when I was alive."

Osmund let out a chuckle and nodded. "I suppose we'll have to see. Shall I continue?"

"Sure thing."

"Haunting spirits stay in an area designated by their attachments. Some can move to two or three different areas if they have that many attachments that feel like home to them. This can be especially true with celebrities and politicians, people who moved around a lot in the course of their lives. Some stay where they died, others may have attachments to a certain place or person or even a thing, and that is where they haunt.

"There are three general types of haunting spirits," he continued. "The first type is a haunting that really no longer has an intelligent spirit behind it. It's almost a kind of psychic record that plays at specific times or dates."

"A residual haunting?"

"Is that what those ghost experts call it?" Osmund asked.

"If I remember it right, yes. Where it's not really them, they just go through the motions, never interact intelligently with anyone. Like, come in, look out the window, leave the room. No matter how much they try to talk to the spirit or get the ghost to deviate from that path, they never can."

"Yes, exactly. It's like trying to interact with a movie or television show. You can perhaps see, smell, or feel the spirit, but you'll get no interaction at all. Right. Very good. The second is a normal spirit. They will interact with people they come into contact with, but oftentimes, they see their surroundings as they were when they died. They feel that these living people are perhaps ghosts themselves, or at the very least, intruders. They will interact with them, and sometimes will have moments of clarity when they recall that they are dead, but then they lapse right back into seeing things as they were when they died."

"Okay, got it."

He nodded, pausing just a moment, then continued. "The third kind is a little bit different, and we tend to have them any place that has an abundance of spirits, like hospitals, prisons, and very old buildings. They are intelligent, aware that they are dead, and they see things as they really appear. If the place where they are has degraded due to abandonment, they see it that way, though they do have the ability to see it as it had been when they lived. They actually help us in a way. They handle the day-to-day stuff, making sure none of the other haunters actually harm living people. If a team of ghost hunters comes in, they contact us so we can be there to exercise a little bit more control over the situation."

"So, they are basically the hall monitors, and we're the teachers that get called in when people are playing with the big guns."

"That … would be one way of phrasing it, yes." He conceded her point.

Cadence nodded again. "Okay, so we have residual hauntings, intelligent but not aware hauntings, and then the intelligent and aware hauntings, who are our contacts at the haunting sites. Right?"

"You catch on very quickly, yes." He smiled and nodded his approval.

"Now, how do the haunting spirits affect the living world? I mean, you always see in the movies that they are slamming this door or throwing that plate. Yet, at Andy's place, we were passing through all of the solid stuff. Is it all just Hollywood bullshit, or is there actually truth to it?" she asked.

"There is truth to it, actually," he replied. "We're basically just energy, Cadence. We can use that energy to make our presence known in the living world. I'll be teaching you how to use your energy to do just that, in fact. Focus and direct your energy, and you can move items, open and close doors, turn electrical items on or off, even make yourself seen and heard. That can be a handy thing if you are trying to lead a ghost hunting team off course and away from something or someone we don't want them to be around."

"And do we just sit here shooting the shit until we get a call that someone is investigating a building in our area?"

"Well, there would be other reasons for one of the Monitors to call in."

"Such as?"

"Well, we do ask that they check in once a month or so, just to make sure all is well."

"They're dead, haunting a building; what wouldn't be well?"

"If one of the other spirits tries to stir up too much trouble, drawing attention to themselves, or causing things to happen that would induce a living person to call in a ghost hunting team. And then there are the non-humans. But those are often few and far between, and given how small an area we have, I doubt we'll have to worry about anything like that for quite some time."

"Have you ever encountered one?"

"A non-human entity?" he asked, as he wanted to clarify that she wasn't topic jumping again.

"Yes."

"Yes, I have, once or twice, now."

"And?"

"And, what?" Osmund asked.

"What do they do? I mean, I grew up seeing all this stuff in movies and on TV, poltergeists, possessions, all kinds of gruesome things."

"Well, while I'm sure a lot of it has been made incredibly more dangerous and dramatic by the cinema, that is, in effect, what they do. What they can do to the living, however, pales in comparison to what they can also do to the dead. They are incredibly dangerous to us since we exist on the same plane as they do. They can consume the essence of the haunter, leaving it no more than a residual haunt, or not even that, causing it to cease to exist. It can rip apart an unaware spirit's image of home and use that to torment them. They thrive on torment and grief, of both the living and the dead."

"Sounds like a few people I knew when I was alive," Cadence quipped, then clapped a hand over her mouth. After a moment, she lowered it, then gave him a sheepish smile. "Apparently, I'm going to have to work on that filter thing."

Snow laughed and shook his head. "It sounded perfectly alright to me. I knew a few like that in my lifetime, as well." A sudden ringing from Snow's person gave pause to the conversation. He pulled something that looked like a cell phone from his jacket pocket, which caused Cadence to gawk.

"Snow," he answered. He paused as the person on the other end of the phone spoke. "Alright, we'll be there shortly. Goodbye."

As he hung up, Cadence finally spoke. "You have a cell phone?" she asked, incredulous.

"We need to go," he said, either evading or ignoring her question, as he rose from his seat.

"You died in the sixties; how do you have a cell phone? And for that matter, how the hell did you know who Gallagher is when you were yelling at me yesterday? He's not dead, and he was popular in the seventies and eighties."

"It's not really a cell phone," he said with a sigh as he urged her out of her seat. He led her out of their shared office and down a hall she hadn't noticed before. "Some of the more recent members of the force were aware of the technology and thought that a kind of visualization of it would be helpful in communications. You have to understand; this plane of existence is all about mental images and visualizations. As for your Leo Gallagher, just because we're dead doesn't mean we can't keep up on some things. Personally, I find the man very funny."

He opened a door that had their monikers on it. That door opened onto a long hallway full of other doors. "This is our equivalent of a police car." He offered the explanation before she had the chance to ask. "Each door opens into a haunted structure or a place near it. This is how we travel to where we need to be."

"We can't just teleport or something like we did last night? Just poof and be there?"

"This tends to be less ..." he said as he paused and searched for the right word, "involved. It takes less energy and gives way to fewer complications. It's important, especially with the newer spirits, that things be a bit simpler. You have a lot to deal with as it is."

"What happens if we get a new haunted place?" she asked as they made their way down the long hallway of doors.

"Then a new door will appear in here. The hallway can extend itself if it needs to."

"So, where are we going?" she asked, apparently accepting his explanation at face value.

"There's an old asylum in our area."

"Lexington Hills?" she asked as she recalled the asylum shutting down being big news in the area when she was in her teens. She had been there once when she was in high school, a few years after it had shut down. She had gone on a dare with some other kids. They had been supposed to stay in the lobby for one hour. They had made it maybe ten minutes before they all collectively chickened out. One of her friends swore up and down that she had seen a ghost that night, but Cadence had never believed her. Of course, given her current situation, she was now more than willing to believe what her friend had said.

"The very place." He nodded as he moved down the hall, looking for that door. Cadence noticed that each door had a plaque beside it, denoting the name of a house, institution, or crossroads. "Come along," he urged. "I had planned a much different first day for you. Just going over things and maybe taking you somewhere to practice using your energy. It would seem, however, that we'll have to postpone that and have a more practical lesson today. It seems that a team of ghost hunters has taken an interest in Lexington Hills. And the monitor there has called on us to come and be present while the team is there."

"So, what do we do while we're there? I mean, how do we stop them from saying too much?"

"Sometimes our presence is enough. Other times, other methods need to be employed."

"It would be those other methods I'm asking about. I don't imagine handcuffs and duct tape are going to be worth anything."

"You might be surprised." The impish grin he graced her with as he replied pulled a smile and laugh from her as well. He stopped at a door marked "Lexington Hills" and began to flip through a ring of keys he pulled from his pocket.

"Yeah, that's the thing, Ozzie. I'm not so big on surprises. The last one ended up with me being dead. Not something I'm keen to repeat."

"Look, I wish we had more time to run through a few scenarios, but we don't. Just follow my lead. I'll try to be as communicative as I can. But please try to keep any questions to yourself until we get back. Believe it or not, they can get a bit twitchy if they think someone entirely new is on the job and they don't know what they are doing."

"Wouldn't want to give that impression," she said as she rolled her eyes. He arched an eyebrow and gave her a pointed look. Then he turned the key in the lock and opened the door.

CHAPTER 5

Lexington Hills

Lexington Hills hadn't functioned as an asylum or hospital in almost twenty years, though, at one point in time, it had been both of those things. It closed its doors in 1998 when it could no longer afford to remain open, and no one had looked back. The building showed signs of deterioration from its abandonment. Most of the windows had lost their glass and were either boarded up or just left open, with plants and ivy crawling inside the window. The roof had sprung leaks that weren't tended to and the ensuing water damage had brought down some of the ceiling panels on the second floor of the two-story building. It had rotted a good portion of exposed wood. It was dark, damp, and dusty, with mold growing in just about every corner. And to a collection of former patients and employees, it was home.

Cadence looked around the lobby of the place and wondered, wisely in silence, how anyone could choose to remain in this desolate place. The staircase immediately on their right still stood just fine, but the railing had given way in segments. The linoleum floor seemed mostly intact in here, but you couldn't tell what color or colors it had been due to the layers of dirt, grime, and dust on it. The same could be said for the majority of the walls as well. The windows in here had been boarded up, but there were gaps in the boards, and some ivy vines had crawled inside. There were four doors off of this room. One stood immediately to their left on the wall behind them. A double door was on the wall to their left and was obviously the front door, as it was far more ornate than the others. Across from them was another door and to their right, beneath the balcony of the second-floor landing, was the last. A shadow detached itself from the corner of the lobby and materialized as a perfectly normal looking male orderly. He looked to be in his mid-twenties, had dark brown eyes, close-cropped brown hair, was of Latino descent, and wore a white uniform.

"Officer Snow?" he asked, extending a hand. Osmund reached out and shook the other man's hand firmly.

"Yes, indeed," he confirmed. "And this is my partner, Officer Riley." Cadence reached out and shook his hand, in turn, noting that for ghosts, they still seemed to have a good grip. But maybe that went in with the whole mental image or projection thing. She would have to ask.

"Pleased to meet you. I'm Ramon Suarez," he replied in a pleasant baritone. He then got down to business. "I heard the team out front this afternoon. They came into the lobby, but no further. They made mention of getting dinner and their equipment, then coming back tonight. They'll be back soon, I'm sure. Thank you for coming."

"Not at all," Snow replied. "That's what we're here for. Is there any particular area of worry?"

"There was a patient who has managed to give this place quite a reputation. She died in the fifties. She is very aggressive to men when they go into her room. She always was, even when she was alive. She would always lash out at the doctors or orderlies when we would go into her room. When she killed me with her fork … Well, that's when they started locking her down in a feeding chair for the day."

Cadence pressed her lips together, forcefully trying to not ask the questions that kept springing to mind. It was strange trying to control her impulses again, something she thought she had overcome in her young adulthood. But oh, so many things kept leaping into the forefront of her brain.

"Is she able to physically harm the living when they come in here?" Snow asked, either ignoring or unaware of Cadence's struggles.

"She has been known to scratch and punch, and she screams a hell of a lot. My apologies for the language, ma'am." He added with a bit of a rueful smile to Cadence.

"Is there any way we can keep them out of her room?" Snow asked.

"I don't know. From the things I have overheard, she has become something of a legend to the living around here. They may be coming in specifically to look for her."

"Lock her door?"

"Her door rotted through. She was on the second floor, and the water damage up there took out most of the wooden doors."

"What's her name?" Cadence asked suddenly. She may be new, but she was smart enough to figure out that if a person, or spirit, were averse to men, the female responder would be the one to handle the person.

"Ruby Jones."

Cadence nodded. "Why don't we see if I can calm Ruby down a little bit or distract her while you guys create a distraction of some sort away from her room? That way, she stays quiet, and you can lead the ghost hunters away from her."

Osmund turned and smiled, pride in his eyes. He nodded. "Excellent plan, Riley. Excellent."

Cadence smiled and nodded to him, but she couldn't help but feel a pang of hurt. It felt a little wrong working with a new partner and not Andy. She lowered her eyes, studying the floor instead of feeling sorry for herself. A car door thumping shut brought her attention once more to the here and now.

"Mr. Suarez, please make sure any others who need to be prepared are ready. Riley and I will take a look at this team as they enter. See what kind of danger they pose, if any at all." Ramon nodded and seemed to disappear from the spot he had been occupying. Cadence blinked, then looked to Snow.

"When do I get to do that?" she whispered, knowing they had to maintain the image that both of them were well trained and not brand new to the afterlife.

"In time, in time," he assured her. "We need to see what kind of equipment this group is bringing in. And by the way, good job on the plan. It's solid. I just hope you're good at dealing with irascible people."

"Okay, number one, do you know her? And number two, who talks like that? Irascible? Really?"

"It means ..."

"I know what it means," she said with impatience as she interrupted him. "It's just that no one speaks like that anymore. Most people would just say grumpy, or cranky, or bitchy."

"I can see that standards for vocabulary have declined in America since my time."

She thought about that for a moment, taking into consideration slang and modern-day text speech using only letters. "Yeah," she said, "I suppose they have."

"And as to your first question, no, I've not been to this institution before. As I alluded to before, we were given this territory because of your familiarity with it. Have you been here before?"

"Once," she replied. "When I was about seventeen, I came here with some friends. We didn't stay long." More would have been said, but the door being pushed open cut off any more discussion. Their attention became focused on sizing up the team that was lugging equipment in.

The first person through the door was a mountain of a man with black hair that was graying at the temples. He wore glasses over watery blue eyes. He was followed by a far more athletic man who looked like he was young enough to still be in college. He was lugging in coils of cords over his shoulders and had a case in each hand. Two more people followed them in. One was a woman who seemed to be in her late thirties or early forties, with dark brown hair and green eyes. The last was a very tall, thin man with shaggy, brown hair and brown eyes, as well as a goatee. They both carried in cases and set them down before going back outside to get more equipment.

"Are they here to hunt ghosts or move in?" Cadence asked under her breath to Snow, who chuckled softly in reply.

"You know you don't have to whisper until they start recording. They can't see or hear us right now."

"What about when they get those cameras and audio recorders out and going?"

"Unless you attempt to materialize, which you don't know how to do yet, they won't see you at all. And with the audio, as long as you aren't too close to the recorder or talk too loudly, they won't pick you up. Why don't you go up and introduce yourself to Miss Jones? See if she can be reasonably spoken with."

"Alright. What about you?"

"I'll follow them. I'm sure I'll be meeting up with you soon. Especially if Mr. Suarez is right and Miss Jones is the reason they are here. Otherwise, keep her as calm as you can until I come for you. Do you think you can manage?"

"I'm on it," she said. Since she couldn't teleport herself around yet, she was forced to go the mundane route and took the stairs up to the second floor.

As she reached the second floor, she began to feel like her vision was swimming. The decrepit, abandoned hospital kept disappearing to be replaced by images of a cleaner, brighter, and more functioning hospital. She wished Snow was there so she could ask him about it. It was disorienting at the very least and a glimpse into the past at best. It didn't take her long to figure out which room was Ruby's. She could hear the yelling from the top of the stairs. She followed the sound of the voice to room 219, where Ramon was waiting outside the door.

"I know you're out there, you little piss-ant," an old woman's voice yelled from within the room. "What's the matter, Ramon? Don't feel like getting beat up by a woman today? Don't want to hit back today?" she asked.

Ramon looked almost stricken. "I never …" he began to say to Cadence, and she shook her head.

"Didn't think you had," she said in order to reassure him. "I've got this. Go meet up with Snow downstairs in the lobby. He's looking after the team." Ramon nodded and disappeared.

"Jealous." Cadence sighed at the ease with which Ramon moved around the hospital.

"Where'd you go, you coward?" The old woman shouted from her room. The door was shimmering in and out of existence, and Cadence braced herself. She wasn't sure that the woman was going to behave any better for her than for a man. She took a deep breath, reminding herself to not show fear or inexperience. Confidence and a commanding presence were what she needed to convey to get through just about every situation.

She breezed through the doorway with her head held high. "Miss Jones," she said as she greeted the woman with a smile. The room swam viciously in her vision until she made the conscious decision to stick with one view. She chose to give in and see it the way Miss Jones would see the room—as it had been when she lived. The walls and floors were whiter and brighter, and there were lights. The bed was made and there was a chair against the wall that seemed like a kind of high chair for adults. The tray was locked in place with a padlock; in the chair sat the diminutive form of Miss Jones, her wrists strapped down to the arms of the chair.

The woman, had she been alive, looked to have been in her eighties. She had a wrinkled face and deep-set blue eyes that glittered with malice. She had lost her teeth, so her mouth was crabbed and clenched in a grimace. Her eyes narrowed as she regarded Cadence.

"I don't know you, girly," she stated. Cadence was relieved that the volume had at least lowered a bit with her presence.

"No, you don't. I'm Libby Riley, an administrator here," she said, using her middle name instead of her first. She didn't know why, but instinct told her to hide her first, more unusual, name. If her gut bothered to tell her something, she usually went with it.

"What do you want with me?" Ruby Jones asked, a dangerous edge to her voice.

"I just want to talk, Miss Jones."

"Are you going to untie me?"

"Maybe, but from what I've heard, you've not been very nice to some of the employees here. People who just want to help you."

"They're useless. They never do anything right. I've got more anything in my pinky finger than the whole bunch of those stupid assholes does."

"A woman doesn't get to your age without having a whole ocean of knowledge and talent and drive to draw from." Cadence complimented her in the hopes of getting her to be calm and reasonable. She had a plan of attack for this particular job. She just hoped that she would be allowed to carry it out without much complication. "Where were you born?"

"Wisconsin," she said, sitting up a little bit more in the chair. Cadence grabbed a chair that was in the corner of the room for visitors and dragged it over. For a moment, she wondered if she would be able to sit in it or not, whether or not it actually existed in the real world. At that moment, the room wavered back and forth from the room that Miss Jones occupied to the abandoned room in the derelict building. She closed her eyes a moment and reminded herself to be where Miss Jones was, and when she opened her eyes, the room was back in full view, white and clean.

"You okay, girly? Look a bit green."

"I'm alright, thank you," she said as she sat down in the chair. "What did you do in Wisconsin?" Cadence was relieved that her plan was working so far. She got the old woman talking about her past, picking up stories of old friends, family, and sweethearts. She encouraged the woman to talk and tell all the stories she wanted. If there was a lull in the conversation, Cadence made sure to ask more questions. They spent about an hour and a half there, with Cadence asking her to tell story upon story of her life. When she heard the team come up to the second floor, she let Ruby finish the story she was telling, and then she changed direction.

"Miss Jones, do you know what is going on here today?"

"No, what?" she asked.

"The hospital is being inspected."

Ruby's eyes narrowed again. "Is that why you come in here all nice like? You want ole Ruby to keep quiet about all the mean faggots you got working over here?"

"No, Miss Jones. I actually wanted to talk to you like we've been doing, and I want to continue for a while. You've had a very interesting life; someone should write a book about you. Or, better yet, a movie. Who would you want to play you in a movie?"

"Elizabeth Taylor," she answered without hesitation.

Cadence thought the fact that Taylor was dead was a moot point. "Excellent, there is no one like her on stage, and she has a great presence, just like you. But you know what she would do now?"

Ruby seemed mollified by the fact that Cadence hadn't argued with her choice. "No, what?"

"She would be very quiet for the inspectors, so they would not come into this room."

"And why should I?" she asked, her back straightening, her jaw getting set into a defiant look once again.

"Because." She leaned forward to whisper conspiratorially. "They're men. Men who would come in here and not even see you or pay attention to you. And I don't want that to happen. I want them to just pass this room by because you deserve the peace and quiet. You've earned it. Now, why don't you quietly tell me about your son?"

Cade could see Osmund outside the door, out of Ruby's view. He nodded, acknowledging the fact that

Cadence had managed to keep Ruby quiet all this time. Now they were both crossing their fingers that she could be placated into remaining so.

Ramon was there, too, with someone whom Cadence assumed was another spirit. She didn't recognize him as one of the investigators. The two of them started making noise and darting here and there. They were making passes around and through the investigators, which set off their instruments, filling the hall with a cacophony of beeps and alarms. They were trying to draw the investigators down the hall and away from Ruby's room.

The overweight investigator was holding both a camera and some kind of device that was apparently taking measurements. At least, that's what Cadence thought the device was doing since the man kept calling out number variances to the others. The big man paused and looked at the college-aged guy. "Derrick, be a sport and go into 219. I want you to try EVP and the infrared camera. Lauren and I'll continue going down this hallway, since there seems to be some activity down here."

The investigator named Derrick nodded, and Cadence's heart sank. They were sending a guy in. If Ruby saw him, she would start screaming.

Crap, she thought to herself. She looked to Snow for some kind of guidance; he just gave her a nod, then turned to follow Ramon. *Well, double crap,* she thought. She was on her own.

She turned back to Ruby and saw the old woman eyeing her suspiciously. "They're making an awful lot of noise out there for people who are supposed to be quiet," she said.

"They are showing the inspectors how poorly sound-proofed the rooms are. We're trying to get added insulation so you all aren't bothered by sounds from the nurse's stations and such." She pulled the chair closer to Ruby. "Now, why don't we whisper so that we don't disturb their demonstration?"

The suspicion in the elderly woman's eyes did not abate. "If you want to show them how much sound carries around here, I could just start yelling."

"But then they would come in here," she replied, somewhat relieved that Ruby hadn't yet seen the ghost hunter that was already in the room. She was not, however, thrilled with the fact that the woman was starting to work herself up again. It had been going so well. "And I know you aren't comfortable around men. I don't want you to be uncomfortable, Miss Jones."

"Then untie me from the chair!" Her voice rose as Derrick set the digital recorder on the tray of the feeding chair that Ruby was tied to. And that's when the house of cards Cadence had been building crashed in flames.

The image of Ruby's room vanished and was completely replaced by the building as it was now. Ruby stared at the recording device, then at the man who placed it there, then at Cadence. The old woman shook with rage. Ruby tried to use what little leeway she had with her bonds to lash out at Cadence. Cadence sprang to her feet and ducked out of the way of Derrick, narrowly missing him. The force of Ruby's lunge caused the chair, the real chair, to move a little bit. Derrick looked shocked for a second, but recovered quickly and grabbed the camera, taking pictures of the chair and the room.

"You fucking bitch!" Ruby screamed. "You tricked me! You let me loose this minute, you skinny little bitch!" Her hard eyes glittered with unconcealed rage as they turned to the man. "And you," she said, her voice trembling with rage growled, "you cock sucking homo! Get out of my room or so help me; I'll make you bleed."

To feel for cold spots, Derrick unfortunately put his hand too close to Ruby. Her hand angled up, and she managed to scratch the young man on the arm. "Ow!" he exclaimed, flinching back and inspecting the two newly formed red lines running down his arm.

Snow ran into the room, and Cadence looked at him helplessly, having completely lost control of the situation. She was in over her head now and knew it, and she was pissed off about it.

"Can you tell me your name?" Derrick asked. The poor man was completely unaware of the chaos taking place around him.

"I don't have to tell you my name. You don't get to know crap about me, you coward," Ruby replied, but thankfully didn't scream.

"Miss Jones, I think you ought to just not answer the man," Ramon suggested as he came in as well.

"How many spirits are here in this room?" Derrick continued after a lengthy pause.

"FOUR!" Ruby screamed, mostly to spite Ramon. Snow ushered Ramon out into the hall, then returned and came close, but not too close, to Ruby.

"Thank you, Ruby," he smiled coldly at her. That caused the old woman to stop and regard him for a moment.

"Are you trapped here?" the ghost hunter asked, but right now, none of the ghosts in the room were paying attention to him.

"Thank me? For what?" she asked suspiciously and in a much quieter tone.

"Thank you for yelling. You see, Miss Riley here was indeed trying to keep you quiet. Ramon and I, however, we want you to scream your head off," he growled. "Nothing makes us happier than hearing how angry and miserable you are, you old witch. So, go on. Yell and scream until the walls crumble down. Your anger and misery are the things we thrive on."

"What do you want?" Derrick asked.

Cadence blinked in shock at the change in her new partner. Gone was the unassuming and proper Englishman. There was a hard edge to his voice, and his eyes were almost as hate-filled as Ruby's. The two stared each other down for a moment. There was a cruel smile on Snow's face and uncertainty on Ruby's. The old woman looked to Cadence, and for her part, Cade nodded.

"I'm sorry, Miss Jones," she said, feigning sadness. "I was just trying to help protect you from them." She shrugged helplessly as she played her part in the good cop/bad cop routine.

Ruby Jones looked between Cadence and Snow. She then slumped back in her chair. She was angry, but apparently not about to give the men the satisfaction that they wanted. "Well … you're a good girl, Libby." She gave Osmund a venomous look and turned her head decidedly away from him. She then faded from view.

Cadence gave Osmund a quizzical look. Snow gestured for Cadence to follow him from the room and she did so. As they left Ruby's room, she noted that Ramon and the other spirit she had seen before were down the hall a few feet. They were keeping an eye on the female member of the ghost-hunting team. Ramon nodded to Snow, an indication that all was well within control there. Snow nodded back and then led Cadence back down the stairs to where the ghost hunter group had set up their so-called base camp. There was one person there, the tall one with the goatee. He was watching some monitors that had been hooked up, but there was no one there that was actively investigating the lobby.

"I'm sorry," she said to Snow before he could even turn around and look at her. When he did, there was surprise on his face.

"Sorry for what?"

"For losing control of the situation up there."

Snow shook his head. "Actually, you did far better than I would have thought. And that's not based on your ability, but the history and disposition of that patient. You found a way to get to her. You were able to keep her calm for a very long time. From what Ramon tells me, the last officers were unable to control her. That's why the legend of her haunting has become such a tale. She is what made Lexington Hills infamous for being haunted. You managed to accomplish what they could not."

"Not entirely. I may have kept her calm longer, but when it counted, I couldn't keep her in line."

"Cadence, would you please relax? And here I thought I was supposed to be the more uptight one in this partnership. Miss Jones acted out far less than she usually does, according to Ramon. And when hunters come here, they are expecting to get some evidence because of what has gone on here before. We also don't yet know what evidence they have exactly. So why don't we simply wait and see before you panic?"

"Wait and see?"

"Oh yes," he nodded. "This is only the first part of the case, so to speak. Next comes something I'm sure you'll be very familiar with. We go on a stakeout."

"A stakeout? Really?" she asked as she crossed her arms over her chest. "How does that even work?"

Snow shrugged. "We follow them to wherever it is they intend to examine their footage, photos, and recorded tapes. We watch and listen in as they review what they have to make sure that nothing truly out of the ordinary … well, as concerns us … was caught."

"What about the chair moving and everything Ruby was screaming?"

"The boy had only a still camera and a digital recorder. So, it is very unlikely he has any actual images of the chair moving. As for Ruby's yelling, well, it depends. We'll have to see what was caught."

"What was with her disappearing like that?"

"When spirits cause a physical disruption, as she did by scratching the boy and making the chair jump, it drains them. So, she has depleted her energy and will likely remain in a kind of sleeping state until tomorrow."

"Why was she cuffed to the chair?"

"I think because she murdered Ramon. She spent a good deal of her last days tethered to it for the employees' safety."

"Yeah, I get that. Ramon talked about that. But she's dead now. She shouldn't need to ask me to untie her from the chair. She should just be able to get up, right?"

"It's all about your state of mind and how you perceive yourself as being. She likely perceives her existence like that because she spent so much time there in life."

"So, if I perceived myself in a cop car or handcuffed, I would be?"

"If you believed it strongly enough, but please don't experiment right now. I'm not sure what physical reactions a sudden manifestation of a police cruiser might have." He offered her a smile and a quick wink to show he was teasing and was rewarded when she smiled back.

They were interrupted by the sound of feet descending the main staircase to the lobby. Derrick, whom Cadence noticed looked about the same age her brother had been when he died, was coming downstairs. He was accompanied by the overweight investigator and the lone woman on the team, who seemed to be paying more attention to her camera than anything else.

"How's it going?" asked the shaggy-haired late twenty-something man seated at the bank of glowing computer monitors.

"Hey, Aiden, pretty good," the overweight one replied. "Lauren's camera battery drained suddenly, however, and Derrick got scratched."

Derrick reached out and presented his arm to Aiden. Aiden turned on a flashlight and illuminated the two angry red scratches on Derrick's forearm. "Nice," Aiden commented. "You get pics already?"

"I took them," Lauren said as she set about replacing her battery pack.

"So, what now, Dan?" Aiden asked. He looked over to the overweight man. "Keep going, or pack it up?"

"Well, the place is definitely active, but since we have a minor injury, I want to make sure Derrick is okay. We can come back again. It's not like this place is going anywhere."

"Dan, I'm alright, it's just a scratch," Derrick said in protest.

"I know you're okay, and I know it is just a scratch. But this is a big place, and it's already proven it has a bite to it. I don't want anyone getting hurt worse, either by spirit or by the mundane. This place isn't in the best repair, and it is getting late," he said.

Aiden nodded, and the group began to pack up. Thirty minutes later, the cords were coiled back up, and all of the equipment was back in the cases. As Derrick and Lauren took things out to the van, Aiden moved over to Dan.

"I'll take it all back to my place and go over it. I have the next couple of days off from work. I'll let you know if we get anything."

Dan, the hefty leader of the group, nodded. "Sounds good to me."

Snow motioned Cadence to follow him, and they both moved outside the hospital to the van the group was using. Snow got in and motioned for Cadence to, as well. "We'll hitch a ride since this is going to take us to that one man's place."

"Aiden," Cadence reminded him. "His name is Aiden."

"Do this long enough, Cadence, and you'll stop trying to remember everyone's names," he said as he took a seat in the back of the van.

"Mental, right?" she asked, looking at the van apprehensively. "Just believe that you won't go through the van, right?"

Osmund smiled and nodded. "Right."

Cadence took a deep breath and let it out slowly, then climbed in. She was very relieved when she didn't sink through the floor of the vehicle and back onto the broken pavement of what remained of the hospital's driveway.

Snow chuckled softly and shook his head. They settled into the back of the van amidst the equipment and went off with the oblivious group of hunters.

CHAPTER 6

Stakeouts and Conversations

Aiden's apartment was a gadget geek's heaven. Laptops, desktops, cameras, and video editing equipment took up most of the living and dining rooms. There was a couch, and a large flat-screen TV that had two different console games and a computer hooked up to it. A bookshelf, in what was supposed to be the dining room, held cases of cameras, camcorders, and other equipment. An open drawer on a filing cabinet revealed a multitude of neatly coiled wires and cords for charging equipment. The man had driven the others to a strip mall where they had parked their cars and dropped them off before heading back to his own place. He had lugged in the equipment from the investigation at the asylum. Some items he put away after retrieving memory cards, other things were sitting next to a computer in the dining room. Then the tall investigator had gone to bed. Snow was sitting on the couch in the living room as Aiden slept in his bedroom. Cadence paced the apartment restlessly.

"And here I thought you had done a stakeout before," Snow commented dryly after spending five minutes watching her pace back and forth.

"I've done plenty of them," she retorted, her arms crossed across her chest as she walked.

"Then why on earth can't you settle down?"

"Because on my stakeouts, we watched for things; we didn't just sit around and wait while the guy slept."

"Now, I'm sure that's not true. A great deal of most stakeouts is simply waiting for some sign of the person you are watching."

"Ugh, fine, whatever. I'm bored."

"Well, you know you could talk to me instead of storming back and forth around here."

"About what?"

"About whatever is on your mind that has you so worked up. You wouldn't have kept the rank of detective if you hadn't been able to handle a stakeout, Cadence. So that leads me to believe that something is troubling you other than simple boredom. You can talk to me, Cadence. I'm not simply here to work cases with you. I'm here to help with your acclimation to this life, as well."

"You know, I was fine with all this back in the ghost world, or wherever it is we're usually at. I was fine with it at the hospital, if mad at myself for not having total control over the Ruby situation. But this? I can't do anything with any of this," she said, gesturing helplessly at all of the technology. "No checking headlines or playing Angry Birds on my phone. No grabbing coffee or a snack."

"No life," Snow concluded. "And being here around all of this stuff is a stark reminder of what you've left behind."

Cadence turned and looked at him for a moment, then nodded. "Yeah," she said and sank down to sit on the floor in front of the couch. "Yeah, no life."

"I know this will sound trite, but I do understand. I've been there. I do remember."

"How do you cope? How do you just sit around and not do anything?"

"Well, we are doing something."

"We're sitting in some guy's living room. We're haunting his apartment until he gets his ass up and we can see what he got from the hospital as evidence of a haunting."

"Yes. There is that. But we're also talking. That seems to be something that goes more and more by the wayside as years and technologies progress. People talk to each other and listen to each other less and less. I've gone around the streets lately. I've seen it. People sit in coffee shops and bars with other people, but their eyes and fingers are glued to those phones. And in a stunning turn of irony, they rarely use those phones to actually talk to people—text message, play games, post those infernal status things, yes. But, to actually sit face to face and talk to someone or listen to them talk? It's becoming a lost art form.

"That's one reason you were so successful with Miss Jones. It's an art form you have talent in. It's an art form a lot of officers possess a talent in, to one degree or another, because they have to pick up on clues from speech and body language. They have to discern what people are really saying or when they are lying. And when we don't have a case, I'll take you out and show you what we can do in our spare time. It's not all sitting around back in the ghost world, as you called it. There are ways to keep up with what is going on in the living world. I promise you, Cadence, your life will not simply be about working or waiting in your new home to go to work. We'll be able to do more, but that will come in time as you get more settled.

"I believe there is more to your temper than simply being bored, however. I think you think you are trying to spare my feelings by not mentioning it, but I am aware that I'm not your Mr. Halleran." He held up a hand as she opened her mouth to protest. "No. When I started with my mentor, it was the same. He wasn't the partner I was used to. The partner I'd spent so much time with on the job. It was difficult at first to not make comparisons. It was difficult to talk to him the same way I had with my old partner. You and I are virtually strangers, Cadence; we met only yesterday. Now we may not know much about each other yet, and we may not have the rapport that we each had with our previous partners; however, this is an excellent opportunity to build it."

He paused as his words sank in. "So, with that in mind, I have a question for you. Libby? What made you give that as your name?"

Cade paused and smiled a bit at the change in topic. "It's my middle name. Or a nickname for it, at least. I didn't think her knowing my real name would be that good if she did end up screaming it and getting caught on tape. Especially since it's not exactly a common name," she shrugged.

"You're right, of course. Cadence isn't a common name. What is your middle name? And why did your parents choose it?" He turned a bit on the couch, shifting position to be able to look at her better as she sat on the floor by the other end of the couch.

"Cadence Liberty Riley," she replied with a somewhat embarrassed smile and chuckle. "I come from a heck of an army family. Both grandfathers were in the service, even great-grandfathers, I think. My dad was, too. So, he named me Cadence after the chants they do when they are training. Liberty is because that's what soldiers fight for."

"That's a very unique and lovely name."

"Thanks. What about you? Where did your folks get Osmund from?"

"It means God's protection. You see, I was a second son, and my family never intended me for the police. They wanted me to go into the church, thinking it was a far more righteous and proper profession."

Cadence arched an eyebrow and looked him up and down. "I don't know … I just don't see you as a church guy."

"No," Snow laughed. "I didn't either. The declaration of which apparently broke my poor mother's heart. It took a while, but she seemed to get over it tolerably well."

"What made you choose the force?"

"Doyle."

"What?"

"Not a what, a who. Sir Arthur Conan Doyle. He's the man who wrote the Sherlock Holmes stories. I had been fascinated with them ever since I was a boy. I loved mysteries and puzzles. It was sort of a natural progression into police work. What about you? What drew you to it?"

"Well, I told you my family was very military," Cadence said. Snow nodded in response. "But the women of the family had always been wives and stay-at-home moms. Well, I didn't want to just sit on my ass and wait to get married and pop out kids. And I grew up hearing all the talk about pride and patriotism, protecting the people, doing your duty, and serving your country. But when I talked about following in my dad's footsteps, he forbade it. He didn't want his daughter in a war zone, especially after we lost my brother, Sam."

"Named for Uncle Sam, I presume?"

Cadence nodded. "Samuel Patrick. The Patrick is for Patrick Henry of the Revolutionary war. He gave the 'Give Me Liberty or Give Me Death' speech."

"Can't fault them for following a theme, I suppose," Snow said. "Sorry for the interruption. Go on."

"When we lost Sam, he was a freshman in college, and I was a junior. My parents were very into the idea of me staying in college and taking a nice, safe job as a secretary or a teacher. But I didn't want that. And I figured if I couldn't protect and serve in the armed forces … Well, they hadn't said anything about me going into law enforcement," she said as she smiled and lifted her shoulders in a casual shrug.

"I can imagine they likely had a good deal to say about it when they found out."

"Yeah, that they did," she said. "I think my dad shouted so loud he could have put a drill sergeant to shame. Mom just cried. She was convinced I was going to get myself killed." She paused and looked down at the floor. "At least they both died before I proved them right."

"Everyone dies sometime, Cadence," Osmund said gently. "But you died serving the citizens of your country, trying to make it a better and safer place. That is a noble death."

"Noble or not, it doesn't keep it from being final."

"True. However, the term afterlife does apply. This is your life after your previous life. And once you've had time to grieve the loss of things you did and people you knew, you will come to find that this life can be as fulfilling as your other one."

She looked up to Snow, the hurt shining in her eyes, but it wasn't the pure, incomprehensible grief he had seen in others. "I'm trying."

"And doing a wonderful job of it, I assure you," he said. "To change the topic for a moment, if you'll let me, good job staying on your toes tonight." Cadence tried to wave the compliment away, but Snow persisted. "No, I mean it. This was your first day on the job, really. Yet you managed to come up with a brilliant plan of attack for a very difficult spirit. A plan that worked quite well until her room was actually entered. Then you were able to go with the flow and slip into the bad cop/good cop routine I threw at you without warning. I must say I'm impressed."

"Well, thanks," she said. "Andy always said I was good at keeping up. We could switch up tactics with suspects or victims on the fly, and we could always keep up with each other."

"Well, if tonight was any example, it looks like you and I will be able to do that as well. I find myself truly looking forward to what this partnership will bring."

They spent more time chatting and getting to know each other a bit better. Cadence talked about her time at college, though Snow was careful to keep the conversation away from the topic of her brother. Cadence asked Snow about what working for the Yard had been like and what life in England had been like half a century ago. Before Cadence knew it, it was light out, and Aiden was shambling out of his bedroom in his boxers to his coffee maker. "So, we don't dissolve into nothing during the day, huh?" Cadence asked.

"Not at all," Snow said with a laugh as Aiden shuffled back to his bedroom. "The myth that we're only active at night is something we have no problem keeping living people believing. I mean, would you want to think about ghosts perhaps popping in and watching you at any time of the day?"

"The thought that they could do that at all is a little creepy. It doesn't matter if it is day or night."

"Exactly. Besides, if our goal is to make people uneasy, it is far easier for us to unnerve them at night. Think about it. During the day, nooks and crannies for things to hide in are lit up, easily discernable. In the dark, they blend into shadow, making what is in them, or what could be in them, unknown."

"Why do I get the feeling you've scared off a few living, breathing humans in your day?"

"Sometimes it's part of the job. Sometimes we have to keep the breathers away from certain areas for their own good. Occasionally, the most effective way to do it is to prey on their fears."

Cadence grinned at Snow. "Breathers?"

Osmund had the grace to look a bit embarrassed. "That is a common term among our kind for the living."

"Well, Ozzie, looks like you might be some fun after all," she said. Her voice held a teasing tone, and in return, he grimaced.

The smell of coffee filled the small apartment and brought a longing groan from Cadence, who rose and made her way to stand by the percolating machine and gaze at it longingly. Aiden emerged from his room a second time, this time in jeans and a T-shirt. He flipped on a computer and began hooking equipment up to it.

"Well, this chap doesn't waste any time. Good," Snow said.

"I have just come to the conclusion that I really, really, really miss coffee," Cadence said. She gave a wistful sigh as she stood over by the coffeemaker.

"Focus, please. The job is at hand," Snow said.

She begrudgingly left the coffeepot and came over to hover by the computer with Osmund. "Alright," her partner said. "He seems to be starting with young Derrick's still camera. Good. We'll get to see what shots he caught."

Other than a very vague streak of light in the feeding chair in one shot, the camera came up with nothing. That was a fact that relieved Cadence greatly. Aiden saved the one shot and moved on to the camcorders after he got himself a cup of coffee. He perused the tapes from the three cameras, and other than some orbs, which Snow seemed unconcerned about, he moved on.

"Good," Snow commented as the tech began switching equipment around. "All we have left is the audio recordings. Orbs, light anomalies, those things are fine."

Cadence nodded and shifted position a little bit. The first tape, which was Lauren's, began to play and had nothing of any consequence on it. The second tape, which was Dan's, had two EVPs on it. One was very clearly Ramon yelling, "Over here!" It must have been when they were trying to distract the others away from Ruby's room. Aiden marked the time, copied it over to the computer, and then wrote down what he thought it was, along with a "Class A" notation. The second EVP on that tape was simply a bunch of footsteps that apparently were happening while Dan was standing still.

Then both Snow and Cadence tensed as Derrick's tape was put in. This was what they had been waiting for.

They heard the tape set down on the metal tray of the feeding chair. They heard the metallic scrape and thump as the chair was moved, and a raspy female voice could be heard saying "bitch." Cadence threw a concerned look to Snow, who shook his head, indicating she shouldn't worry.

Then Derrick's voice was heard, crying out as he was scratched. That was quickly followed by the sound of footsteps and Derrick's voice, asking if the spirit could tell him its name. There was no answer.

"How many spirits are in this room?" Derrick asked.

"Four!" The raspy response was quick and clear. Aiden didn't react, as if what he was hearing was just your ordinary, average, run-of-the-mill conversation. He simply made notes about what he heard and let it continue playing, pausing if he needed extra time to mark a note down.

"Are you trapped here?" Derrick asked through the recorder. There was a long pause, with nothing heard. Then, once more, Derrick's voice rang out in the supposedly empty room. "What do you want?"

Very faintly, the name "… Libby …" came from the recorder. Cadence gave Snow a stricken look, and he shook his head.

"It's fine. Good thinking using your middle name," he said in order to calm her.

"But they weren't supposed to get anything," Cadence said.

"No." Snow corrected her. "They aren't supposed to get anything too conclusive. No solid apparitions, no disembodied voices spilling all the secrets of the afterlife. A few words, some footsteps, a vague shadow, orbs, these things are fine. Relax, Cadence. We did a good job last night."

Cadence nodded slowly, letting out a slow breath. "Alright, if you say so. Just don't want to get into trouble on my first case."

"You won't, trust me."

They watched Aiden for a little while longer, making sure that no other evidence had been captured. Once they were satisfied that he was done, Snow gestured for her to come close. "Take my hand. I'll get us back to the office."

"You could teach me how to teleport on my own, so you don't have to do it for both of us."

"Yes, I am going to. Though I'll still keep with you until I'm positive you have it in hand. I just need you to think of the clear area right outside our office door. Can you do that?"

She gave him a wry look. "I'm a grown woman. I think I can concentrate on a location for a moment."

Snow shrugged. "With the stream of consciousness thought you experience as newly dead, I wasn't sure. Now close your eyes and concentrate."

"Sure thing, Ozzie," she said. Her grin as she said it provoked a bit of a frown from her compatriot.

They disappeared from the apartment. Aiden, the intrepid ghost hunter, was never even aware of their presence.

CHAPTER 7

Baggage for One Please

There was a weird pressure shift, and when Cadence opened her eyes, they were standing in the open area, with people at their monitors, in front of their office door. No one seemed to look up or even take notice of their arrival. Cadence blinked a few times, feeling a bit dizzy.

"You'll get used to it," Snow said. "But I know it's very disorienting the first few times you do it yourself." He turned and opened the door to their office.

"You could say that," she said. She followed him into the office and eagerly sank down into her chair. "So, the case is over, right? Or is there more? And by the way, what the hell is that room out there called?"

"That's the observation bay."

"Observation bay? You have a whole office full of people just watching for people playing with Ouija boards? Seems excessive. Or do they do something else?"

"Some of them watch out for people using Ouijas and other communication devices, yes. Others are dedicated to watching haunted locations that have only one haunting spirit. With no monitor in those places, we need to have eyes on them. Still others monitor the living, more importantly, those who are likely to be of use here in the afterlife." He had already gone over some of this with her before. However, she had been thrown so much information in the last couple of days he didn't blame her for forgetting.

"Those people who would be of use in the afterlife? People like me?"

"Yes," he said. "People like you."

"Wait. There were people out there who were charged with watching me? Like spying on me or guardian angel type watching over me? Because I have to tell you, neither answer is going to make me particularly happy."

"You wouldn't be happy with a guardian angel?"

"Considering I'm dead? They did a shit job, so no."

"Then I suppose you can relax because, to use your term, it was more the spying type."

"That doesn't make me very happy, either. When were they watching me?"

"It depended really, though mostly when you were working."

"Mostly?" Her voice sharp as she asked this.

"Cadence, what's bothering you so much? You've been pricklier than a porcupine since we left the asylum."

"The idea that some weirdo could have been watching me in the shower or on the toilet or something even more private is a little troublesome," she said.

"Well, rest assured, nothing like that happens. During a person's more … private … times, we leave them alone and unwatched."

Cadence still didn't look happy, but she settled down a bit. He watched her for a moment, debating what to do. She'd had her initial cry after saying goodbye to her former partner, but since then, she had clamped down on her emotions hard. She had focused on trying to adjust and learn her new role. Originally, he had thought that was all well and good, but now he realized maybe it wasn't. Maybe she still had some things to deal with that she was ignoring. Things that were apparently still eating away at her. But until he could figure out the best way to approach it, he supposed it was best to just continue on.

"Now, to answer your other question, the next step is the same as it was in life."

"No. No way."

"Oh, yes."

"There's paperwork in the afterlife?" she asked.

"Indeed," Snow said. His sigh echoed her sentiment for the chore.

"You're sure this isn't hell?"

He chuckled and pulled two files from his desk, and passed one over to her. "You'll find pens in your center desk drawer."

She grumbled something that was mercifully incoherent and opened the drawer. "I don't get coffee, but I have to do paperwork. This sucks."

Snow chuckled. They started in on the files. The paperwork was required because there needed to be a record of what transpired during the case and what evidence was captured by the breathers. How detailed the report became depended on how successful the living were at capturing proof of the ghosts. Snow and Cadence sat at their desks, bent over their files. They had been working for about twenty minutes when they were interrupted by a knock on their door, which swung open before either of them had the chance to say anything.

In the doorway loomed a large, muscular, bearded man. He was easily over six feet tall and built like a football linebacker with very dark skin. Osmund got to his feet with a broad smile on his face.

"Alistair," he greeted the bald man. He crossed the small space between the desk and the door and shook the newcomer's hand heartily. Cadence recognized the name as Osmund's old mentor and partner, so she, too, got to her feet.

"Sorry for the interruption, my friend, but I couldn't resist the urge to meet your new partner." Alistair spoke with a heavy accent that sounded almost like cockney.

"Of course. Alistair Croft, it's my pleasure to introduce you to Cadence Riley."

Cade strode forward and offered her hand to him. Alistair took it and kissed the back of it; Snow had to suppress the urge to chuckle at Alistair's use of old-world manners on his very modern partner. Cade, for her part, looked awkward and embarrassed. "Um, nice to meet you."

"Ah! American! Good, I was hoping they would have given you someone with fire in them, Osmund. I'm glad to see they did."

"She does seem to have plenty of that."

"Yes, I've heard about how you two handled yourselves at Lexington. You both did a very good job."

"How did you hear?" Osmund asked, surprised that someone of Croft's rank would have heard about their investigation, let alone how that investigation went before they even filed the paperwork.

"Well, I watched, of course. I had to see how the two of you got on together."

"You set that up, didn't you?" Snow asked. He knew that Alistair had far more important things to do than just watch officers work and look in on random investigations.

He had the grace to look a bit embarrassed. "Let's just say I put a bug in the ear of that Dan fellow to go check out Lexington. Thought it would make a good first run for you two. You did me proud, Osmund. You as well, Detective Riley. Quick on your marks, you are. Very good, very good. Well, I won't keep you. I know you've got work to get on with." Alistair turned and left, closing the door behind him.

Cadence turned to Osmund, mouth open, the look on her face somewhere between stunned and confused. "So, he set us up?" she finally asked.

"He set the case up, yes. It would seem I was being tested as much as you were."

Cadence shook her head. "Well, hell, if they watched it all, why are we doing paperwork?"

Snow chuckled. "Nice try. Set up or not, it was still a case. We still have to record what went on."

"Shit." She sighed and sat back down, picking up her pen once more. Half an hour later, she passed her file with completed paperwork over to Snow. Leaning back in her chair, she rubbed her wrist, more out of habit than any actual pain. "Yep, paperwork still sucks."

Osmund chuckled as he finished his. "Indeed. Why don't you wait here? I'll go turn these in." She nodded her agreement, and he got up and left with the files. Cadence leaned back in the chair and closed her eyes for a moment. Then she opened them and looked at the map on the wall. A thought occurred to her, and she opened her desk drawer.

And there, just what she was looking for, was a case of push pins. "Huh … Guess there really is something to this whole mental image thing." She grabbed the case and opened it, taking out a green push pin and then faced the map. She found the area where Lexington Hills was and sunk the push pin into the paper. Then she took a blue push pin and found where Aiden's neighborhood was. Glad that she had paid attention to the street signs and direction they had traveled while they rode in the van to his house, she pushed the pin into that spot. A ghost hunter marked by blue, a haunt marked by green. For now, it would do.

Her eyes ran over the map, going over streets and locations. She paused over places she knew, idly wondering if perhaps they harbored ghosts somewhere in them. Eventually, her eyes fell on the university. She frowned.

"Sam," she said. Her voice was soft and sad as she reached out and touched the spot on the map. "Are you there?" She didn't even realize that she had wondered that out loud until she heard Snow answer her.

"That's not an area we're to go to yet, Cadence. Not until we get a call to."

"Why?"

"I explained this to you before. You're not ready."

She hadn't taken her eyes from the map when he had entered, but she did now, turning to look at him. "How am I not ready? He died a decade ago. I've dealt with it."

"You may have dealt with it, but you are also still dealing with losing your own life."

"And so that prevents me from going to the college?"

"When the college is your own alma mater, as well as where your younger brother lost his life, yes. It's best for a while that you be removed from the things that remind you of your mortal life, unless the job requires you to be there. You're also not allowed to go to your apartment building or the police precinct yet. And for the same reason."

"Yeah, but we aren't talking about the station or my apartment building. Osmund, please, I just need to know. I never used to think that ghosts were real. I thought when he died, he went to heaven or whatever else there was out there in the great beyond. But now that I know better, I need to know. Is he a ghost now?"

"And why are you so focused on him? Why not your father? He died a violent death, too. Or your mother? Her sudden stroke? Why are you so focused on whether your brother is out there somewhere haunting?"

"My father died in the war, in the middle east. He told me, 'Any day you wake up and get to go back to bed at the end of it was a good one.' I always figured he was prepared to go. Mom had been sick; she'd had surgery. The stroke was a risk of the surgery, and both she and I knew it. Both of those situations are different. They were my parents, yes, but he was my brother. He was my best friend from the time he was born. I'm pretty damn sure my parents have moved on. Him, I'm not so sure of."

"It's natural for you to want to make sure your loved ones are alright, and they are, I assure you."

"But assuring me that they are alright isn't answering my question. He is, isn't he? He's still there. That's why you are avoiding the question. That's why you avoided it before when I asked if any of my family were ghosts. At first, I thought it was that you just didn't know, but now I can see that you do actually know. That's why we won't be going there. It has absolutely nothing to do with me being ready or not. It has to do with him being there. Am I right?"

He sighed and clenched his jaw, looking away. Cadence's eyes dropped, knowing she had her answer. She looked back to the map, turning her back on Snow, eyes riveted to the spot on the map where the university stood. Finally, she selected a yellow push pin and stuck it in there. She then turned and stormed out of the office.

It was quiet in her new apartment. After the argument with Snow about her brother, she had just needed to go home. She had needed to get away from him. They had been working for 24 hours together, and she needed a break. With nowhere else to turn, she simply wandered back to her apartment. Now she was beginning to wonder if it had been a smart idea.

It was too quiet. No city noises, no radio, no television. The silence left her alone with just her thoughts. That was not likely to lead to good things. She paced the apartment, too restless to just sit down. She wanted to yell, to scream and throw things. The logical, adult part of her knew that a temper tantrum would accomplish nothing. The emotional part didn't care. She had been awake for a long time, but she wasn't tired, and, of course, she wasn't hungry or thirsty either. There was nothing to do to distract her from her emotions. The lack of things to do was just as frustrating as having no one to talk to.

A soft knock sounded on her door; she closed her eyes and rubbed her forehead. The only person it could be was Snow, and she wasn't sure she wanted to see him right now. She ignored it.

The knock sounded again, followed by his voice. "Look, I can hear you fuming from here. I know you're in there. If you'd just open the door, I think you'll be happy you did."

She sighed and debated just to continue ignoring him. Then it occurred to her that maybe he had brought her brother to her or was going to bring her to him. Maybe he just wanted to talk, and at this point, she was ready for a distraction from doing nothing. She went to the door and opened it. Snow stood there patiently and extended his cell phone to her. "You have a call."

She opened the door wider and let him in, taking the phone as he handed it to her. "Hello?"

"Cade."

That single word in her brother's voice brought tears to her eyes. The floodgates of emotions she had been keeping such a tight lid on opened and tears fell freely from her eyes. His voice, in just that single word, brought back vivid images of what he had looked like when he had lived, as well as the terrible emotions of when he had died.

"Sam," she said. She tried to control the trembling of her voice and failed as the tears began rolling down her cheeks.

"God, Cade, I'm so sorry you're on this side." It sounded like he was crying, too. "But I'm real proud of you. I always knew you'd be a hell of a cop."

"I'm sorry you're stuck," she said. She wondered for a brief moment how he had known what she had gone on to do. Then she realized that he likely had his own version of the television set that sat dark in her living room. He had been watching over her.

"No, don't be. I'm not stuck. I made the choice to stay. I'm good. And your partner there says we'll be able to get together, eventually. I know it's got to be hell for you right now, but hang in there, sis. Just hold on, and we'll be able to get together real soon, okay?"

"Sam ..." They had always been each other's best friend; they always had each other's backs, and they had always been able to be themselves with each other. With him, she felt she would not have to be strong for once. "I don't know ..."

He cut her off. "Yes, you do, and yes, you can. You were always strong, Cade. You were strong enough to fight Dad when he went nuclear about you becoming a cop. You were strong enough to fight back against those guys in the academy when they thought you were some weak chick they could push around. You're strong enough to fight this, too. I know how hard this is, but it gets better. Once you get your phone, we'll be able to talk more. Just hang in there, and don't let this get the best of you. I love you, sis."

"I love you, too, Sam."

He didn't say goodbye; he just hung up. That had always been his way. He never said goodbye. She slowly sat down on the couch, the phone in her hand, her other hand covering her face as she cried. Snow simply sat in the armchair facing her, letting her finally have her cry out. He wanted to go over and help her, comfort her, but he knew that would likely only make her clamp down again and stifle the emotions she had to get through to accept her situation here. After a while, he went to a closet by the front door and pulled a box of tissues and a wastebasket from it. He set the basket down by her and the tissues on the coffee table. He then resumed his seat in the armchair.

It took about half an hour for her to calm down enough to reach for the tissues. Another few minutes were spent blowing her nose and reigning in control of herself before she could look at him. "I'm sorry. I didn't mean to have a meltdown in front of you."

He waved a hand dismissively. "If you think I didn't have one or two myself, when I was new, you're mistaken. In fact, I managed to completely trash my flat once, throwing things about. It was a right proper temper tantrum. I was so angry. Cadence, I do understand. I know you think I don't, that it's been so long I've forgotten, but I haven't."

She nodded and slid the phone across the coffee table to him. "Here, this is yours. Thank you for that. I needed that. I didn't realize how badly I needed to hear him. He sounded good." She paused and chuckled, shaking her head. "It seems really strange and wrong to say that since he's dead."

"He is doing very well. He's the monitor for the dorm where he was killed. I doubt I'm supposed to tell you that, but then I wasn't supposed to arrange for the phone call either." The phone call had been highly against the rules, and he knew it. However, when they had the argument in the office, the thought had occurred to him. Her brother would be able to get through to her when no one else could. She had seemed so stuck on needing to know he was okay. Maybe now, she would be able to move on and start living her life here, such as it was.

"Well, thank you. I appreciate it, and I'm sorry for being such a bitch earlier. I'm assuming he's been watching me? He knew about the fight with Dad, which happened after he died. He also knew about stuff that happened at the academy."

Snow gestured to the television set, which sat unused. "I'm sure he watched over you when he could."

She smiled a little. It made her feel better, a little closer to her brother. It made her feel a little more whole. "I'm really sorry I went off on you at the office. I know you have rules you have to go by."

"Doesn't mean either of us has to like them," he said. "Hence my calling your brother as I did. I'd dare say it worked, too."

"Worked?"

"Yes. You weren't dealing with your feelings."

"I'm a cop, Ozzie. Warm and fuzzy isn't my thing."

"Truly? Or are you clinging to a tough girl stereotype that helped you get through some very trying times? Cadence, you can be tough all you want. In life, you were able to go back to your room, or your home, and curl up and cry about it. You hadn't let yourself do that yet. You were clinging to our job, your boredom, and other small details as things to be angry and frustrated about. You had to stop doing that and start dealing with being you and all that entails. Façades are useless here. I know you are so used to living behind one that this makes you uncomfortable. You had to come out from behind your wall and face your emotions. All of them."

"So, you used my brother against me, in effect." There was no anger or venom in her voice as she stated it.

"In a way, yes, I did. It became clear to me as you were going on about how important he was to you that if anyone was going to knock through those walls of yours, it would be him. And it worked. Congratulations, you're beginning to accept things now."

"I wasn't before?"

"Well, after the whole candid camera bit, where I ended up having to yell at you to get you to see reason, you did, in a way. But mentally accepting something and emotionally doing so are two different things. Even after Mr. Halleran, you cried for a moment, but then you found you could concentrate on work, and so you simply closed down."

"So, you had to do something to kick me in the ass."

"Your words, not mine," he replied, but he did smile a little.

She tossed the used tissues into the wastebasket and sighed. "Well, thanks. I actually do feel a bit better."

Snow nodded. "I'm glad. Now get some rest. I'll meet you at the office tomorrow." He rose to his feet and grabbed his phone from the coffee table. He offered her a smile and a salute before letting himself out the door. In the quiet that followed, her exhaustion took hold, and Cadence fell asleep on her couch.

Training Day

"**S**o, what are we up to today, fearless leader?" Cadence quipped as she left her apartment the next day to find Snow waiting for her in the hall. She offered him a smile, and he relaxed. He had been worried about any lingering animosity she might have had about him using her brother to force her to deal with her feelings.

"Well, first things first. How do you feel?" he asked.

"I'm actually doing alright, I think. I feel much better than yesterday. Still a little … I don't know … soft? I'm not sure if that's the right term for it or not."

"Right term or not, I do understand what you mean by it," Snow said. "For what it's worth, I am glad you are doing better. It's good to see."

Cade smiled and nodded a bit, feeling a little self-conscious. "So," she said as she tried to move the focus of the conversation off of her and onto something else, "what's the plan for the day?"

"A little training if you are up for it," he replied as he offered his arm. "We're going to go out into the breathing world to teach you how to operate within it."

"Field trip, nice." She nodded, taking his arm so he could teleport them to wherever he had planned.

They arrived in the living room of a nice, middle-class home. It was obviously lived in, although it seemed no one was home right now. It had been decorated in light-colored wood, cream, peach, and blue. The walls were painted a peach color that seemed to glow in the sunlight that the windows were letting into the room. The cream-colored sectional had decorative throw pillows and blankets on it, and it faced the wall-mounted television. It looked as if it had once been a pristine, almost showroom-like home. However, that pristine home décor had given way to a bit of brightly colored plastic chaos; the couple that lived there had a baby.

There was a bright blue playpen in one corner of the room, right next to two toy boxes filled to overflowing with stuffed animals, along with all kinds of colorful bits of plastic and wood. A motorized baby swing with a happy jungle animal pattern was near the couch. A couple of pacifiers sat on the end table between the couch and the swing.

"We're in an empty home because …?" she asked as she looked around.

"You're going to learn how to move things and manipulate items," Snow said.

She took a deep breath, then nodded. "Sure, okay. Shouldn't be too hard, right?"

"Sometimes learning to control your energy can be tricky. Let's start small. Try to move the pacifier."

Cadence arched an eyebrow and debated being insulted for a moment. At length, she shrugged and moved around the end table to where the nearest pacifier was lying. She reached down and tried to grab it. Her hand passed right through the pacifier without making it so much as wiggle.

"A good effort," Snow said, "but you need to put some energy into it. Not all of it, of course; we don't want to send it sailing across the room. Just a little bit. Focus on your finger. I want you to try to focus just on that and to really feel it. It'll start to tingle a little when you've got the energy there. Then try to just use that finger to knock the pacifier to the floor."

Cade closed her eyes and did as he instructed. She focused on the pointer finger of her right hand. After a moment of concentration, she actually could start to feel it tingling a little bit. Once the sensation was steady, she opened her eyes. Snow intently watched as Cade reached down and knocked the pacifier off of the table and onto the cream-colored carpet.

"Very good!" Snow complimented as Cade smiled. "Now you just need to pick it up and put it back."

"Don't people notice when you move things around on them?" she asked as she hunkered down to the floor, concentrating now on her entire hand.

"Most of the time, they don't. They chalk it up to having a faulty memory or that they must have bumped the item or some such thing. People do tend to go out of their way to find perfectly rational explanations for things that are out of the ordinary. Even when they are faced with how improbable their rationalizations are."

"Such as?" Cade asked as she tried to pick the pacifier back up. She made it wiggle a bit, but couldn't get a solid enough hold on it yet to pick it up.

"Let's say, for instance, that we were to move their television remote and put it in the freezer."

"The freezer?" she asked, as she picked the pacifier up a few inches off the floor before her concentration faltered, and it fell back to the floor.

"The freezer," Snow repeated. "They would tear the living room apart looking for the remote, of course. Toy boxes emptied, couch cushions strewn about. Now they know they left that item on the coffee table because they always do. It's a carefully constructed habit, you see, so that they don't lose the remote."

"Do you know these people?" Cadence asked. She took a moment to look at him as she asked the question, before once more returning her attention to the pacifier.

"That's beside the point," he replied, sidestepping the question. "Now, when they find the remote later that night, they may wonder how it got there. They may construct false memories of being very tired and putting it in the freezer when they went to get ice for their drink. They may accuse the other one of playing a practical joke. But neither of them will conclude that it was a ghost. Especially as this house is not haunted by anyone other than us right now."

Finally, Cadence was able to pick up the pacifier and drop it gently back onto the end table. "There, back where it started. You should really see someone about your freezer fixation," she said to tease him.

"I'm merely illustrating a point. These people could be home, and if we turned on a toy, they would simply think it was a glitch in the wiring. Most of the time, you have to do something big to get them to start thinking that they may have a ghost around. The exceptions to the rule on that one are the ghost hunters. Depending on the depth of their interest or obsession in the topic, they might make even the most mundane of occurrences a ghost's fault."

He gestured for her to try the pacifier again. This time, she very easily knocked it off the table on the first try. She bent over where it landed, and it only took a couple of tries this time before she had picked it up. Once she had put it back on the table again, he gestured to a colorful, blocky toy remote on the coffee table.

"Now try to make that work," he said. "The same principles apply. You'll focus your energy and reach out to the toy. For this first time, I simply want you to set it off by pushing a button on it."

Cadence nodded and knelt in front of the coffee table. "Hey, what about toys?"

Snow blinked, not following her line of conversation as she jumped topics. "I'm sorry?"

She shook her head for a moment, aware that she had jumped tracks on him without warning. "Sorry, working with the toys made me think of one of those ghost shows I saw once. They were claiming that a doll was possessed by a spirit. The show was going over haunted items. There was an old piano and, I think, an old wine rack or something. Can items be possessed or haunted?"

"They can, actually. As I said your first night here, sometimes people can have such strong attachments to items that their haunting is tied to that item. Wherever it goes, they go. Wonderful!" he said as she managed to set off the toy on her second go at it. "Try again, a different button this time."

"Is there a difference between possession and haunting?" she asked as she continued to play with the toy.

"Yes, there is. Let's say you were tied to that stuffed bear on the couch. You would have to be in the general vicinity of it always. It is here in this house, so you might have free range over the home, but your energy would be stronger the closer you were to the bear. If the child takes the bear out to the store, you would be compelled to go with it. If the child loses the bear, you would have to stay where the bear was. Now, if you possessed the bear, you would be in control of the bear. You could animate it, make it walk, wave, turn its head, etcetera."

"That makes sense for the doll and the hypothetical bear. What about the wine rack and piano?" she asked as she set the toy off again on the first try—while holding it above the table. She had gotten the hang of it, so she was showing off. She grinned at him, then set it back down.

"Show off." His tone was one of admonishment, though his admonition was lessened by the fact that he was smiling and trying not to laugh. "The furniture pieces might have been items that the spirits were banished into if it was indeed an actual possession. Breathers tend to have the wrong information where the spiritual world is concerned. Sometimes what they assume is a possession of an item is simply a very strong spirit, usually ill-natured in those cases, that is attached to the item as a haunter."

"Okay, well, I'll use the piano as an example. This family said the piano had an effect on the mother. That she started obsessing over restoring it, then playing it. It got to the point where she ignored other responsibilities, even her kids, because of it. They said her personality changed, and she got mean, even vengeful. The whole family would have nightmares. It was also said that if anyone other than her touched the piano, they would wind up attacked by something they couldn't see. They had pictures of the kids and dad with scratches and bruises, and it wasn't the mom attacking them."

"Ah. I think I know of the piano you're talking about. This took place in Ireland, yes?" Snow asked, so absorbed in their discussion now that he forgot they were there for practical training.

"Yeah, I think so," she said.

"That piano was not possessed; it was haunted. The spirit was a wife and mother who was betrayed and murdered by her husband. She had lived a hard life, and her only solace was in the music that piano produced. Somehow, she identified with the woman and actually began trying to possess her. When she felt that her possible possession or attachment to the woman was threatened, she retaliated. See? Simply misinformation."

"So, what happened to this piano, then?"

"I believe a paranormal collector has it now."

"A what?" Cade asked as she moved over to the toy box and began randomly making toys go off.

"A paranormal collector," Snow repeated. "They are people who, for whatever reason, have the unique ability to handle haunted or legitimately possessed artifacts. A rather famous one is that American bloke, John Zaffis."

"Never heard of him," Cadence replied with a shrug and a shake of her head.

"Ah, well, you could say he comes from a line of those who are paranormally gifted."

"How so?"

"He is a nephew to Ed and Lorraine Warren, who investigated that famous New York haunting. Amyville or some such?"

Cadence laughed. "You mean Amityville?"

"That's the one. But we are getting off track. We're here so you can learn to manipulate things. I want you to reach into the television and turn it on. No remote this time."

"I'm not an electrician, Ozzie," she said, protesting. "I have no idea which wire to tug on to make it work."

"You don't need to. Just concentrate, and you'll feel where the power builds up in the set. You just need to manipulate that power." Sadly, this was something that was a little harder to explain and nearly impossible to show.

Cadence reached into the television with her brow furrowed. "So, was that real, anyway?" she asked.

"Was what real?"

"Amityville." She frowned as she felt around in the television set, trying to concentrate on feeling for power.

"In some respects, yes. There was a non-human creature influencing people there. However, it was not what Hollywood made it out to be."

"It usually never is." She sighed in frustration. "Ozzie, I don't feel anything."

"That's because you're busy talking and not concentrating. Try again."

She made a grumbling noise and tried once more. Five minutes passed, then ten. After fifteen minutes, Snow called a halt to the exercise.

"God, that is frustrating," she said.

"Relax. We don't all have the same talents. Some of us are better at manipulating electronics; others are stronger at communication. Just like breathers, we all have different strengths. One last exercise and then we'll call it a day."

The light coming in from the windows had changed from the bright white light of morning. The shadows had stretched across the room as the sun changed position in the sky and now the light coming in was the warm golden glow of late afternoon. Cadence shook herself out as she tried to release the tension that had been building as she had continued to fail at the television experiment.

"Do you see the plants up there on the ledge?" he asked. She looked and nodded, seeing the silk plants on the ledge of the wall that divided the living room from the kitchen. "Good. I want you to focus your energy and create a ball. It doesn't have to be very big, perhaps the size of an orange. This will just be a ball of your energy. Once you have that in hand, I want you to throw it at one of those plants and knock it off the ledge."

"They aren't going to notice that?" she asked.

"Breathers rationalize things," he said.

She shrugged and figured if he was fine with it, she would be, too. As she closed her eyes, she cupped her hands in front of her. Snow began to smile as he saw the faint silvery white light begin to flicker in her cupped hands. At first, it was a wisp, but after a few moments, it was the size of a rubber ball; then, a few minutes after that, it was roughly the size he had asked for.

Cadence opened her eyes and blinked in surprise as she saw the ball of light in her hands. It felt smooth in her hand, but had almost no weight. She lifted her hand up over her shoulder and threw the ball. It sailed across the room and into one of the dusty silk plants, knocking it off the ledge. They heard the wicker basket that the plant was in land, first on the counter, then on the floor.

"See?" Snow said with a smile. "You might not have as much of a touch with manipulating electronics from within, but you seem to definitely have the touch with using your energy. You got that on the first try in just a few minutes. And that is a very useful skill. You can manipulate your energy to make all kinds of things. The more energy you put into something, the more real it becomes in our plane of existence. Just be careful; you don't want to drain too much of your energy at once."

"Okay." she nodded and looked happy that she had managed to get it right on the first try that time. "What happens if you drain too much energy at once?"

Snow paused, thinking about the best way to explain it. "It can have detrimental effects. You have to rest long enough to regain the lost energy, or it can put you out for a longer time."

"Gotcha," she said. She was still miffed about not being able to figure out how to work the television, but she was pleased she had managed the rest of it as well as she had.

"Let's check in at the office now, make sure all is well, shall we?" Snow made the suggestion, Cadence nodded, and they teleported back to the office.

CHAPTER 9

Ding Dong! Chaos Calling!

Cadence found it a bit easier to adjust to her new life after the phone conversation with her brother. She found herself opening up to Osmund a little more, as she finally understood that she didn't always have to put up the façade of toughness to have his respect. She got her stream-of-consciousness thinking under full control and was able to better focus on conversations without going off on tangents. Snow took her out occasionally to roam the streets of their region, giving her a little more to do than just sit in her room and stare at the walls. He was even given clearance to teach her to teleport herself from place to place without his chaperoning her.

A little over a week passed from the Lexington Hills case. They were both in the office when there was a knock on the door, followed by the door opening. The large figure of Alistair loomed in the doorway.

"Snow, Riley. Just wanted to stop by and let you know the paperwork on Lexington went through fine. No follow-up with the ghost hunters required."

Snow nodded. "Good to know, thank you." They nodded at each other and Alistair closed the door again.

"What's wrong?" Cadence asked. She had noted the odd look on her partner's face.

"Nothing's wrong, per se."

"But ...?" she asked.

"Well, ... It's just a bit odd for the State Director to come down and tell a regional officer that everything was fine. Unless there was some sort of investigation into the events."

"Maybe he felt he owed it to you since he set the whole case up in the first place. Maybe there was an investigation into it since he set it up. Or maybe, since you were his protégé, he wanted to let you know you had done a good job. We have a state captain? You've never gone into the hierarchy here, and I've never really thought to ask. He has all of the officers for the entire state under him? That's a lot of cops to be responsible for."

"His actual title is State Director. Calling him a captain is something of an old habit from our living jobs. Our efforts are something of an international effort, you see. And since every culture has different ways of dividing authority and different titles, we do things just a little differently. We're given regions to watch over, as you know, or a jurisdiction, as you would like to say. Our separate region is in a larger region, which in turn makes up a region of a state, or in another country, or a county."

"Oh, wait, I think I've got this. We're like the city police, there's county police, he's state police, and then there would be someone higher up that would equate to federal?"

"In American terms, yes."

"Is there anyone who is a global director?"

"The country directors form a council which oversees things on a global scale. That way, there is no one person in charge of it all."

"So, like the United Nations."

"In effect, yes," he replied.

"Cool." She was going to say more, but Snow's phone began to ring. Osmund pulled it out of his coat pocket and answered it.

"Snow," he said. "Ah, Mr. Suarez, how are you?" His face darkened after a moment, and he was out of his chair in an instant. "We're on our way," was all he said, and he hung up.

Cadence stood as he hung up, not liking the sudden shift. "What is it?"

"Probably nothing," he replied.

"But, possibly?" She prodded as she followed him to the hall of doors, walking fast to keep up with him.

"There are apparently strange people lurking about in Lexington. They're wearing hooded robes and have candles and chalk."

"What, like some kind of cult?" she asked in disbelief as Snow unlocked the door and stepped through. She followed right behind, and they were in the lobby of the defunct hospital once more. Ramon stood at the base of the main staircase and looked relieved to see them.

In the lobby, over where Aiden had sat, not long ago, in front of tables full of equipment, a circle had been drawn on the floor. That circle was currently being carved into the floor by one of the robed people for more permanency. The typical pentagram associated with these types of things was there, also some other form of writing. There were five people of varying shapes and sizes in black robes and hoods. Candles were lit all around them, flickering here and there when a stray breeze blew through the open doors or the cracks and gaps in the boards that covered the windows.

"Cultists," she muttered the answer to herself. Then she looked at Snow. "Can they really do any harm?"

"It depends on what they are here to do. Ramon, have you heard them talk about anything?"

"No," the orderly answered. "They've been quiet since they came in. None of them have spoken much other than directions."

"Any one of them seem to be the leader?" Cadence asked.

"The portlier one seems to be in charge. He was pointing to where to put the candles. He also has a note-book in his pocket that seems to have the directions for whatever they're doing." Of the robed figures, two were heavy, but one was heavier than the other. They all seemed to be male, or at least Cadence couldn't discern a female-like figure there. Even loose robes usually show whether a human form has breasts or not.

"I'll follow your lead," she said to Snow.

"For now, we just watch. I've seen a few of these in my time, and these figures they've written aren't anything I've seen before. I think we might just have some amateurs here playing at being witches. But I don't want to leave until we've seen all they are going to do."

The three ghosts stood and watched as the five breathers chanted their chant around the circle. One of the figures, the heaviest one that Ramon had pointed out before, turned and produced a wriggling bag from behind him. From the bag, the cries of a cat could be heard. The figure then bent down and drew a knife from his boot.

"Shit!" Cadence exclaimed and moved, but Snow grabbed her hand.

"You can't stop them, remember?"

"Well, wouldn't this be a good time to try and scare them away?"

"I don't know if anything will scare them."

"We could let Ruby loose on them," Ramon suggested with a slight grin.

The yowl of the cat was suddenly cut short as the figure stabbed the knife into the bag. He stabbed the bag a few more times and cut a small hole in the bottom of it, through which blood began to trickle. The figures then began to pass the bag around, making sure the blood trickled into the groove of the circle they had carved into the old linoleum. When the circle was completed, there was a subtle snapping sound and an almost electrical hum in the air.

Snow's eyes widened as the wind outside seemed to pick up. It was a real circle, capable of real magic. Snow felt the icy cold fingers of dread spread through him. "Ramon, go upstairs. Alert everyone to stay in their rooms, please." Ramon didn't ask why; he just nodded and disappeared. Snow didn't hesitate before looking at Cadence. "Get upstairs as well. Stay with Ruby until Ramon or I come for you."

"Snow, what's ..."

"Questions later, please, do this now!" he said. He had to raise his voice to be heard over the howling that was growing louder in the lobby. An acrid odor was beginning to emanate from the area where the ritual was being performed. Cadence nodded and teleported upstairs. Despite the fact that she no longer had a heart to pound, she felt as though there was one pounding in her chest. She skidded into Ruby's room and turned to close the door before remembering that the doors up here had mostly all rotted away.

"Libby?" Ruby's voice croaked from the feeding chair where she was cuffed. "What's wrong, girl? Is that son of a bitch, Ramon, after you?"

Snow, for his part, stayed. He had to make sure of what was happening. He really hoped he was overreacting, and that nothing was going to come of this. But the group had managed to close a real working circle, and whatever it was for, it was doing something. Shadows in the room seemed to jump as if they were as nervous as Snow was. The howling got louder until it sounded like a train was pulling through the lobby. A tendril of dark smoke began to drift up from the center of the circle, quickly joined by other tendrils and puffs. The sour smell grew more pungent, sharp, and unpleasant. More and more shadows seemed to pour from that one spot on the floor, coalescing and congealing until, finally, they formed a vaguely humanoid-like shape in the center of the circle. The dark shadow creature was visible not only to Snow, but to the five cultists around the circle as well.

Apparently, Snow had been right about the group being amateurs, as several swear words were dropped, and the group began to run. One of the men, again the heaviest one, ran across the line of the circle, smudging the blood and chalk, breaking it with a snap. They ran out into the yard screaming, leaving Snow and the shadow in the lobby. The winds outside rose to a fevered pitch and blew out the candles in the room.

The creature roared and began to advance on Snow. When a spirit came through the back-lobby doors, asking what all the noise was, the creature whirled and bore down on the poor woman before Snow could call out to warn her. The creature grabbed the ghostly woman with sharp-looking tentacles, and she cried out in pain as Snow edged up a couple of stairs. It began eating her, taking the bits of her it tore off and shoving them into a gaping hole in its shadowy face that served as its mouth. Snow was powerless to stop the creature as he stood there frozen, witnessing the horror. His mind was blank, unable to come up with a way to try to help the poor spirit. When it had finished consuming her, leaving no trace of her behind except for splatters of silvery "blood," it powered through the swinging doors she had come through and disappeared with a final terrible howl.

As the howl faded into the night, Snow's mind seemed to unfreeze, and he immediately teleported himself to the second-floor hallway of the asylum. Ramon was there waiting. The silence, after all of the deafening noise from downstairs, was eerie. "Who haunts downstairs, behind the lobby?" Snow asked him, trying to keep both his body and his voice from shaking.

"Maggie, she was a housekeeper here. Also, Carl, he was one of the patients, but he's residual. They're the only ones in the area you're talking about. Why? What's happened?"

"Maggie is gone. Let me get Cadence. Then we'll talk."

He walked over to the door to Ruby's room, but didn't step inside. He started to call for Cadence, then remembered that she had used the name Libby with the old woman. "Miss Riley," he opted for formality, "could you come out here, please?"

Cadence emerged from the room, looking a little shaken and wide-eyed, but thankfully unharmed. "What happened?" she asked apprehensively. "I could hear all the noise from downstairs. And even for a ghost, you look pale."

Snow gestured for them to follow him into a room that was once used to keep medication. It was a long narrow room with a desk running the length of the room and shelves up above it. The wood of the shelves had rotted to the point that it looked like a single bottle of aspirin would make them collapse. "I'm sorry to say Lexington Hills has lost one of its ghosts," Snow said gravely, as Cadence and Ramon both looked at him expectantly.

"Maggie?" Ramon asked needlessly. Snow nodded.

"How is that even possible?" Cadence asked.

"The cultists apparently stumbled onto a real summoning circle. Only it would seem that they weren't prepared for what they summoned. A shadow creature appeared. When they saw it, they ran. In doing so, the largest one of them broke the circle they had cast, which set it free."

Ramon muttered a few choice words in Spanish. "What do we do now?" he finally asked.

"Riley and I will have a look below. We'll check to see if Carl managed to get away from it. Then see what direction it took out of here."

"Out of here?" Ramon asked.

"Creatures like that rarely stay where they are summoned. I will warn you; it will very likely come back here. This is like a base camp of sorts for it. It will go out exploring, but it will come back here to consume more energy."

"More of us, you mean," Ramon muttered in a sour, matter-of-fact tone. Snow nodded.

"Yes. At least until it can find a new home to claim. We're going to research what it is, see if we can find any pattern or habits we can exploit, and deal with it. We will be in contact with you frequently; feel free to be in contact with us as well. Advise everyone that if it comes back, they are to hide. Do you understand? No heroics. Just hide. We'll take care of it."

Ramon nodded. Snow led them out of the medicine closet, and Cadence followed him downstairs.

"Now would be the time for us to be armed, yes? I wish guns were useful," Cadence said as they crept down the staircase to the lobby. Snow didn't respond. He just kept carefully moving inexorably forward, turning the corner at the bottom of the stairs and moving toward the doors that Maggie had come through. Unlike a human murderer, which would leave behind remains, the creature had consumed all of Maggie. There was no evidence of viscera, of bones. There was precious little to mark her passing, let alone the brutality of how her end had come. She would never come back, never move on, never be seen or heard from again. Her demise was final, and it frustrated Snow to no end that he had not been able to prevent it.

The two partners passed through the door into the dining hall of the asylum, and Snow pulled them to a stop to listen. The large room still held two tables and a few mismatched chairs, a couple of which were obviously broken. The paint was peeling from the walls, and one of the large arched windows had been broken, but not boarded up. Areas of the walls had been spray-painted with graffiti. It was silent in the room. There was no howling, no growling, none of the noises or smells that had accompanied the creature before; it must have left. Snow closed his eyes for a moment and allowed himself to relax just a little bit. That was when he heard it. There was a faint voice off in the distance.

"Help!" the male voice called.

Cadence and Snow exchanged glances and ran in the direction of the voice. They followed it through the dining room and then into the kitchen. Halfway through the kitchen was a door that led down to the basement. That's where the voice was coming from. They passed through the door and into the stairwell, and there, at the bottom, was an elderly male spirit tangled up in what seemed to be a spiritual wheelchair.

"That must be Carl," Osmund said.

"It is." Ramon's voice came from behind Cadence and startled the hell out of her, making her jump.

"Jesus! Don't sneak up on people."

Ramon couldn't help but grin a little despite the seriousness of the situation. "Kind of my job, Ma'am."

Snow was in a less than jovial mood, and did not play along with the two. "Is he normally like this?" he asked as the spirit called for help again.

"Yes. In the twenties, there was a nurse who was not precisely the Florence Nightingale type. I've heard she liked to take out her frustrations on a few particular patients. Carl was one of them. The story is that one day she got fed up with everything and shoved him, in his wheelchair, down the stairs. She went to jail for it, not that it did poor Carl any good. He's more residual than anything. We can never get a response from him. He just lays down here and calls for help."

"Which would be why the creature left him alone." Snow nodded, his mind going through what he knew of those kinds of creatures and their feeding habits. "A residual spirit has far less energy to consume than an intelligent one." He turned and led them out of the stairwell and into the kitchen. "Alright, Ramon, we have to get back and put in a report for this. Call us if you need us; we'll keep in touch with you, too."

Ramon nodded. He looked around the kitchen a moment and frowned. He already missed the warm presence of Maggie down here. He then disappeared. Snow turned to Cadence.

"Back to the office we go." Cade nodded, and they both teleported back to the observation bay right in front of their office.

"I know you have questions," Snow said as he opened the door to their office, "but right now isn't the time."

"Honestly, it seems to be the perfect time to me," she said as she followed him into the office. "We're partners. I need to know what's going on to help you."

"You can't help me. Not with this."

"Bullshit. Just because you have more experience with it ..."

"I don't have a great deal more experience with it, but I am an older spirit than you," he said. He rounded on her, frustration and anger in his eyes. "That makes you a far tastier meal for that thing than I am. You still have a lot of energy from your life left. That would draw it straight to you, Cadence. And I am not about to serve you up on a platter to a monster."

"That's why you sent me up to Ruby. Not to keep her safe or keep her quiet, but to get me out of the way, out of its line of sight."

"I had no idea what was coming out of that circle at the time, so when I sent you upstairs, it was in effect to accomplish both of those things, to keep you safe and to keep her quiet. Had I known, yes, it would have been for the first reason entirely. Only had I known what was coming, I would have sent you back here instead of upstairs to Miss Jones. That is also the reason you are going home now. You're not on this case."

"Bullshit, I'm not. This is my job now, too, Ozzie. Like it or not, you are stuck with me. So, the best thing you can do is teach me."

"No, the best thing I can do for you is to send you home. Failing that, perhaps I should see about getting you transferred."

"What the hell is up your ass about this?" she asked, as both of their voices rose.

"I'll not see a partner of mine hurt."

"I'm not going to get hurt if you would just teach me what I need to know for this like you've done before."

"It's not that simple!" he yelled.

"Yes, it is!" she shouted back.

"Is there a problem?" asked a quiet, velvety baritone. Alistair stood in the doorway, looking between the two of them. He'd been drawn over by the yelling coming from their still open door.

"Yes," they replied in unison.

"Alistair, she can't be on the case I have now. She's too new, and it's too dangerous."

"And with all due respect, Sir, Snow needs to get the stick out of his ass." Cadence shot back her retort with a sidelong glance at her partner. "I may be new to being a ghost, but I'm not new to being a cop. If he would just tell me what I need to know, I can handle myself on this case." Cadence and Osmund glared at each other for a moment before Alistair cleared his throat, drawing their attention.

"What is so all-fired dangerous, if I can ask?" the large man rumbled.

"There's a non-human spirit, Sir. Some occultists released a shadow at Lexington Hills tonight," Snow replied to his former mentor.

"I do see your concern, Osmund. However, while they can be dangerous, I do agree with Detective Riley. If you take a few moments to teach her, she can perhaps be of help to you."

Snow practically sputtered in response. "B-b-but her safety is my responsibility!" he said.

"Wrong, my safety is my responsibility," Cadence said, countering his argument.

Alistair looked at them and chuckled. "Yes, you definitely have yourself a spitfire, Osmund. While it is commendable of you to want to keep her safe, if you shield her from everything, she will learn nothing. I never took you off of anything when you were new."

"We didn't deal with a non-human until I'd been dead almost five years," he said.

"Granted, but there were some pretty nasty human spirits we had to deal with. Teach her, Snow. That's an order."

"But, sir!"

"That's an order," he said, in a tone that no longer brooked any opposition. With that, he turned and left.

Snow frowned and sank into his chair, defeated. Cadence practically beamed triumphantly and moved to sit down in hers. "So," she said. "Teach me."

He glared at her once more and pulled the phone from his jacket, dialing a number. He waited for someone to answer, but when they did, all he said was, "Snow and Riley, non-human shadow." Then he hung up, returning his phone to his pocket. Cadence was about to ask what that had been about, but then he finally spoke.

"Did you see all the blood left behind when the creature killed the female ghost, Maggie?"

Cadence paused, thinking back, running over the sight of the lobby in her mind. "No, I don't think I did."

"And do you know why you don't recall seeing any?" She shook her head no. "It's because there wasn't much to see. It consumed her completely. Her spirit, her memories, her energy, all of her essence, everything she was. There is nothing left of her. She doesn't move on to another plane; she isn't going to be reborn; there is nothing of her left at all. Everything that made her what she was was consumed by that thing to give it the energy to continue being. And right now, you would smell like a holiday feast to that shadow. That is why I am so concerned for you. That is why I was fighting to keep you safe."

"Look, Snow, I appreciate the sentiment. I do. But you can even ask Andy, the more someone tries to protect me or keep me safe, the more determined it makes me to do what they don't want me doing. People have tried to shield me, to shelter me, whatever you want to call it. Look at my father. He was so resolute in protecting me from going into the services that he never saw law enforcement coming. People going out of their way to 'protect me' just pisses me off."

"It pisses you off that they bother to care?" he asked.

"No. I'm touched that they care. I am. But it pisses me off to no end that they think I need protecting in the first place. I've fought my whole life not to be characterized as some stereotypical girly girl. My life doesn't end if I break a nail. As a teen, I would rather play sports than go to the mall. And I never back away from something just because it is hard or dangerous. I can handle myself if you teach me what I need to know for this. I'm sure having a rookie on a dangerous case is a lot to handle. But take the twenty minutes to fill me in, and maybe it will save you hours in the long run. A rookie only stops being a rookie with experience."

He was still fuming a bit, but he nodded.

"Thank you. So, what was the phone call you made?"

"I had to call NHD," he replied, then realized she wouldn't understand what that stood for. "The Non-Human Division. They specialize in non-human creatures and help us figure out what they may be and how best to handle or dispose of them. They'll send an agent down."

"Okay, so we won't know how to tackle this shadow thing until this guy gets here, then?"

"Well, there are general guidelines for handling things until we know how to get it caged or how to eliminate it."

"Caged? You can cage a spirit? We walk through walls; how on earth can you cage the ethereal?"

"That's something we'll have to discuss with the NHD agent. There are special items that can trap or perhaps even kill the creature."

"Nice. So, honestly, this isn't going to be too bad, then. We get the gizmos, go after it, and get it gone."

"That's like a child saying calculus will be easy because they've learned how to add."

"Gee, thanks," she said sourly.

"Look, you need to understand that this thing will devour you if it gets half a chance. Plus, the more spirits it consumes, the stronger it gets. It's out there," he said, pointing to the map. "And we don't know where."

Cadence looked at the map and frowned. "Oh."

Snow nodded, grimly satisfied that he had finally gotten through to her about the way things stood right now.

"Okay, but you said it would come back to Lexington. Use it as a sort of base camp, right?"

"Yes, but we have no idea where it has gone in the meantime, or even how long it will be before it returns."

"Which is why I'm here," a smooth female voice said from the doorway. Snow rose to his feet in an instant, and Cadence followed suit, figuring she should. The woman had a similar build to Cadence, but in contrast to Cade, she had dark hair, eyes, and skin. "Veronica Banks, NHD."

"Agent Banks, it is a pleasure to meet you. I'm Officer Snow, and this is Officer Riley." They each took turns shaking hands.

"Time is of the essence, officers. I need you to take me back to where it was summoned, please." They nodded and headed out of the office once more, trekking back down the hallway of doors to the one marked "Lexington Hills."

They went through the door and into the lobby of the abandoned asylum once more. The first rays of sunlight were streaming through the doors, which had been left open when the cultists fled. Agent Banks strode straight over to where the circle was and took a notepad from her pocket, as well as a pen, and began to take notes. It wasn't long before Ramon appeared next to Snow.

"An NHD Agent?" Ramon asked in a hushed voice, and Snow nodded. "That was fast," he said.

"This isn't something to let lie," Snow replied, although he, too, thought the speed at which Agent Banks had appeared was a little unusual. NHD was usually bogged down with cases, suffering from the age-old problem of too much work and not enough people to do the job. They would usually get back to an officer within a day of the initial report, but further action might take longer.

Agent Banks had arrived within half an hour of his call. Usually, they simply asked the officers what they had seen, and then they went from there, yet here Agent Banks was, at the scene and taking notes. He hoped that meant that positive changes were afoot in the NHD.

The three of them watched in silence as Agent Banks went slowly around the circle, drawing a representation of it in her notebook, including all the runes and the position of the candles. Several minutes passed, the sunlight became stronger as dawn passed into early morning. Finally, she finished and walked back over to them.

"What was sacrificed?" the agent asked.

"A cat," Snow answered.

"And you didn't think you might want to stop it?"

"There wasn't time," Cadence said. "The guy didn't hesitate at all." Ramon nodded, confirming what Cadence said.

The agent frowned but nodded and looked over her notes, taking a moment to note that the animal sacrificed was a cat. "How many living people were taking part in this?"

"Five," Snow replied. Banks noted that as well. She then noted the time of year, date, and phase of the moon.

"Do you know what we're dealing with?" Snow asked. He was doing his best to rein in his impatience at her silence.

"Not yet. I'll take this information back to my department and we'll cross-reference the runes. See if we can determine if this is a specific non-human or a general one. I'll get back to you as soon as I know. Has it come back yet?" she asked, looking at Ramon.

"No, Ma'am," he replied.

"It will. Do your best to keep everyone in their rooms and call these two if it comes back."

Ramon nodded in reply. Agent Banks finished a few more notes, then said a quick goodbye before disappearing. The three remaining ghosts relaxed a little bit.

"Never did like working with the FBI," Cadence said. She shook her head and grimaced.

"She's not FBI," Snow said.

"Oh, I would be willing to bet she was when she was alive. I would bet a lot that she was either that or the CIA. Trust me, the way she holds herself and acts just screams that she was a Fed." Snow arched a brow, and she shrugged in response.

Snow clapped Ramon on the back. "Is everyone here doing alright?"

"As well as can be expected," he said.

"Alright, we'll call as soon as we learn anything." And with that, Cadence and Snow teleported back to their office.

"So, is there a general rule of thumb as to how long the creature will wait before going back to its base camp?" Cadence asked as she sat back down at her desk.

"No. It could be a few hours, could be a few days. If it finds a place or a person to latch onto, it could be never," Snow answered.

"Is there a way to lure it back there?"

Snow looked up and over at her. "Lure it?"

"Well, if you want to trap something, one good way is to lure it into the trap, right? You bait a fish hook; you put cheese in a mouse trap."

"Until we know what it is, we won't know how to trap it, let alone what kind of lure would work. But I'm curious as to what you're on to. Please continue as if I'd said yes."

Cadence chuckled. "Well, I was thinking ... I know this is probably very childish or too simplistic an approach, but my knowledge on this is limited. In the movies, all it takes to get rid of a demon, or demonic entity, or evil spirit, whatever you choose to call it, is an exorcism."

"Have one of those handy in your pocket, then?" he asked.

"No, not quite," she replied. "But what if we could arrange for one to be done after luring and trapping the thing there?"

Snow blinked. It was simplistic and had problems. But it was brilliant. "There is one major flaw there," he said.

"Okay, what?"

"How do we, as non-corporeal people, manage to arrange an exorcism with what would have to be a very corporeal priest?"

"Aiden."

"I'm sorry?"

"Well, think about it. Croft set up our first case by making some suggestion to Dan, the leader of that ghost hunting team, right?" Snow nodded. "I'm not sure, but I'm assuming that he spoke to Dan in a dream like I did with Andy to say goodbye?"

"That is usually how we influence breathers, yes."

"Well, we don't know where Dan lives, but we do know where Aiden lives. What if we get them to be involved in the trapping and get them to set up the exorcism?"

"Usually, appearing to breathers in dreams has to be approved, as a final goodbye was in your case."

"Did Croft get his little dream time to influence Dan sanctioned?"

"I … I don't know. I would assume he did." Now that he thought about it, however, he had his doubts. He really couldn't see the higher-ups approving communication just so that Croft could set up a test.

"Well," she paused, thinking. "Well, you have flaunted the rules before."

"I never …" he began to protest, but she waved his argument away before he could really get it started.

"Yes, you did. You let me talk to Sam."

"But that was different, it was …"

"For my own good?" she asked.

Snow nodded, then saw where she was going. "Of course, what could be more for the good of others than stopping this thing?"

"Exactly," she nodded. She was glad he had been able to see where she was going.

"Alright. While I like where your head is at, and I heartily applaud your quick, if out-of-the-box, thinking, why don't we wait until we see what NHD uncovers? Give them a little time to come up with a solution before we go breaking rules that are there for a perfectly good reason."

"Fine, fine. But don't knock out-of-the-box thinking. Sometimes it's the best way to think."

CHAPTER 10

Enter the NHD

Snow had insisted they go home. They wouldn't be able to move forward with anything until Agent Banks got back to them, and he had no idea how long the NHD's research would take. It had been a stressful day, and while Cadence loathed leaving the case just hanging there, she couldn't really find any reason to argue with taking a breather, so to speak. They walked through the quiet halls to their doors, right across from each other, and stopped.

"Why is it always so quiet?" Cadence asked suddenly. "Other than the other people at work, I never see anyone. There's never anyone in the halls. No coffee shops or parks, not that you've shown me, at least. Are we all just solitary?"

Snow blinked, a little surprised at the sudden question. "No, we're not solitary. Most just tend to stay with spirits they know. Family, friends from their old life, friends they make here if they do work on this side like we do."

"Yeah, but even college dorms have common rooms. I get that we don't eat or drink, so there isn't a need for a bar or a coffee shop, but surely a game room or something exists, right? So people can unwind and do something?"

"A lot of the time, people just go to places among the living. I like to go to the movies myself. Of course, it's frowned on for you to do something like that until you get your phone."

"But what about getting to know your neighbors?" Cadence asked.

Snow stopped in the hallway between their doors. "I've never really thought about it, to be honest. However, right now, you need to focus on getting some rest so you can be on your game for this case. This is a dangerous case, Cadence. I need you in top form."

"Come get me if you hear anything," she said. "No leaving me behind on this, you got it?"

Snow nodded his agreement. "I promise. The second I hear anything, I will come get you."

"Thank you. G'night." It seemed the appropriate thing to say, even if time had no real meaning, no clear definitions like day and night here.

He smiled and nodded, and they both entered their doors. Cadence sighed as hers closed and the lights came up. Only then did she realize that he hadn't answered her question. She sighed and shook her head. She began walking through to her bedroom, but something on the coffee table caught her eye. She walked over to the table and realized it was two things.

The first was a phone, looking much the same as Snow's phone did. She grinned and picked it up. She was going to call Snow to tell him she had gotten it and to jibe him for evading her questions, but realized she didn't have his number. She put the phone back down and picked up the second item. This item produced a much larger smile.

It was a television remote. She had finally gotten the remote and she could look in on people. She immediately clicked the television on and was instantly treated to a view of her old precinct. Her desk had been cleared and still stood empty, but Andrew was there, filling out paperwork on something. He still didn't look like his normal old self, but he didn't look as awful as he had the night she died. A picture of the two of them at the Police Athletic League softball game the previous year was framed and on his desk.

It hurt a little bit to see, but it felt better just to see him. To know he was doing okay. That he wasn't still sulking around his apartment with a case of beer and her cat. "Oh, Andy," she said. "What would you say if you could see me now?" She smiled to herself as she thought of comments he would likely make. Eventually, she hit the channel up button to see what else there was, and she saw her cat curled up, sleeping on Andy's sofa. She grinned a bit. Life went on. There were a few more channels, and she looked in on a few other friends she had before. Eventually, it cycled back around to Andy, and she turned it off.

She didn't even realize she had fallen asleep until the knock on her door woke her up. She rose, unfolding herself from the couch, when her phone rang. "Really? I got nothing for a couple of weeks, now door and phone at once. Lovely," she said. She was not really as annoyed as she was pretending to be.

She grabbed the phone and answered it as she moved to the door, knowing it would be Snow. Because who else would show up at her door? "Hello?" she asked, as she answered the phone, opening the door at the same time.

"Cadence, good to see you have your phone," Snow's voice came over the wire. She tried to make a sound as a reply, but the sound was less an affirmative sound and more a shocked sound. There, in front of her, stood her father in full uniform.

"Uh, Oz, gonna have to call you back." She hung up, feeling almost as numb as she had when she first found out she was dead.

Her father smiled at her and reached out his arms, enveloping her in a hug. "Cade," he said.

She smiled and fell into his arms, hugging him tightly. "Dad." She heard Snow's door open, but she didn't open her eyes. If she was dreaming, fine. It was good to see him again after five years.

She heard Snow's voice as he said a quiet but surprised, "Oh!" She then heard his door close again. When she opened her eyes, she didn't see him there, so she assumed he had disappeared back into his apartment to give her some space. She ushered her father into her apartment and closed the door behind him.

"What … How …" she started trying to ask, but could not find the words to finish the sentence or question.

Her father simply smiled that indulgent smile he always had for her and patted her shoulder.

"I was informed. Sam told me. I'm sorry about what happened, sweetheart."

"It's okay. I mean, I guess this means you get to say you told me so, right?" she asked.

"I wouldn't do that. I was very proud of you, you know. You fought hard to strike out on a path of your own, and you were a hell of a cop. I have always been proud of you. In death now, too, it turns out. Most people wouldn't turn down a piece of heaven to stay a cop."

She shrugged as she said, "It's what I do. It's what you raised me to do. To do what was right and help people out. Besides, I've always loved my job. I wasn't about to let a tiny detail like death stop me."

"I know. Look, I can't stay long. But since you were cleared to get your tools," he said, gesturing to her TV and phone, "I got the okay to come and see you. Your mother didn't get clearance to come, but she wants you to know that she loves you. She also wants you to know she is grateful to you for taking care of her right up until the end. So am I, for that matter, since I couldn't be there."

"That sounds like mom," she said. "Give her a hug and a kiss for me? Tell her to come and see me after this case I'm on is done. Or if I can figure out how to see you two ..."

"No, it will have to be us seeing you, Cadie, if we can." Cadence nodded and was sure there was some rule or reason for that.

"Okay, well, tell her I love her, please."

"I will. And be careful. I'm not sure of all the details of what you're doing, but stay safe."

"I will, Daddy." He gave her a hug and a kiss and turned. She returned the affection, then followed him back to the door. "I miss you guys a lot."

"We miss you too, Cadie-bug." He opened the door and stepped through it. "Remember, we love you, honey, always, and we're all so proud of you." He smiled and then disappeared from the hallway. Cade leaned against the doorframe and sighed softly, a sad smile on her face. She stood there for a moment before she shut her door and crossed the hall to knock on Snow's door.

"Come in," he called. Cadence touched the door, and it swung in easily.

Snow's apartment was very different from Cadence's home. Her home was all soft carpet and softer fabrics. Snow's was all a beautiful hardwood. Hardwood floors, paneled walls, even the majority of furniture seemed to all be matching hardwood. The fabrics that were visible were richly colored hunter-greens or deep maroons. He had shelf upon shelf of books, and over in one corner of the living room stood his television.

Snow sat in an armchair, his legs crossed, with a book open on his lap. He looked up from the book and regarded Cadence carefully. "Are you alright?" he asked.

"Yeah, I am. It was good to see him. To know they are okay."

"They are. And I'm happy for you that you got to see him. But I've heard from Agent Banks."

That brought her mind back to the present, and she stopped looking around the apartment and looked sharply over at Snow. "And?"

"We're to meet her at the office. Come on." She took Snow's hand, more for ease of transport than anything else, and they teleported.

"I expected you two five minutes ago," the velvet voice of Agent Banks said from their office as they appeared outside their office door.

"Sorry," Cadence said as they stopped in the doorway to regard the agent. "It's my fault; I had an unexpected visitor."

"Mmmmhmmm," was all Agent Banks said on that count. "Fine. Come in and close the door." Cadence was once again reminded of why she hated working with the FBI. They entered their office and sat down. Banks had some charts she had pinned up to the wall of their office.

Agent Banks began her speech without preamble. "This rune is for chaos," she said. She pointed to each rune as she named them. "The next rune is for evil and then force, shadow, and the final for life. The summoning circle is very old, although it is more appropriate to call it a creation circle. We haven't seen anything like it since the 1700s of the breather's time."

"The 1700s!" Cadence exclaimed.

Agent Banks frowned at the interruption. "Yes, as I said, the 1700s. Now there are, to our knowledge, no actual accounts of how to create this circle left in circulation. No books, no diaries, no pamphlets—they have all been destroyed."

"Then how did they get hold of it?" Snow asked.

"Unknown. It is possible that they were simply practicing. It's possible that they didn't know what the runes were. However, the runes are too precise for that to be a reasonable explanation. It could have been trial and error, a process of throwing things at the wall and seeing what sticks. I'm not so sure about that, but it is a far cry more believable than they were practicing runes and didn't know at all what they were writing down. And the fact that they had the correct supplies, the right color candles, the cat. It all leads me to believe they somehow found an instruction or instructor as to how to do this."

"Do you think the creature itself could have influenced one of them?" Snow asked.

"No, they summoned it into existence. The runes they used created it out of nothing."

"They can do that?" Cadence asked.

Veronica turned to Cadence. "How new are you?"

Cadence was a little taken aback by the question. "I've been on this side for a couple of weeks now. Why?"

"Just trying to gauge how much you should know and why I'm wasting my time trying to talk to you."

"Well, that was uncalled for," Snow said.

"What's uncalled for is a rookie on this case," Agent Banks retorted. "Officer Snow, I've heard your name. You are well liked and respected, so I have no problem working with you on this one. Her, however? She has no place on this case. She needs to be on a milk run, some easy case to break her in. This is a serious case, the big leagues. I'm not going to waste my time holding her hand."

"How many years did you have in the FBI before you were killed, Banks?" Cadence shot back.

"Twelve, but I fail to see how that has anything to do with this."

Cade shot Snow a quick "I told you so" look before shrugging to Veronica. "I just wanted to gauge how big the stick up your ass was," she said. She took particular enjoyment in throwing the NHD Agent's words back at her.

"Excuse me?" Banks asked, drawing herself upright.

"No, I don't think I will. You don't get it because you spent over a decade on earth pretending you were better than any other cop out there. Preening yourself and standing over them just because you worked for the FBI. You aren't or weren't any more important than the cop who puts his life at risk any time he pulls over a car for speeding or shows up at a domestic dispute situation. Because you sit behind a desk and do your profiles and your research. Meanwhile, the cop on the street never knows if the guy driving the car has a gun, a stash he wants to hide, or a warrant he is trying to outrun. Your badge may grant you the right to swoop in and take cases and evidence away from the cops who were working the job in the first place, but it sure as hell does not give you the right to think you are any better than me just because you have been dead longer. Now just answer our questions about the shit we don't know and stow the fucking attitude because, quite frankly, all you are doing with the holier than thou attitude is pissing me off and wasting our time."

There was a stunned silence in the room for a moment before Agent Banks turned and simply walked out the door. Cade looked to Snow, expecting disapproval and for him to scold her. He had an eyebrow arched, but the look in his eyes was not one of disapproval or anger. "I'm impressed," he said. "I don't know that anyone has ever stood up to an NHD agent like that."

"Yeah, well, my mouth may have just screwed us, but God, it felt good to say it." She shot him a guilty smile, then looked up, closing her mouth, and Banks walked stiffly back in.

"The runes were placed here like someone places the ingredients to cook a recipe," she said, in answer to the question Cade had asked before their argument. "You don't simply pull bread out of a hat. You have to make it, right?" Cade nodded. "Well, that's what these runes are—ingredients. They created the shadow creature. He wasn't a previously existing entity. One of them somehow got their hands on this particular recipe to create a shadow creature from scratch."

"Alright, so we're looking into how they got hold of this recipe, then," Cadence said. "How do we go about it? They all wore hoods; we have no idea who they are."

"They left some of their things. The candles, the chalk, they might come back for it," Banks replied.

"All right, Ramon will call if anyone comes back to the asylum. What about the creature? Does this recipe have a particular order to it? Any set time before it comes back to base camp? Any particular direction it goes or things it looks for?" Snow asked.

"No, being created out of chaos, one of the runes used, we have no way of predicting what it would do."

"How about what it wants?" Cadence asked.

"Again, chaos ..."

"No, that's not what I meant. I meant, is there something that might hit its radar? Is there something that it would go looking for if it caught a whiff of it?"

Banks arched an eyebrow and regarded Cadence for a moment. "Like bait for a trap, you mean?"

"Exactly," Cadence said with a nod.

"As something like this, it would be drawn to chaos, like to like. But for energy needs, it would always be drawn to some kind of vibrancy. The newer the dead, the better. Volunteering?" she asked in a sickly sweet voice.

"Uh, no," Cade replied. "But there has got to be something we can do."

"Short of going out in the street and canvassing your entire region, no. And even then, there is no guarantee that it has even stayed in your region. It may have moved on and be in someone else's region now."

Snow got up and began looking at the runes and the sketch Banks had made of the circle. "I believe the man who broke the circle was the same man who made the sacrifice to summon the creature. Agent Banks, would the creature be drawn to turn its own summoner's life into chaos?"

"Follow the one who summoned it? Especially if that person is the one who set it free? Yes, it might. But you said you have no idea how to track down this person, that you have no idea who it is."

"No, we don't. But the fact that this group very likely lives in our territory gives me the belief that it would remain in our area."

"That may narrow down the search territory, but still makes the search itself nearly impossible. A door-to-door search ..."

"A door-to-door search wouldn't be needed," Cadence said as she interrupted. "This thing needs energy to cause havoc, right? And it gets that by consuming spirits. Snow, what are our most densely populated haunts?"

"Lexington Asylum, the University, there are two prisons and an old mansion. Those five places harbor the most spirit presence. And since," he said, pausing as he moved to the map, "the prisons are on opposite corners of our area, the University is over here, and the mansion here," he explained, pointing out areas. Cadence quickly stuck her colored push pins into those areas. The three of them studied the map silently for a moment.

"So, you see," Snow said, "it was summoned at Lexington Hills, and Lexington Hills is going to be the closest place it can go for plentiful food."

"So, it will be the easiest place to try to set a trap," Agent Banks nodded. "Very good. Let me go and get some supplies dispensed to us and we can begin." She turned and walked out the door of their office.

"Funny how the atmosphere seems to lighten right up when she walks out the door," Cadence remarked as she sat back down at her desk.

"Normally, I would chastise you for a comment like that, but I have to say, I agree. And brilliant work, by the way."

"Not really. You figured out that it would likely be going after the guy that summoned it. I just kind of followed your path and figured out the best place for it to make pit stops for food. And I may well have been heading in the wrong direction. As people love pointing out, I'm the rookie here."

"A rookie to being dead perhaps, but definitely not one to police work. I have to say I am quite happy to have you as a partner."

Cadence smiled under the praise. "Wow, thanks."

"You are very welcome. I must say, I was surprised your father came to call."

"Why?"

"Getting dispensation to travel from where he is at to you is rare."

"Why?" she asked again as her brows furrowed. "Where is he at?"

"I suppose the best and most accepted term for it is heaven. He definitely served his time in hell while he was on earth, with all those battlegrounds."

Cadence paused and smiled softly. "It's good to know that's where they ended up."

Snow smiled and settled into his seat behind his desk. "So, any more brilliant plans? You do know she won't approve of your idea of the exorcism, right?"

"Oh shit, I forgot to ask if an exorcism would even work on a created evil spirit. And by the way, what is with that? There's not enough evil in the world? Someone had to go and make a recipe to create some more?"

"It is unfortunate, but there are some who are never convinced there is enough evil in the world, just as others are convinced there isn't enough good."

"Well, from what I saw when I was alive, there really wasn't enough good. Not enough to balance out the evil."

"That's what I thought when I was on the job, too," Snow said. "I think most cops are that way. But there is a balance. I promise you."

Cadence arched a skeptical eyebrow. "I think I'll have to take your word for it."

An hour later, Agent Banks walked back into the office with a dagger, a spear, and a net. Cadence looked at the so-called tools, then back to Agent Banks skeptically.

"Are we going spear fishing?" Agent Banks shot Cadence a withering look as Snow did his best to hide his smile.

"I don't have time to indulge your humor, Officer Riley," Agent Banks replied. "We need to get back to the asylum. You will, however, be pleased with one thing."

"What's that?" Cadence asked.

"I'm going to be following your suggestion."

"Which suggestion was that?" Snow answered, having a feeling he wasn't going to like where this went.

"To use our young rookie here as bait." And with that, Agent Banks swept out of the office with the supplies and all they could do was follow her.

The darkening colors of sunset were streaming through the still open doors and whatever cracks there were in the boarded-up first-floor windows of Lexington Hills as the trio appeared within it. Ramon appeared a few feet away from them in the middle of the lobby. Cadence offered the harried looking orderly a smile, which he returned.

"Officer Snow, Officer Riley," he greeted them. He then added, "Agent Banks," and a nod to her as a greeting for the NHD agent. "No sign of the creature yet. It's not been back."

"Well, buckle up," Cadence informed him. "Because we think it is going to be. How's everyone doing around here?"

"Those who are aware are nervous. But we're handling things alright."

"We're going to need you to make sure everyone is securely out of the way," Agent Banks said, cutting into the conversation.

"Sure, just tell me where you think the danger areas are and I'll do my best to keep everyone out of them."

"It will retrace its steps to return, so what door did it exit?"

"The back door from the kitchen," Ramon replied.

"Then it will more than likely come back in via that door as well. If it follows the habits of others of its kind, then it will retrace its steps back to the summoning circle. Then it will simply look for food. How long has it been since the youngest of the resident haunters here died?"

Ramon paused for a moment, thinking. "The youngest of the dead here died about thirty-five years ago, I think? Give or take." He shrugged.

"Good, then our plan still holds." Agent Banks nodded.

"What plan?" Ramon asked, and Snow frowned, apparently not liking the plan.

"I'm bait," Cadence said with a sigh.

Agent Banks looked out the open doors and nodded to herself. "It's last light. We need to set up."

"Wait, why is anyone acting as bait?" Ramon asked in concern.

"Agent Banks believes ..." Snow began, but was cut off by the agent herself.

"It will be lurking nearby because it will be hungry. When it smells the energy of a newly deceased spirit, it'll be like offering a starving man an all-you-can-eat buffet. When it comes for her, Officer Snow and I will dispense with it."

Ramon cast Snow an uncertain look. An obviously unhappy Snow just shrugged.

"No one has explained this stuff to me yet, by the way," Cadence said, changing the topic as she fingered the net until Banks pulled it out of her grasp. "I get that the dagger is to chum the water, so to speak. But what about the net and spear? Apart from some strange secret desire to look like King Triton, I don't get it."

"You wouldn't," Agent Banks said. She sniffed dismissively before turning back to her work.

"I didn't think weapons worked, anyway."

"Conventional ones, those in the corporeal world won't, of course," Banks said. "But these have been made in our world, fashioned out of energy for this specific purpose. That net is specifically made with energy to trap a shadow creature. The spear is made specifically to disperse negative energy."

"So my spear-fishing analogy wasn't that far off, then?"

"No, it seems it was quite accurate," Snow answered.

"If elementary," Banks said. Her voice still carried that haughty, holier-than-thou tone as she spoke to them from where she stood over by the summoning circle.

Cadence rolled her eyes and stuck her tongue out at the former FBI Agent when her back was turned. Snow somehow managed to look both amused and disapproving all at once. That look changed when there suddenly came a bang from the back kitchen area.

The officers all froze, eyes glued to the set of doors that screened the back of the hospital from the lobby. It seemed to get noisier around them as a phantom wind began to rise. Ramon cast them an uneasy glance, then disappeared to make sure everyone upstairs was still sequestered.

"Heads up," Veronica called and, in a smooth motion, tossed Snow the dagger. Cadence took a deep breath as she readied herself for this.

The noise started picking up even more—howls and screeches and a general cacophony, one that was slowly growing louder as the creature grew closer. The wind in the building seemed to pick up as well; loose pieces of debris began to swirl and skitter across the floor. The same acrid smell that Snow and Cadence had noticed at the summoning began wafting into the room from the back of the asylum.

Snow caught the blade easily and looked at Cadence apprehensively. "You're certain?"

Cadence nodded. "I'm sure." She wasn't, really. The last time she had blithely gone along with a plan, it hadn't ended too well for her, and she found herself a little anxious now that the time had come.

"Do it!" Banks yelled over the noise as the floor and walls began shuddering.

Cadence pushed up her sleeve and presented a bare arm to Snow. He hesitated, knife in hand, and she frowned. "No time like the present, Ozzie," she urged. He laid the blade against her bare flesh and hoped that this would turn out alright. He pressed and drew the blade down swiftly.

Cadence hissed as she felt the blade bite sharply into her skin. She honestly hadn't thought it would hurt. She was dead. She didn't have nerve endings anymore, since she was incorporeal. Then she recalled Snow's many references to expectations, mental images, and such. Her mind expected it to hurt, so it had. The realization of this did little to stop the throbbing and stinging. Silvery blood flowed from the fresh cut, dripping down her arm to splatter on the floor. There was a sudden pause in the previously steady growth of the noise that this creature seemed to bring with it, and the building stopped shaking for a moment. Then a scream of anger, anguish, and stark hunger broke through the hospital, shattering any of the glass left in the building.

"Oh …" Snow began.

"Shit!" Cadence finished for him. She suddenly went from not being sure it would work to being terrified it was working. Agent Banks moved swiftly over, net in hand, passing the spear to Snow. Cadence stood frozen between them, fear immobilizing her as if she were a deer frozen in the headlights of an oncoming train.

The double doors to the back flew open, one door tearing off its hinges completely, flying a few feet into the lobby. It landed with a thud and kicked up a large plume of dust. Swirling dark shadows heaved upon themselves as if the creature was regarding them, staring at them, studying them. Then it moved, shadows collapsing, coalescing, swirling in, and tangling around themselves. A tendril reached out as if grabbing and tearing down the wall, but the wall remained.

"It's feeding on the memories of the building, what the spirits remember the hospital looking like," Snow said in an awed voice.

"If it can feed off the building, what does it need from me?" Cadence asked. She hoped she managed to hide some of the fear in her voice. She had no problem facing down a bad guy, even if they were armed with a gun or a knife. She knew how to fight back against humans. Waiting to be attacked by some unearthly shadow thing while unarmed and bleeding was an entirely different matter. Shadow hunting was in a totally different league.

"Living energy is different," Agent Banks replied curtly, then amended her answer as if anticipating Cadence's argument. "You were a living being."

During this brief discussion, none of them took their eyes off the slowly approaching creature. It looked bigger to Snow than he had remembered it, but then it kept changing its shape as it moved, so it was hard to judge. The thing crept closer and closer, the noise that seemed to accompany it growing to deafening proportions. The wind gusted, bringing with it the now overpowering stench of the creature.

When it got within range, Agent Banks hefted up the net, preparing to throw it. Cadence shrank back a few steps, both to stay out of the NHD agent's way and to simply be further away from the terrifying creature. Before Agent Banks could throw the net, however, a shadow tentacle snapped out like a whip and wrapped around Agent Banks, trapping the rope against her.

Smoke rose from the shadows where the appendage touched the rope that Veronica still held. She struggled, trying to get free, or at the very least get the net free to sling over the creature, until another tentacle reached out and ripped Agent Banks' throat out. It shoved the flesh it had torn from her into a gaping hole in its middle. Veronica's eyes were wide with pain and fear, and her mouth moved as if to speak, but she was mute.

Osmund and Cadence stood still; eyes wide in shock. The creature hadn't played by the plan. It had been supposed to grab Cadence, leaving the others free to capture and spear the thing. It wasn't supposed to grab Banks and the net as well. Snow shook himself, leaping into action. Net or not, he began driving the spear into the thing, more smoke rising from it where it was injured.

Agent Banks kicked at the creature. She released the net, as it seemed the tool was useless against the thing. The net remained pressed against her, as it was in between her and the tentacle that was tightening around her waist. Her hands beat against the shadows as she tried in vain to free herself from its grasp. Silvery blood dripped from the grotesque hole in her neck, the ragged flesh around it dancing obscenely as her body jerked as she fought.

The creature screamed shrilly again, and Cadence involuntarily clapped her hands over her ears to muffle the sound. Then it did something none of them had thought it would. It tore Agent Veronica Banks in half and began consuming her, shoving her incorporeal and still twitching body into its shadowy mass.

"Run!" Snow ordered, shoving the dagger into her hand and yanking her away from the creature before teleporting himself. She momentarily forgot the tricks and trades of being a ghost and ran. Back through the double doors, she went. She remembered she could teleport once she hit the middle of the dining room, but she had no idea where Snow had gone. She heard the creature scream behind her, and she turned. She could see it through the door that it had torn down when it entered the lobby. It was turning around and seemed to be searching. A tendril of shadow hit a splash of her blood on the floor, and it let out a howl.

That's when she decided she wasn't going to teleport. She was going to continue running. She was still bleeding, and she wasn't about to leave the inhabitants of the hospital alone, with no protection. If she could draw the creature away from the ghosts of the hospital, then maybe they'd be safe for a time. She probably still smelled yummy, and if it was still hungry, there was the hope it would chase her out and away from the smorgasbord of ghostly vittles. Of course, what she would do with it once she got it away from the hospital, she had no idea. An NHD agent and an experienced officer had just failed at defeating this thing, but defeating it was no longer her main priority. Her main priority was just to get the denizens of the hospital safe.

She flew out of the kitchen door and ran across the yard toward the tree line. Her arm still stung and throbbed, but the bleeding had slowed. That was good, she hoped. She could see a faint flicker of lights through one of the windows on the second floor that wasn't boarded up and, for a moment, her heart froze. What if her plan had just backfired? What if, instead of leading the thing out of the hospital and away from the haunting spirits, she had simply just left the building, leaving the spirits alone with a monster?

A sudden increase in noise and a howling scream from the back door both relieved and frightened her. It seemed to be following, to be coming for her. She raised the dagger in her hand and braced herself. With a primal bellow, the shadow creature began to charge her, moving faster and appearing more solid than she had seen it before. She wasn't expecting the hand that grabbed hers, making her jump. Snow nodded briefly, and then reality swam, and she was suddenly in the hospital, on the second floor, in a room that looked out over the back. Through the broken window, she watched as the creature crashed right over the spot where she had stood and did not stop, moving back into the trees.

She stood there, watching the trees in the forest twitch and move despite the lack of wind, her body trembling. A gentle touch on her injured arm made her jump, and she looked to find Ramon there with gauze. He offered her a silent smile, then began to bandage her arm.

"That was very brave, what you just did," Snow said solemnly after a moment. "There was a modicum of stupidity to the plan, but it was very noble."

"I just … The only thing I could think when our plan went to hell was that I needed to get it away from everyone here."

"Well, believe me, we all thank you," Ramon said.

"How did you know where to find me?"

"I told them," an elderly voice said from across the room. Cadence looked over and saw Ruby, still cuffed to her chair. Cadence was speechless.

The old woman gave her a genuine smile; then she shifted herself in her seat as her usual curmudgeonly demeanor fell back into place. "Not about to let these cock-suckers throw away the only good person we have running this joint." And just like that, Ruby was back to being Ruby. "God knows the peckers between their legs are the only brains they got between them. Once you get her patched, you get the hell out of my room."

Cadence tried to hide the smile at the old woman's rambunctiousness and word choice. "Come on, I think Miss Jones has had all of the uninvited guests she's going to tolerate tonight," she urged, gesturing for them all to leave.

"They go. You, I want to talk to." Ruby's tone brooked no opposition. Ramon finished the bandage and nodded to Cadence. He and Snow both left, leaving Cadence to face whatever Miss Jones had to say alone.

Ruby squinted up at Cadence for a moment. "Not that many people would be willing to sacrifice themselves for us. Even when we were all alive. Some here may be too lost in their memories to know it, but what you did was mighty rare. I saw you ready to face down that thing. You're one hell of a woman, Libby."

It took Cadence a moment to remember that she had introduced herself by her middle name to Miss Jones. "Thank you, Miss Jones. Don't worry; we'll take care of that thing, so no one here has to worry about it again."

Ruby nodded and gestured with her head. "Go on, they don't deserve you, but I reckon they're waiting for you."

Cadence smiled and nodded. "Goodnight, Miss Jones," she said and then left the room.

A wave of weakness and exhaustion passed through her as she made her way down the hall toward the nurse's station, where Snow and Ramon stood talking. The world seemed to start spinning a bit. They stopped speaking as she approached.

"You don't look well," Ramon commented, concern crossing his features.

"Don't worry, I'll take care of her," Snow said, moving to help support her as she leaned on, and nearly passed through, the desk. "You'll be safe for now, and we'll concoct a plan for the next time it comes back."

Ramon nodded, looking back at Cadence. "Thank you again, Officer Riley."

"Cade," she said dismissively, waving a hand at the thanks. "Call me Cade." She felt a little drunk, like the world was spinning, even though she hadn't had anything to drink. For some reason, it made her giggle.

"Alright, time to go home," Snow said, recognizing what was happening. He nodded to Ramon; then they disappeared from Lexington Hills and reappeared in the hallway in front of her apartment. She laughed again at the transition and lazily slapped her hand against the door and grinned when it popped open in response.

"That is the neatest thing," she said. She chuckled a little, finding the door funny. Snow maneuvered her inside and to the couch, unsure if he could help her get any further.

"Why am I drunk, Ozzie?" she asked as she flopped down onto the sofa. "Did you get me drunk? Did Ramon get me drunk?"

"No one got you drunk, dear; you just spent a little too much energy tonight. Get some rest and you'll feel right as rain in the morning, I promise."

She laughed, even as she slid sideways on the couch to a lying down position. "Right as rain!" she declared. "Is rain right? Are…Are we like…On the right, and when we think rain is falling down, it's falling to the right?"

"Oh my, you are power drunk, aren't you?"

"Power drunk? Who spiked the punch with power?" she asked loudly, as if there was someone else in the apartment to ask. Then she burst out into another fit of giggles. Snow watched in a mixture of concern and amusement as the giggles subsided and she fell asleep.

He looked down at her arm, at the bandage that had a silvery mark on it as blood, or at least what constituted their blood, seeped from the healing wound. He sat down in the armchair, weary. "I hope the cut isn't too deep," he said. He pulled his phone from his coat and dialed a number, settling back with a sigh.

"Non-Human Division." A female voice answered with velvet professionalism.

"This is Officer Snow. Sadly, I need to inform you that Agent Veronica Banks went down in the line of duty tonight."

There was a slight pause of comprehension, then, "I'll tell her superior. Thank you, officer. We'll be in touch." The line clicked dead before he had a chance to hang up his end. The loss of the agent was going to be a sticky thing, but they hadn't done anything wrong. There had been no reason for the creature to go after the agent like it had. But on the other side, he was very glad it had chosen her over Cadence. He'd grown rather fond of his brash young partner.

He hadn't expected her to run out the back doors. He thought she would teleport back to the office or to the second floor for safety. She had still been trailing blood, and being young as she was, it was a certain draw for the creature. The creature had indeed been drawn to her and followed her blood splatters out of the asylum. Her plan had created an unforeseen consequence, however. The energy that replaced human adrenaline she had used in luring the monster away, the fear she felt and the pain from the wound, had all combined to make her very solid and visible. So much so that Ruby had seen her from her window and voluntarily called the two men into her room. He shuddered to think what would have happened if she hadn't called them.

He settled more deeply into the armchair. He had no intentions of leaving her alone tonight. He had never had a younger sister, despite his having constantly pestered his parents for more brothers and sisters as a child. He realized now that he thought of Cadence as the little sister he never had. Or perhaps as a daughter. With that, and the events of the evening still rolling round in his head, he fell asleep.

CHAPTER 11

Trouble? Trouble.

"**P**lease explain to me," Alistair Croft said as he entered their office without knocking, "how an NHD agent, a supposed expert in the field, winds up down the gullet of a shadow creature?" He leveled his gaze at both Riley and Snow.

"We were just discussing that, actually. The truth is, we're not sure," Snow answered.

"It was supposed to come after me," Cadence said as she showed off her bandaged arm. "It just suddenly switched tracks and grabbed her before she could get the net over it."

"I tried stabbing it with the spear she had supplied me with to get it to let her go. That weapon, however, as well as the net, seemed to have practically no effect. The creature made sounds as if it was injured, and smoke rose where they touched it. However, they seemed to do little else to it other than cause it mild discomfort. They certainly did not stop it."

"So it would seem," Croft replied gravely. "Well, it turns out that Agent Banks was something of a rogue agent."

"Come again?" Snow asked sharply.

"The NHD is having something of a troubling time coming up with free agents for training their rookies. Agent Banks was as new as your partner here," Alistair said, indicating Cadence. "Younger, I think, by a day or two. They hadn't assigned her to an agent for partnership yet, so they had her inventorying their arsenal. Apparently, she grabbed your case request off of a secretary's desk and ran it herself, without dispensation to do so."

"Seriously?" Cadence asked. Alistair nodded.

"I knew some of her speech was too modern," Cadence said and shook her head. "There she was, all high and mighty, giving me hell about being a rookie? What a fucking hypocrite."

"Was she? Well, it would seem she was more the rookie and paid dearly for her inexperience. In any case, you two have been cleared of wrongdoing in this unfortunate business."

"Thank you, Alistair," Osmund said. He stood and shook his old mentor's hand.

"You're welcome, Osmund. You, as well, Riley. I hear you had a moment out there last night."

"A moment of stupidity," she said with a chuckle.

"If that were true, I wouldn't have recommendations from two of Lexington Hill's residents sitting on my desk." Cadence blinked, and he chuckled at her surprise. "Well, you two try to have a less eventful day, yes?"

"Yes, Sir," they both replied in stereo.

"Well," Osmund said, retaking his seat after Croft left, "I would hazard a guess: one is from Ramon and one is from Miss Jones."

"Just surprises me that they would go to such trouble."

"Not too surprising. Miss Jones seems to have really taken a liking to you, Cadence. And I think your selflessness last night made quite the impression on both her and Mr. Suarez."

"I guess," she said, as her shoulders lifted in a nonchalant shrug. "Still, going to the lengths of writing up compliments or recommendations? I don't know … so few people take time out of their day to do nice things for people anymore. I guess it just surprises me when they do."

"Ah yes, the pessimistic cynicism of the modern day rears its ugly head."

"It's not pessimistic, Ozzie. It's just how the world works anymore. People are so caught up by their schedules that they just don't have time to think outside of their little bubbles."

"Were you like that?" he asked as he looked over at her.

"Probably," she conceded after a moment's thought. "I mean, I tried not to be. There was this old lady in my building and I tried to look in on her when I could. She was nice, but she was alone. Her husband had died; her kids had moved away. She had friends and would go out and meet up with them, but I always liked to check in on her. So I would go out of my way for that. However, if I called the cable company about my bill, I wouldn't do the survey they ask you to take about their service. I don't know that I ever gave a waiter or waitress a compliment beyond a good tip."

"At least you made efforts not to be so self-absorbed. Plus, you need to remember that both Mr. Suarez and Miss Jones come from a time when people weren't so caught up in their day-to-day lives. Most people had time for their neighbors or to pause and compliment others. These were very deserved, given what happened last night."

Cadence shrugged, feeling uncomfortable under the praise. She resettled herself in her seat and went about changing the topic. "So, no NHD agent. What are we going to do?"

"We'll figure out a way. Maybe you were on to something before."

"Before what? When? Which idea?"

"You had previously suggested an effort in concert with the breathers, using the ghost hunting group. Perhaps we should work a bit more on pursuing that?"

"Well, maybe, but if Banks was spouting nonsense, how do we know anything she had to say was the truth? We could go working on the assumption that it's some generic shake-and-bake monster, but instead, it's some form of old demon that has to be handled a particular way. Without an agent, one that truly is an agent, we have no way of determining the truth."

"Perhaps we can get a few moments of an agent's time for research purposes if we promise to take care of it ourselves." He paused and pulled his phone from his pocket, dialing. "Yes, Officers Snow and Riley requesting research information only." He hung up, pocketing his phone once more.

"I guess we'll find out then, huh?"

"Yes, they'll be in touch soon, I'm sure. Perhaps we should use this time to try to construct a plan of attack."

"I don't see how we can do that yet. I mean, I know I'm supposed to be the one that's all guts, and you're the brains, but without knowing if what Banks told us was true or not, we can't move forward yet. It sucks, but until we get confirmation, we're back at square one."

Snow sighed. "Yes, I suppose you're right."

"To which part?" She chuckled.

He made a slight face and rolled his eyes. "To not being able to move forward until we get confirmation about the particulars of the shadow. You should stop putting yourself down, you know. You've had some brilliant plans."

"Hey …"

"What's on your mind?" he asked as he noted both the hesitance and preoccupation of his partner.

"Last night … I don't recall that much after leaving Ruby's room. I know you said that we don't have adrenaline. We simply use energy to compensate for the fight-or-flight instinct. And I know you said that between the wound and the energy I used up last night, you weren't surprised I was out of it. But seriously, how obnoxious was I?"

Snow chuckled softly. "Don't make yourself uneasy. You were fine, if not amusing."

"Amusing? Oh God, that's probably not good," she said with a frown.

"It's as if you were a little drunk, Cadence. You even said you felt as if you were. It's not uncommon in new spirits who use that much energy in such a short time."

"Yeah, but I've never really been a good drunk."

"What do you mean?" Snow asked.

"I always tended to be a mopey or depressed drunk. I was never one of those happy drunks like you say I was last night. Unless you find mopey amusing, I suppose."

"No, you were funny. Alcohol is a depressant, so it's not a huge surprise it would affect you in that way. But since alcohol wasn't involved last night, it's natural that your reaction would be different. Relax. You didn't embarrass yourself. I brought you home, and you fell asleep. It's as simple as that."

"If it was that simple, why did you say I was amusing?"

"Suspicion really is part of your makeup, isn't it? You were just laughing about things you thought were funny, like my saying the phrase 'right as rain.'"

"That's all?" she asked, a suspicious eyebrow rose.

"I swear," he said, his voice solemn. They were interrupted by a knock on the door. "Come in," he called.

A somewhat harried-looking middle-aged man entered the office. He wore navy-blue slacks and a white, button-down shirt with a navy-blue sweater vest over it and had short but wild ginger hair. "Officers Snow and Riley?" he asked unnecessarily. They both nodded in response. "I'm Agent Whitfield from the NHD. I'm here to take a look at the research Agent Banks brought you and to retrieve the tools she checked out for you."

Snow gestured to the wall where they had pinned up all of the pictures and notes Agent Banks had gone over with them. "Here is the research. You can see the pictures and the tags for what we were told the runes meant." He paused, giving Whitfield time to look over the notes.

Whitfield walked over and immediately began perusing them in depth. Cadence said nothing but arched an eyebrow at Snow, who shrugged. The silence went on for a time as the agent made his way along the wall, reading and looking at everything. Once done, he turned to look at them.

"Just so you know, I've been with the NHD for five years. I'm not a rookie."

"We didn't think you were," Snow replied calmly.

"It's just … I heard what Banks pulled. I didn't want you guys thinking I was another one."

"Not at all," Snow said. He wanted to dismiss the idea to ease the somewhat nervous-looking agent. "Now, please, can you tell us if she was right?"

"Well, that depends."

"On what?" Cadence asked.

"On what she told you to begin with. I have no idea what she said."

"Ah, right," Snow said and nodded. "She told us that this was some old, long-lost ritual, not used or found since the 1700s, to create a shadow creature. That this did not summon an already existing non-human spirit, but created one from scratch."

"Too bad she's gone; she was right," Whitfield said, impressed. "I don't know about the circle or the ritual becoming lost. I would have to look that up, but I know the runes and the way they were cast. Yes, it's a recipe to make something that isn't very nice."

"Do you know the best way to get rid of it?" Cadence asked.

"Dealing with these things in the field is not my area of expertise. I'm strictly doing the research. But I can tell you that you may have trouble."

"Why?" they asked in unison.

"This one, right here," he said. He pointed to one of the rune drawings. "It was at the top of the circle it looks like, which means it is the most dominant trait. Chaos. That means it might not always react the way you think it will, or the way you want it to. It's going to be chaotic, unpredictable, and possibly not play by the rules. Whoever threw this together was definitely trying to summon something that was going to be a challenge to get rid of."

"Do you think it is possible the group came up with this on their own, a kind of trial-and-error thing?" Cadence asked. "Because when they summoned this thing, it freaked them out enough that they ran. It didn't look to me like they were expecting anything from it."

"It's possible, but one of them had to have seen the circle in a book or something. It's too detailed and too correct to be something haphazardly thrown together or guessed. Maybe one of them remembered seeing it once and just didn't know what it did?"

"Maybe," Cadence said.

Snow set out the spear, the net, and the dagger on his desk while Whitfield and Cadence were talking. "Could you perhaps do the research to find out the origin of the circle and the ritual? If it is as old as Agent Banks first told us, and whether the ritual was removed from breather circulation? And if it was removed, why and who ordered it?" he asked.

"Yeah, I guess. The whole department is inundated right now. Since I'm research and not field, I should be able to get a little bit of time to look into this for you."

"I don't suppose you could leave the dagger?" Cadence asked. "I'm not real keen on going up against this thing without a weapon."

"I'm sorry …" He said. "I wish I could. But I have to make sure all of this gets checked back in."

"It's alright, Agent Whitfield. You have your job to do, we understand," Snow said and reassured the obviously stressed man.

"I'll see what I can come up with on the ritual. Can I take a couple of the pictures?"

"Sure," they both replied. He nodded and grabbed the drawing of the circle that Agent Banks had done, as well as the drawings of the individual runes.

"I'll call you as soon as I have something."

"Thank you, Agent Whitfield." The NHD agent nodded and scurried out of the office, drawings and weaponry in hand.

"I'd forgotten about the net," Cadence said after the door had closed.

"Mmm …" Snow nodded. "I recalled Agent Banks having it, so when the noise from the creature began to subside, indicating it was leaving, I went back down to the lobby to see if the net had been left behind. I didn't think the creature would consume it since, obviously, the thing did have some small effect on the creature. It was on the floor, and I grabbed it right about the time Miss Jones started screaming for us to get you."

Cadence chuckled and shook her head. "Still can't quite believe the old lady would voluntarily call you guys into her room."

"She was concerned for you. Apparently, you made quite the impression on her."

"So it would seem," Cadence said. Snow chuckled a bit, then pulled his phone from his pocket after it began to ring. "That was fast, Whitfield," she said.

"It's not Whitfield," Snow replied gravely. He frowned, answering the call. "Snow." He paused as the other person spoke. "We'll be right there, Mr. Suarez." The two of them were on their feet and out the door before Snow had even hung up the call.

The lobby of Lexington Hills was dark, save for the flashlight beams sweeping the place as Dan and Aiden entered the building. Osmund and Cadence stopped inside the lobby at the stairwell just as Ramon stepped over to them. They surveyed the situation silently for a moment as the two other members of the paranormal group came in with cases of equipment.

"Woah," said Aiden as the flashlight beam cut across the area of the dusty lobby where the ritual had taken place. "What the hell is that?"

"What?" Dan asked as he turned around suddenly, seeming a little jumpy tonight. But then, given the tension that all the spirits in the building were feeling, Cadence wasn't surprised that maybe the ghost hunters would be picking up on it, too.

"Look at this," Aiden said. He hunkered down and touched the groove of the circle. "Dude ... I think this is blood."

"Blood?" Lauren asked sharply as she and Derrick brought in some cases of equipment. "We were here just a couple of weeks ago. Are you telling me that in between our investigations, someone got in here and got hurt?" she asked, then moved over to see what they were looking at on the floor. "Or got creepy with the dangerous stuff," she said. She found herself more than a little discomfited by the new decoration in the lobby.

"Whoever did this, they're gone now," Dan said brusquely, barely paying attention to them. "Let's just set up."

Lauren and Aiden exchanged glances, then began setting up the equipment. Cadence, Snow, and Ramon watched, waiting to see if they talked about a plan of attack.

"I'm betting they go for the downstairs areas," Ramon murmured. "They did patient rooms last time."

"So, Ruby might be safe," Cadence said. "Good."

"Or, they might be heartened by the evidence they got upstairs the last time and be chomping at the bit to try for more," Snow said.

"Yeah, okay, Mr. Party Pooper," Cadence said quietly teasing.

"Derrick, you got good stuff upstairs last time. You want to try again, or do you want to go with us to the medical suites?" Dan asked.

"We can always come back to redo hot spots," Derrick said, and pocketed a digital voice recorder while picking up a camcorder. "I'd like to go with you guys."

"Man, you just don't want to get scratched by cranky ass ghosts again," Aiden teased.

"Don't see you running upstairs to volunteer," Derrick jeered back.

"Enough." Dan snapped at them, his voice harsh. He shook his head and went back out to the van to get the rest of the equipment.

Aiden quieted, and, frowning, began to set up his monitoring station. Derrick joined him, and Cadence crossed the room to listen in while Snow began quizzing Ramon about spirits that might be haunting the medical suites.

"Is it me, or has he been on edge for the last few days?" Aiden asked Derrick under his breath.

"It's not just you," the youngest member of the group said.

"What's up his ass? Do you know?"

"He doesn't really talk to me that much. I dunno, man. I'm the new guy, remember?"

Aiden nodded a bit and shrugged. "Don't take it personally, kid. I wish I knew what's got him so wound up lately; he is usually laid back."

Cadence made her way back over to Ramon and Snow. "Game plan?" she asked quietly.

"None yet," Snow replied. "They may not be able to get down to the medical suites."

"How come?" Cadence asked.

"My fault," Ramon said. "When we were dealing with the shadow creature, I locked the door to the basement to try and protect Carl, in case the creature decided to add him to the menu as a side dish. It turns out the lock is so old it's now stuck like that."

"Which means if they can't get down, they'll go up," Cadence said.

"For one of two reasons," Snow said to explain. "One, in giving up, they will go back upstairs to investigate the patient rooms. Or two, there is an old elevator that goes down to the medical suite. It's how the doctors would take the patients up and down. Mr. Suarez says that the elevator itself crashed about eight years ago. However, if they are feeling particularly reckless, they could try climbing down the shaft."

Dan came back in with spools of cords, then went back outside with Derrick to get the last couple of cases from the van. Aiden moved over to Lauren, who happened to be over near the staircase.

"Hey, Lauren, you have any idea why Dan is so edgy?" he asked.

She made a face and shrugged. "I don't think I should talk about it," she said.

"Come on; we're all friends here. What's up?"

"He thinks something followed him home from here last time. Please don't tell him I told you. He doesn't want any of us getting scared off."

Cadence glanced over to Ramon, who shook his head. "Everyone here is accounted for. No one left to follow anyone." Snow and Cadence frowned at each other.

"Why on earth would we get scared off?" Aiden asked her. "If something did follow him, we could try to help him. Did you do your clairvoyant thing for him? See if there is anything?"

"No, he won't let me. He also suggested I stay shut down here tonight so that nothing can try to come at me," Lauren said, but she looked doubtful.

"Lauren …" Aiden started, then paused as he thought. "When we were here last, it was Derrick who got scratched. If anything here was going to follow anyone on the team home, don't you think it would have been the kid? After all, it had 'marked' him," he said, using air quotes as he said the word *marked*. "Or you, as the psychic?"

Lauren was at a loss and just shrugged. "Weird," Aiden muttered to himself as he turned and headed back to finish setting up his equipment. Dan and Derrick came back inside a moment later. Within a few minutes, everything was up and running, and the group was ready to go hunting.

The three spirits followed the three hunters, and Aiden stayed behind, as usual, to monitor the video feeds that the team would set up as they went. All three had their camcorders going and their flashlights on, sweeping the floor for any dangers. They crept through the back double doors, crossing over to where the ghost Maggie had been consumed. Snow shuddered a bit as they crossed that bit of floor.

"Hey, weren't both doors here last time?" Derrick asked as they approached the double-door entryway to the dining room that was now lacking one of its doors.

"I guess the floor in the lobby wasn't the only thing those vandals defaced," Lauren said.

"Dining hall," Dan commented in a terse voice as they entered the large room. Their flashlight beams passed over the few dust-covered tables and cob-web-laced chairs.

"EVP?" Lauren asked.

"Yeah, I think I recall another local group got something in here," Dan said.

"Yeah, there is a story that one of the hospital's housekeepers was killed by a deranged patient in here," Derrick said.

The three spirits exchanged looks, knowing that they were referring to Maggie. "Well, guess we don't have to worry about them catching too much on that count," Cadence muttered.

"Sadly, no," Snow replied.

Ramon nodded and frowned, standing next to Cadence. "They have the story wrong. She had a heart attack. She wasn't killed by a patient."

"Gotta love urban legends," Cadence said with a shrug. "People look at this place and see creepy. Therefore, they're going to make up shit about it."

"Shhh," Snow admonished. He pointed to Lauren, who had her digital recorder out. Cadence and Ramon both mouthed "sorry" to him.

"Is there anyone here who would like to speak to us?" she asked. She paused for a few moments before continuing. "We're here to help you, but we can't help you unless you give us a sign of your presence."

A few minutes passed with the three living beings and the three spirits standing around in the dining hall, the living ones asking for answers from a spirit who wasn't there and getting nothing from the spirits who were. Finally, they decided to move on and made their way into the kitchen.

Two old stoves remained in the kitchen, but those seemed to be the only appliances that had remained. Stained pieces of the wall were gaping reminders of where the refrigerators should have been. A dark cavernous hole beneath the counter on the wall opposite the stoves stood as a silent reminder of a dishwasher. The sinks were large, deep, and rusted. One of them was beneath a boarded window, and the other was next to the hole where the dishwasher should have been. The boarded window still boasted the tattered remnants of a floral curtain, though the colors were too far gone to tell what they had initially been.

The group of investigators made their way over to the door down to the basement. "This is our best way over to the medical suites," Dan said.

"Does something smell bad in here to you guys?" Lauren asked, making a face. The other two ignored her for the moment as they were fixated on the door.

"Locked," Derrick said after trying the doorknob.

"Let me try," Dan said, setting his camera down on the counter, facing the door. He bent down swiftly to take a knife from his boot. Cadence's mouth dropped open, and she and Snow looked sharply at one another.

"What's wrong?" Ramon asked as he caught the look between them.

"If it follows him, where is it?" Cadence asked urgently, ignoring Ramon for the moment.

"It might not be following. Or we may be jumping to conclusions." Snow tried to reassure her, but he, too, was on edge now.

"Bullshit. You know we're both thinking the same thing, and that we're both right."

"Right about what?" Ramon asked, lost in the conversation.

"The cultist who sacrificed the cat," Cadence said as she gestured to Dan's boots. "He was overweight and pulled a knife out of his boot. The boots Dan is wearing look an awful lot like the boots of the cat killer."

"You think he is the cultist?" Ramon asked, while Dan wiggled the knife in the lock.

"I suppose it would explain why he feels something or someone followed him home from here. It also explains why he doesn't want the psychic on his team communicating with that something and why he was so short with the others about the summoning circle," Snow said.

"Ramon, warn the others," Cadence whispered. "That shadow creature might come back tonight. If it is following him around, like we were told it might, it could come back here again if only to harass the one who summoned it." Ramon nodded curtly and disappeared. Cadence and Snow shared another look and went back to watching Dan trying to jimmy the lock with his knife.

"I think … I got it …" he said, and the knife slid out suddenly, slicing his thumb. "Fuck!"

"Shit, are you okay?" Lauren asked, as the door began to swing open. Cadence could hear the weak cries for help from Carl at the bottom of the stairs.

"I thought he was louder," Cadence said. She remembered being able to hear him from the dining room last time.

"I'm sorry, what?" Snow asked, but then both of their eyes widened in sudden comprehension. It wasn't that Carl's cries were weaker, nor was it that Cadence was mumbling too much. The level of ambient noise was rising, like a howling wind or an oncoming train, and it was rising fast. It could only mean one thing.

"Shit, sometimes I hate being right," Cadence said.

Ramon reappeared in the kitchen and looked wide-eyed as he, too, recognized the noise that signified the creature's presence. The noise became deafening–wind in the room rising as all three spirits began wildly looking around for the violently churning mass of shadows that composed the creature. Then suddenly, from the basement, a shadow tentacle reached up and threw the door open wider, causing the door to pass through part of Cadence.

"Cade!" Ramon yelled. He grabbed her, pulling her out of the way as the shadow creature began to emerge from the stairwell.

"Drain their batteries," Snow yelled. He reached into Derrick's camcorder and began to pull the energy from it. Ramon followed suit, reaching into Lauren's camcorder. Cadence watched the other two to see how they did it. She then proceeded to follow suit, reaching into Dan's camera and trying to suck the energy from the battery into herself. Unlike the exercise with the television, she could easily feel where the power source was in the camera.

"My camera just went dead," Derrick said.

"Mine, too," Lauren said.

There was a vicious wind in the kitchen now, even though the night outside was still. A strong, acrid stench was rising as well, causing the breathers to cover their noses in revulsion. Dan had gone pale and sweaty, staring wide-eyed at the stairwell door, his bleeding, throbbing thumb all but forgotten. Since he had summoned the creature, he had the best sensitivity to it. He could see it.

"Run!" he yelled to the others, dropping his camera to the floor, which let it fall from Cadence's hand. "Get out of here, run!" He had his knife in hand and, without waiting for his fellow teammates, he turned and fled.

"What the hell is wrong with him?" Derrick asked, and Lauren looked after him, each unaware that a swirling mass of chaotic evil was looming behind them. They were aware that something was going on, as Lauren had pinched her nose shut from the stench, and the wind of the creature was assaulting them. They became aware that something dangerous was near them when the shadowy creature ripped the door to the stairwell off of its hinges, threw it over their heads, and across the room. The amputated door landed with a loud clatter on the stoves across the room.

Even in the wan light of Lauren's flashlight, the spirits could see the color drain from the breathers' faces. Derrick and Lauren ran out of the kitchen, high-tailing it away from the bad smell and weird wind. The creature behind Lauren and Derrick screamed and lunged, but not for the two breathers. It went for Cadence. The move was so sudden that Cadence wasn't expecting it, as she had been more worried about it attacking the living ghost hunters.

She felt Ramon's grip on her wounded arm tighten as he tried to pull her away, but the creature already had a tentacle tightly entwined around her leg. She cried out as she fell, and it felt like a thousand needles shot through her where the shadow touched her.

"Teleport!" Snow screamed at her. She closed her eyes, envisioning the lobby where Aiden was, but the pain searing through her leg and arm from the creature and

Ramon each pulling on her like she was the rope in a tug-of-war contest was too distracting.

"I can't!" she yelled back, gritting her teeth against the pain.

"Use the energy you took from the battery, make a weapon!" her partner yelled as he began throwing things at the creature, trying, unsuccessfully, to get its attention.

"Pull from me, too," Ramon said, and she felt a rush of energy as he poured the excess he had taken from the battery into her.

She could easily have imagined a gun or a myriad of other weapons, but what sprang to mind was the dagger. Simple, no moving parts or extra bullets needed. She could almost feel the weight of it in her good hand, the smooth feel of the hilt against her palm. That was when she realized she could feel it. She looked down, and sure enough, the blade was there.

Her leg lifted, and another tentacle snaked around her waist as the creature started to draw her into the dark. She cried out in pain, her eyes closing as the feeling of a thousand hot needles went through her midsection. She slashed with the knife and was close enough to the creature to cut off the tentacle around her waist from where it was coming out of on its body. The creature screamed in pain and anger as the tentacle fell to nothingness.

Despite the searing pain in her middle, she kept going, knowing it was the only way to save herself. Another few slashes with her hastily created knife, and it released her leg. She landed in a heap on the floor and lashed out again, cutting off another tentacle as it tried to come after her again. Scooting across the floor away from the shadow, she hefted the blade and threw it.

The creature howled in agony and anger as the spirit-made blade hit home, lodging in the center of its mass. Ramon and Snow pulled Cadence through the doors and back out into the lobby. It was chaos there, too, as the ghost hunters were quickly packing up to leave.

"Lauren, I need your digital voice recorder," Aiden called, putting equipment swiftly away in cases as Derrick and Lauren coiled up cords as fast as they could. Dan was nowhere to be seen.

"Shit, I left it in the kitchen."

"I'll go," Aiden said. "Dan probably left his camera back there, too, since I don't have it and didn't see it in his hand as he hauled ass out of here. You guys finish packing." Aiden did not look happy at all.

"I'll be right back," Ramon said as they got Cadence settled on the bottom-most step.

Cadence looked at Snow as Ramon disappeared. "Oh God, Snow, the tape. What if they caught ..."

"It doesn't matter." Snow shook his head, concern creasing his brow. "I'm not worried about what they did or didn't catch right now. We'll cross that bridge when we come to it. Right now, I'm worried about you."

"That thing has a hell of a bite," she said, looking down and seeing both her pant leg and the bottom half of her shirt silver with whatever passed for her blood.

"So I see," he said. His voice was quiet, and she recognized his worried tone.

"Does this mean I'm going to be drunk again tonight?" she asked, trying to lighten up the mood.

"I don't know. I hope so. I prefer that to the alternative."

"You don't like me sober, Ozzie?" she asked. She winced as she tried to shift into a position that might hurt less.

"I like you here as opposed to not," he said. "Don't move."

Ramon reappeared with gauze and a medical kit. "Cadence, I need you to just close your eyes for me, alright?" He then looked at Snow. "We need to get her upstairs. Now."

Cadence winced and momentarily debated being a deliberate pain in the ass for them, but decided just to do as she was asked. She closed her eyes and almost immediately slipped into unconsciousness.

CHAPTER 12

Overwhelming Evidence

Lexington Hills loomed before the teenagers as they drove up in Steve's car. Steve was driving, and Jeff was in the passenger seat, while Cadence, Paige, and Shawna were in the back seat. Shawna's eyes were already as big as saucers as she looked at the huge, dilapidated building.

"Are we really going in there?" she asked in a nervous tone.

"You can't be chickening out already," Jeff said.

"Why not? It wasn't my idea to come here," she replied.

Cadence jumped in, trying to interfere before Shawna and Jeff descended into another one of their infamous drama -filled fights. "Shawna, it's just a building. There's nothing to be scared of in there."

Steve parked the car and turned off the engine. "Kinda hoping you're wrong, Cade," he said. Cade reached forward and thwapped him on the back of the head.

"Not helpful, man," she said. Steve flashed her a grin in the rearview mirror and then laughed when she rolled her eyes at him.

"Come on," Paige said, excitement clear in her voice. "Everyone out!"

Cade shook her head and opened the back door on her side. She had one friend who was scared to go in, one friend who couldn't wait to go in, and two guys who were hoping it would be scary enough to lead to extended make-out sessions.

"Look," Jeff said as they all got out of the car, "Mr. Dobbins said our assignment was to try something out of our comfort zone and write a report about it, right?"

"Yeah, but I don't think he had this in mind. I think he meant like trying to befriend someone we normally wouldn't or maybe going bungee jumping," Shawna said as she moved to her boyfriend and slipped an arm around his waist. Jeff leaned in and gave her a kiss.

"What about you, babe?" Steve asked, slipping his arm around Cadence. "You scared?"

"Are you kidding me? Hell no."

"Come on!" Paige urged, heading for the front doors of the old asylum. "Let's do this!"

"Come on." Cade chuckled, leading Steve after Paige. "Let's make sure she doesn't get herself lost."

"How are we supposed to complete this dare, anyway? What were the rules?" Shawna asked, not letting go of Jeff as he led her up the front steps.

"It's not a dare; it's an assignment. We're supposed to spend at least an hour doing something out of our comfort zone," he shrugged. "So, I guess, spend at least an hour in here." Shawna made an unhappy noise in return.

Paige didn't care one bit about the grumbling going on behind her. It had been her idea for them to do this to complete the assignment. She had always wanted to come here, as she had heard all sorts of stories. She was very into the paranormal, so this was almost like going to Disneyland for her. She pushed open the front door and marched into the lobby. Her friends trailed along after her.

"This place is incredible," she said. Her voice was hushed with awe as she looked around at the huge doorways and big staircase.

"It's dirty," Shawna said. She wrinkled her nose a bit as she looked over the grimy, dust-covered floors and walls.

"Yeah, I don't think they get maid service anymore," Cadence said as she brushed a bit of her long hair from her face. "It'll be fine, so what if we get a little dusty?"

"Paige," Steve called over to the girl as she was four steps up the staircase. "I think we should stay down here."

"Oh, come on!" Paige protested.

"No, you come on. This place has been abandoned for years. I don't mind hanging out for a while here, but the last thing we need is someone falling through rotted floorboards or something." Steve had some common sense, which was one of the reasons why Cade liked him so much. "We stay on the first floor."

Paige pursed her lips in a pout and came back down the stairs. "Fine," she said with a heavy sigh. "Hey, want to try a séance?"

"*Are you kidding me?*" Shawna squeaked.

"*Could be fun,*" Jeff said. He hugged Shawna close. "*Besides, I'm here to protect you, sexy.*"

Paige continued, as if she hadn't heard them. "*I don't have any kind of supplies, but we could all just sit in a circle and try to make contact.*"

"*What kind of supplies would you normally need, anyway?*" Cadence asked out of curiosity.

"*Oh, you know, candles, Ouija board, things like that,*" Paige shrugged. "*But if we sit in a circle and hold hands and try talking, they might communicate.*"

"*Sit?*" Shawna asked incredulously. "*On that floor? We'll get covered in all that dirt and dust.*"

Cadence closed her eyes and started counting. Paige was her friend, Steve was her boyfriend, Jeff was her friend. Shawna was Jeff's girlfriend, and Cadence tried hard to tolerate her, but when she acted like that, it made it hard just to not punch her in the face. So, Cadence counted to ten while Steve, who knew his girlfriend's reactions all too well, rubbed her neck beneath her long, dark blonde hair.

"*Dirt washes off, Shawna, even off of clothes. It won't kill you. Sit,*" Cade said as she and Paige sat down cross-legged on the floor. Steve sat beside Cade; Jeff took up residence on the other side of Paige, leaving Shawna sitting between Jeff and Steve. The girl didn't look happy, but she didn't whine anymore, either.

"*Okay, now we all hold hands,*" Paige said, "*and close our eyes.*"

As they held hands and closed their eyes, Cadence could still hear the trembling breaths of Shawna. What the hell was so scary? Cade didn't understand why the girl was so freaked out by an old, empty building.

"Are there any spirits here who wish to communicate with us?" Paige asked, trying to sound like she knew what she was doing. After a few minutes of getting nothing in response, she tried again. "If there are any spirits here who wish to communicate with us, please come forth. We're not here to hurt you; we just wish to communicate."

Jeff snickered. "Paige, I think you've seen one too many scary movies."

"Shhh!" Paige commanded. She could feel the hairs on the back of her neck rising as goose bumps broke out on her arms. "Something's here."

Cadence heard something behind her, like a shuffling. She discounted it, though, attributing it to a rat or some other wildlife scurrying around.

Then Shawna screamed.

"Behind you, Cade!" she yelled, then scrambled to her feet and ran as fast as she could out the front door.

Cade twisted around and peered, but could see nothing. "What the hell freaked her out?"

Jeff was on his feet and followed his girlfriend out the door. Steve had turned to see what Shawna was talking about, ready to protect his girl, but like Cade, he saw nothing. He looked at her and Paige, and he shrugged.

"Can he break up with her yet, please?" Paige sighed. "She ruins everything."

"God, soon, I hope," Cadence said.

"Come on, let's just lie in the report and say we were here for an hour," Steve said. "There's no way we're gonna get her back in here."

The three teens got up and dusted themselves off, then headed out the door.

She could hear someone moving in the room. The footsteps were heavy, definitely male. She could feel the stiff mattress of a hospital gurney beneath her. She shifted in the bed a bit and gasped at the pain that shifting brought her mid-section and her leg.

"Cade?" a familiar male voice asked.

She opened her eyes and saw a very relieved-looking Ramon and Osmund hovering over her. "Remind me not to go toe-to-toe with shadow creatures again," she said. She tried once again to shift into a sitting position.

"Take it easy," Ramon said as he put a gently restraining hand on her shoulder.

"We have to go," she said, shaking her head.

"We have time," Snow said. "Last time, he didn't get round to checking the evidence until the next day. You can take it a little slow."

"We missed our ride."

"I know how to get there," Snow said. He was trying to reassure her so she would take it easy. "Now listen to your doctor."

Cade tried to smile a little and glanced over at Ramon. "You're my doctor now, huh?"

He shrugged, looking a little embarrassed. "Well, I don't know about that. I just patched you up a little."

"Well, thank you. I appreciate it. And thanks for helping me make the dagger."

"I just gave you the extra energy. You needed it more than I did. You made the dagger."

"And thank you for telling me how," she said to Snow. "I don't know …"

He held up a hand to silence her. "Let's not talk about *what ifs* or *what would haves,* please."

Cadence grudgingly nodded. Both of them were acutely aware of just how very badly things went tonight and how much worse it could have gone. She looked down and saw her bloody clothes. "Don't suppose we have time for me to run home and change, do we?"

"You can change without needing to go home," Snow said. He tapped his head to remind her. "Mental image, remember?"

She nodded and closed her eyes, gathering what was left of her energy. When she opened her eyes again, she was wearing a fresh pair of jeans and a comfortable T-shirt. "Not the most professional," she said, "but I figured you would forgive me the desire for comfort this once."

He smiled and nodded. "It's growing close to dawn. Are you alright to travel?" he asked.

Cadence looked at Ramon. "What do you say, doc? Am I okay to travel?"

Ramon chuckled lightly, relieved that she seemed to be doing so well. "Yes, you can."

"Do I have to worry about tearing stitches or anything?"

"Yes, actually, you do. Just move carefully, and you should be alright," Ramon said. "You'll need to be the most careful of the stitches in your middle. Because of where they are, they are going to be the easiest to tear. You'll also need to be careful walking. Your leg was held the longest and took the most damage. It'll likely hurt a good deal."

"And when should she come back to see about the wounds?" Snow asked.

"The way things are going, you two will probably be back sooner than you know it," the orderly, now-turned-doctor, replied.

"I'll call and check in with you, doc," she said, slipping gently out of the bed, wincing a little. She faltered a little as she tried to put weight on her leg, and both men reached out to steady her.

"Just so you know," Ramon said quickly, "You have fifty stitches around your midsection, twenty-seven in your leg, and ten in your arm."

"My arm?" she asked in surprise.

"When I was trying to pull you away from it, I tore the knife wound on your arm open again. I'm sorry."

"Trying to save my life, or whatever this is, versus a cut. Think I'll forgive you this once." She smiled at him.

Snow opened the door for her, and she followed him out, limping, with Ramon on her heels. She was surprised to see they were still at Lexington Hills. The other room had seemed like a legitimate hospital, not a derelict building. She turned, looking back into the room curiously.

"It was a room as I remember them," Ramon explained, knowing what she was confused about. She nodded and smiled and looked back to Snow.

"Hands, please?" her partner asked. "I'll be taking us there, so just close your eyes and focus on me."

"Be safe," Ramon called as they disappeared from the hospital.

They appeared in the parking lot of Aiden's apartment building. The first rays of sunlight were filtering through the gloom of night, and Aiden's van was parked out front. Snow led the way into the apartment building, up the stairs, and then through the door of Aiden's apartment. Cadence limped along, amazed that, as a ghost, it could hurt so much.

The living room was dark as all of the techie toys were turned off or with screen savers. Snow led Cadence around to the couch. "Sit." She opened her mouth to argue, but he held up a hand, cutting her off. "No, you were badly injured tonight. You will sit and rest. I will do the pacing this time."

Cadence chuckled, then winced because even that hurt. She shook her head, taking a seat. "God, I was still so angry last time we were here."

"I was relaxed and watching you pace. This time, we've switched roles."

That caught Cadence off guard. "What are you angry about?"

"I almost lost a partner tonight. What do you think I'm angry about?"

"It does seem to be a habit of mine, doesn't it? Dying on my partners."

"Dying on Mr. Halleran was one thing; you were mortal."

"I honestly thought it was going to go after Lauren and Derrick. I mean, if life energy attracts it, why would it go after me when it had two fully alive people right there? I'm sorry. I didn't mean to worry you."

"No, you don't get it, Cadence," he said as he stopped pacing for a moment and bent over the arm of the sofa, bracing himself with both hands. "I should have known. It can't get nearly as much energy off of a human as it can get from a fresh ghost. It would have to whip them up into a frenzy of panic to get half the energy it can draw from you. I should have known that it would go for you."

"It surprised all of us there. None of us expected it to already be in the basement. Hell, it was only a minute or so between us figuring out that it was Dan who had summoned it and the damned thing appearing. We had no warning at all. It wasn't like before when it came and we heard it coming. We got caught flat-footed. It won't happen again since we know a little better now what to expect. And I'm fine. I'm still here, right? Any day you wake up is a good one. That's what my father used to say."

Snow paused from his pacing and anger at himself to look over at her. "I suppose you're right. I just … I'm the experienced one out of the two of us. I feel like an incredible fool for not having seen it coming."

"Experienced does not mean clairvoyant," she said. "You even said before that you've only dealt with non-human things a handful of times. That's not exactly a lot. Not enough to expect you to have a playbook about how they operate. We can micro-examine this in retrospect all we want, Ozzie. We can both go and turn this into our own fault. But the fact of the matter is, it really wasn't anyone's fault except Dan's. He's the one that summoned the damned thing in the first place."

Snow opened his mouth to reply, but stopped as the door to the bedroom opened and Aiden came out wearing jeans and little else. A towel was hanging around his neck, his hair was wet, and he smelled like he had just gotten out of the shower. He grumbled something under his breath and walked over to his computer desk, hitting the power button forcefully before continuing to his coffeemaker.

"He's up early," Snow said as he looked out the window to see the colors of sunrise still painting the sky.

"Probably couldn't sleep." Cadence shrugged, then winced as she felt the pull on her midsection. "I'd get like that after a rough case sometimes." Their discussion was interrupted by the shrill ringing of Aiden's cell phone, which was by his computer. He left the kitchen and grabbed it.

"Hey, Lauren," he answered. "Nah, don't worry about it. I couldn't sleep anyhow. What's up?" He paused as she spoke on the other end. "I don't know; I have no idea why he just took off like that. He was weird all night. I do know I'm not exactly thrilled about it. Not just leaving equipment behind, but leaving you and Derrick, too." He paused once more; they could hear Lauren's voice coming over the phone line, but they couldn't make out the words she was saying. "Don't worry about it. I got the recorder and camera, alright. Both of them were still recording. I can't wait to see what wigged you guys out so bad."

Snow and Cadence exchanged looks. Cade thought she had drained the battery of Dan's camcorder and that it wouldn't have recorded. Maybe it hadn't gotten anything; she consoled herself. Maybe they would be lucky. She wasn't so sure because nothing about this case had been lucky since the shadow creature had been summoned.

She frowned as Aiden continued his conversation. "I'll go over it all and let you know if I find anything like what you guys say you saw ... no, it's not that I don't believe you, but you know what these things are like; you don't always catch what you see and hear on film or tape. That's why they call them personal experiences rather than evidence."

"Do you think he could be one of the cultists?" Cadence asked as Aiden talked on the phone.

"It is possible, I suppose, but he is very tall. He's well over six feet, and I don't recall any of the five hooded figures striking me as being quite that tall," Snow replied.

"Me either." Cadence sighed. "It would have been nice and neat to peg all of the paranormal group as the cultists."

"Too neat," Snow said as he shook his head. "Not really possible, either. They have a female in their ranks, and it was obvious that the cultists were all male. Not to mention that there are only four in the hunter group and there were five cultists."

Cadence shrugged. "They could have left Lauren out and brought in two more guys, but I think you're right. I think Dan was the only one in on it. Derrick is too young and seems to get a little too freaked out when something weird happens. Aiden seems to be the one interested in the science behind all of this. I really don't peg any of them as cultists."

Aiden hung up the phone and set it back down on his desk with a sigh. "What are you up to, Dan?" he asked. He groaned and stretched as he rubbed his eyes. He went to the kitchen and got himself a cup of coffee, then sat down at his computer. He reached over and grabbed the case of voice recorders. He singled out the one that had been Lauren's and plugged it into his computer.

"Time to see if you've got anything for me," he said to the recorder as he hooked it up.

"Going right for the heart this time," Snow noted. Cadence rose, wincing a bit, and made her way over to where Snow now stood behind Aiden. The tape started out normally enough, recording the fruitless EVP session that the hunters had done in the kitchen, looking for the ghost of Maggie, who would never be there again. Then it went to Dan, trying to jimmy the lock with his knife. Everything was nice and normal until Dan cut his thumb as the lock gave way, and the knife sliced his thumb, the door swinging open a little.

"What the hell?" Aiden grumbled, turning up the volume a bit. There was the sound of the wind and just a bunch of other nonsensical noise.

"The noise of the shadow creature," Cadence said.

"Cade!" They heard the tinny sound of Ramon's voice on the tape, muffled a bit as most spirit voices were. Both officers looked stricken as the tape played.

"Drain their batteries," Snow's voice clearly said. Aiden's mouth dropped open as he listened, forgetting to note down times and mark the recordings.

"My camera just went dead," Derrick said.

"Mine, too." It was Lauren's voice.

"Run!" Dan could be heard yelling to the others. "Get out of here, run!" The background noise of the room had increased on the tape. It wasn't as bad as it was when they were there, in front of the creature, but it still sounded like a freight train.

"What the hell is wrong with him?" Derrick could be heard asking, then came the sound of the door being forcibly ripped from its hinges, followed by another bang a few moments later as it was thrown and hit the stove. A clattering sound was heard, presumably when

Lauren dropped her voice recorder, and then footsteps could be heard as the ghost hunters high-tailed it out of there.

The tape recorder had survived the fall, and it caught the unearthly howl of the creature as it went for Cadence. Her voice was heard as she cried out in pain.

"Teleport!" Snow yelled in the recording.

"I can't!" came her recorded reply; the voice strained. All the while, the cacophony of the shadow creature's presence could be heard, as well as occasional noises of pain from Cadence or the effort from Ramon and Snow as they tried to pull Cadence free.

"Use the energy you took from the battery; make a weapon!" Snow's voice was heard very clearly.

"Pull from me, too," Ramon's quieter voice said. Cadence shivered slightly as she stood next to Snow, behind the stunned Aiden. Reliving all of it was eerie. For a moment or two, all that could be heard on the tape was the noise of the creature and Snow's fruitless efforts to distract it. Then an angry and pained scream came through the tape, which gave all three of its listeners, living and dead, the chills. The noise of the creature's presence faded as it made its escape, and several minutes later, Aiden could be heard coming into the room and picking up the recorder before shutting it off.

"Oh shit," Cadence said. "We're in trouble."

"Yes." Snow agreed quietly. "We are."

Aiden sat there for a moment, looking at the recorder as if he expected it to jump to life. He was stunned. So many intelligent "Class A" EVPs, detailing apparently three ghosts fighting off some other thing. Was it an evil creature or demon, maybe? Whatever it was, it must have been what had scared the others.

"No fucking way," the techie said at length. He jumped up suddenly and sprinted across to the box that held the camcorders. He went through until he found Dan's and he quickly pulled the memory stick from it, moving it to his video editing computer. He hit power to turn that one on and moved over to his computer desk to grab his coffee.

"Are we going to be on film, Snow?" Cadence asked with trepidation heavy in her voice.

"I'm not sure," he replied. "With as much energy as we had surging through us at the time? It's very possible."

"Fuck," she said.

"Indeed." Snow nodded in solemn agreement with her.

"Come on, come on." Aiden coaxed the computer as it booted up. Once it was up and running, he set everything up to play. He fast-forwarded past them walking into the dining hall and through the evidence-less EVP session. Once they got into the kitchen and Dan knelt down with his knife to work on the lock, he hit play.

The door swung open as Dan nursed his sliced thumb. Aiden hit pause a few moments after, his hands shaking. On the camcorder, not only could he see the black shadow form emerging from the basement stairwell, but he could hear the EVPs that Lauren's digital recorder had caught as well. Ramon yelling Cade's name in warning as the creature came up. Not only that, but he could see that Dan was staring straight at the thing with both a look of fear and recognition on his face.

"Son of a bitch, he knew it was there," Aiden said. "He could see it and left the rest of us to deal with it. Left

Lauren and Derrick alone with it." He frowned and sat there staring at the frozen image for a moment more, anger in him building, and then he hit play. He watched as the creature reached over, looking something like a shadowy octopus with its tentacles, and managed to pull the door to the basement from its hinges and throw it. The door went sailing over Lauren and Derrick's heads to land with a crash on the opposite side. Cadence realized that she hadn't done as good a job of draining the camera battery as she had hoped. It kept recording.

"I guess I haven't gotten much better at manipulating electronics," she said with an apologetic look to Snow.

A flash of an image of her was seen as the shadow creature grabbed her leg. The sounds of the struggle were captured on the camcorder just as clearly as they had been on the voice recorder. Aiden watched in amazement as the shadow creature sent out another tentacle to wrap around Cadence, and she could be seen, a pale, translucent, silvery image, as if looking at a person through a fog. Brief flashes of both Snow and Ramon could be seen as well as they fought to free her, and items began flying as Snow picked them up and threw them at the creature.

After Snow had told her to make a weapon, a small sliver of light could be seen in her hand, which grew brighter and sharper, like a large needle of light. The needle slashed at the shadow tentacles, cutting them away, and they fell, dissolving to ash, or so it seemed. Then the needle was thrown, and it pierced the middle of the mass of shadows. The visions of the three ghosts faded and the shadow creature shuddered and screamed, then turned, the blade of light still embedded in him, and escaped out the back door of the kitchen.

"Snow, what are we going to do?" Cadence asked, as Aiden numbly reached out to hit the stop button, trying to give himself time to digest what he had just seen.

"I'm not sure."

"Not helpful," Cadence said. She attempted to pace, but ended up just limping back and forth. "We have to do something, Snow. We can't let him keep that evidence. I know you said some was okay, but those were practically Polaroid-perfect shots of us."

"Well, we can't very well lift it from the apartment either now, can we?" Snow replied.

"Don't suppose we can plead reason with him, huh?"

"You see what he is like after seeing five minutes of footage of ghosts. I don't think he would take very well to us suddenly appearing and flashing badges to confiscate the evidence."

"I think I need sleep," Aiden said hollowly, not realizing that he had an audience. "Sleep would be good."

Snow and Cadence followed him into his bedroom as he went to lie down. "Snow, we have to do something."

"What do you propose, Cadence?" Snow asked. "Because right now all I can see is trouble, no matter what we do,"

"What about dreams?" she ventured.

"What about them?"

"Well, maybe we don't materialize in his living room. Maybe you go in and talk some sense to him, explain why he can't go public with the evidence he has at all, to anyone, ever. Maybe we can get his help with the shadow creature now. Maybe he can talk to Dan and see if he knows how to unsummon this damned thing. The body count, metaphorically speaking, is now up to three. That we know of," she said as she put emphasis on the last sentence. "We've lost Maggie, Carl, and Agent Banks. We have to stop it. This could be a golden opportunity to get some help in accomplishing that goal."

Snow paced, lips pursed, arms folded. "If we do this," he said, and he stressed the "if," "You're going in, not me. You'll do better communicating, I think. You're far more fluent in the modern American way of speaking."

Cadence nodded, limping over to the bed, her leg hurting. "Alright, fine." To be honest, she was a little grateful for the chance to sit down.

"Are you sure he will be willing? This is an awful lot to ask from the poor fellow. Those tapes out there are tantamount to handing him the keys to his future. You'll be asking him to voluntarily give up those keys."

"What if we offer to work with him in the future?"

"What?" Snow gawked.

"Police forces have their advisors and specialists they call in for help on subjects. We could be that for each other."

"I have a feeling Alistair might frown on us having an advisory relationship with a ghost hunter, Cadence. I have a feeling that something like that is concretely against the rules."

"Who says he has to know? Besides, Croft is not the end-all-be-all. You know that, right?"

Snow bristled at the slight against Croft.

"I'm sorry, Snow. I know you have this hero worship thing going for him and I get it, I really do, but what he approves of or disapproves of isn't my problem. Getting the job done is. And right now, my job is to protect both the residents of Lexington Hills and the breathers who go in there from that damned shadow thing that Dan summoned. If some kind of working relationship with a single ghost hunter can help me accomplish this, so no more bodies pile up, I'm all for it."

Snow frowned. He wanted to argue with her, knowing how very against the rules this idea was, but he could also see the reason behind what she was saying. He wanted to get this creature gone as much as she did, and the fact that she was almost its fourth victim did not sit well with him. Then there was also the fact that if those tapes came out, it would cause even more trouble. "Fine," he said. "I'll get you into his dream once he is dreaming."

"Thank you," she smiled.

"Once you are in there, you can create a space, you know. Make the area look how you want to present it to him. Unless he is a conscious dreamer and can control his own dream space, but those people are rare."

"One of these days, you are going to have to teach me how to do this on my own, you know."

"I know," he said. "But I can't teach you all of my tricks all at once."

They didn't have long to wait, as Aiden was very tired. Once Aiden was dreaming, Cadence took his hand and Snow's and then closed her eyes.

Cadence found herself in a bar and saw Aiden's tall, lanky form in a corner, having a drink. "Interesting choice," she murmured to herself. She saw no reason to try to wrest control of the setting from the dreamer, at least not yet, and so she simply moved to the corner booth that he occupied.

"Evening, handsome." She smiled at him. For the moment, she figured she would try to blend in with his dream. At least, until he recognized her, or she figured out a way to delve into the reason why she was there. He looked up from his beer and blinked, not expecting to be interrupted.

"Evening," he replied after a moment. "Care to join me?"

"Sure," she answered, and she eased herself into the seat across from him. He signaled the bartender for a beer for her. "Thanks," she said. She cocked her head to one side, looking at him. "Are you alright?"

"I've had better days," he said.

"Care to talk about it?"

"You wouldn't believe me if I told you."

"You might be surprised," she said. She started to pull the random patrons from the bar, making them leave to give them more apparent privacy.

He looked at her closely for a moment. "Holy shit," he said. "You're the ghost! The female ghost the shadow thing was grabbing."

"Recognize my face, huh?" she asked. She was trying to keep a calm demeanor in order to keep him calm.

"Not easy to forget the first ghost you see."

"I'm the first ghost you've ever seen? Really?"

"The first full-on ghost, yeah. Not one of those things where I kind-of-sort-of see an outline of a face or a body."

"Well, then, I guess I'm honored."

"Who are you?" he asked, looking at her in awe.

"Cade. You can call me Cade."

"That's what the guy in the recording called you. You have more of a name than that?"

"I do," she replied hesitantly, "but no offense, I think we should just leave it at Cade for now. You go looking for who I was, and it might open wounds for people I care about that are still trying to heal."

"Were you a patient or worker at Lexington?" he asked. He seemed to take this all in stride, a little bit better asleep than he had while awake.

"No," she replied, not going further into an explanation unless he questioned her. And she was really hoping he wouldn't.

He nodded then, apparently, something occurred to him. "That thing grabbed you. Did it hurt you?"

"Yeah, it did. But, I'm okay. Others aren't, however."

"The two guys with you?" he prompted.

"No, they're fine. All three of us made it out of there and away from that creature safely."

"What was that thing?"

Finally, the question she had been both anticipating and dreading. "It's what we call a non-human shadow creature. It was summoned to Lexington Hills a little over a week ago."

"The circle, the blood," he replied as he put two and two together.

"Exactly," she said. "Some cultists came in and summoned it. I guess they weren't expecting their ritual to pay off because they panicked and ran, but in doing so, they set it free."

"So now it is haunting the hospital?"

"It comes back to the hospital from time to time, but no, it isn't haunting there. It mostly seems to be haunting the ones that summoned it." Cadence looked at Aiden, meeting his brown eyes with her green, wondering if he would make the leap.

"Dan," he said after a moment.

Cadence nodded. "So far, all of the evidence points to Dan being the leader of the cult, yes."

"Son of a bitch, I knew he looked guilty as hell." By now, Cadence had gotten everyone out of the dream bar, and the two of them were alone. He frowned, looking down into his beer for a moment. "So, where are your friends?"

"I'm sorry?" she asked, confused by his sudden change in subject.

"Well, I figure I'm dreaming. And I figure you're only here because I just saw you on that tape. I figured my subconscious would drag your friends from the tape in as well. Or maybe that shadow monster. I'm kind of really hoping the latter doesn't make a cameo."

"Trust me; you don't want that thing in your dreams," Cadence replied. "And while yes, you are dreaming, I'm really here in your dream. I'm not a subconscious figment of your imagination."

"Don't suppose there's a way for you to prove that?" he asked.

Cadence frowned, thinking about it. "Maybe. But if I do give you a way to look up information about me and you realize that I am really here, that we've really had this conversation, I need you to do something for me."

"What?"

"I need your help in fighting against that thing, Aiden. Talk to Dan and see if he knows a way to destroy it. Or help us get some of the more physical components we'll need to take care of it. That way, Lexington Hills is safe for you to investigate and for the haunting spirits there. Also

..." She paused, knowing this would be the hardest part. "You'll have to bury the evidence that is on those tapes in your living room."

He pressed his lips together in a narrow line as he thought about it. "Don't ask for much, do you? With that evidence, I could practically write my own ticket in the paranormal field."

"I know … I know it's a lot to ask. But we can help each other out here, Aiden. We can help you, as much as it is in our power to help you, with your investigations."

He frowned, then shifted, pulling his wallet out of his back pocket. He tapped it on the table as he thought. "If I do this… if I check out whatever it is you are going to tell me to verify that I am not having a mental breakdown over this and if I agree to help you and your friends in getting rid of that thing. If I agree to bury the evidence we got last night when that thing attacked … I want a favor in return." He pulled a picture out of the wallet. A very pretty young woman with long blonde hair stood against a stone half wall with a garden behind her. "That's Bethany," he said, his voice gruff. "She died a year ago. I want to talk to her one last time."

"Aiden," she said, "I'm not sure it's in my power to arrange that."

"That's what I thought you'd say," he replied, emotion still strong in his voice as he moved to put the picture away.

Cadence sighed, thinking. "I'll see what I can do. I can't make any promises, but I will look into it." He looked at her in surprise, then smiled sadly and nodded his thanks. "As for me," she continued, "I would prefer you do all of this research on the computer and not call anyone. My name is Cadence Riley. I was with the 22nd precinct downtown. My partner was Andy Halleran. I lived in the Windmere building off of West Monroe. I died almost a month ago in the line of duty, in the arrest of Scott Sage."

"The Somerset Strangler?"

"Yes, the Somerset Strangler. My brother Sam Riley died nine years ago in the university massacre. He was a freshman and was majoring in education. He died trying to protect his girlfriend, Eri Takahashi. They were both found in one of the bathrooms of the dorm. Is that enough for you to Google?" she asked.

"Yeah," he nodded. "There's no way I could know all that stuff to plug it into a dream. Right?"

"I don't think so. So, you can research all of that, bury those tapes, and try to find a way to see if Dan knows how to get rid of what he conjured. I'll work on finding Bethany for you. What's her last name?"

"Saxon."

"Bethany Saxon, got it."

"How do I get in touch with you anyway?" he asked.

Cadence paused and thought about that for a moment. She didn't think that her spirit phone would take mundane phone calls. So, she offered him the best way to get in touch with her that she could think of off the top of her head. "Go to Lexington Hills. Just go into the lobby and wait a minute. Then say, 'Ramon, tell Cade I believe.' He'll get the message to me."

"Who is Ramon?"

"He's a ghost at Lexington Hills. He knows how to get in touch with me."

"Was he one of the ones helping you with the shadow thing?"

"Yes."

"Was he the one with the English accent or the other one?"

"The other one," she replied, hoping that she was doing the right thing in giving Aiden this information. "The English guy is my partner."

"You have a partner?"

"You don't stop being a cop just because you're dead," she said with a smile.

"I thought you stopped being everything when you were dead," he said.

"No. You don't believe that. If you did, you wouldn't be in a paranormal group trying to find proof of life after death."

"I guess you're right," he said as he conceded her point. "I don't suppose you want to let me in on the secret of life after death, do you?"

"I can't. Trade secret, sorry," she said.

"It's okay," he said with a slight smile. "I didn't really expect you to be able to tell me anything."

"Maybe one day I can. In the meantime, I'll see what I can find out about getting Bethany in contact with you. I'll be waiting to hear from Ramon. Then I'll come back and talk to you again."

"In my dreams? You can't just show up and talk to me, like EVP or something?"

"Believe it or not, this is easier."

"I'll take your word for it. I guess I'll talk to you again." She nodded and followed the tether she felt back to Snow and out of Aiden's dream.

"Come on," Snow said grimly as she opened her eyes. "We still have work to do."

CHAPTER 13

When Things Go From Strange to Worse

The office was mercifully quiet with their door shut. Cadence cradled her head in her hands. "God, I have such a headache."

Snow didn't even look up from his paperwork as he answered her. "Let's see, you pulled energy from a battery, got attacked, had energy pushed into you from another ghost, got quite a few stitches because you were so badly torn up, then went dream walking for a while. I can't imagine why you wouldn't feel at the top of your game."

"Ooh, nice sarcasm there, Ozzie. Didn't think you had it in you," she said. She looked up and gave him a weary grin.

"Sarcasm? Damn, I was trying for dry wit. I must be spending too much time with you; you're rubbing off on me," he said. He smiled at her, but he looked as tired as she felt.

Cadence shot him a sweet grin in reply. Snow had pulled what looked like a laptop computer out of one of his drawers and had that computer running a search for records of a Bethany Saxon. "Any luck yet?" Cade asked.

"You asked that just a few minutes ago," he said.

"And now I'm asking again."

"You're like a child asking '*Are we there yet?*' every few minutes. You'll know when I've found something; I assure you." She frowned at his snapping but didn't reply. Given the night they had both had, he had earned the right to be cranky.

A knock sounded on their door, and Snow quietly closed the laptop. "Enter," he called as Cadence lowered her hands to appear less ill and more professional.

Agent Whitfield entered the office and closed the door behind him. His brow furrowed when he saw Cadence. "Are you okay?" he asked.

"Just peachy," she replied sourly. "Why?"

"You don't look well, that's all. Sorry," he replied as he fidgeted with his hands. "I found some intel on the summoning circle for you. Agent Banks was right. We saw to it that this ritual, or recipe, as you called it, was removed from the breathers. It's too dangerous and the creatures it created were far too unpredictable and harmful."

"Oh, joy, more good news," Cadence said.

"Ignore her," Snow said as Agent Whitfield looked distressed at her reaction. "She's had a bad night."

"Oh … well … Sorry to hear it. Um, the good news is that it can be undone. The bad news is that it is really hard to undo it."

"But not impossible then? Well, that's good news," Snow remarked. Agent Whitfield fidgeted again, looking unsure. "It isn't impossible, right?" Snow urged.

"Well, the thing is, it was summoned by a breather. But this particular ritual has to be undone by a combined effort from both breathers and spirits in tandem. That, as I'm sure you know, is something that's forbidden."

"How do they do that?" Cadence asked and shifted in her chair, wincing as the motion pulled on sore areas. She hissed slightly as the sting grew more intense, but was determined to do her best to focus on the subject at hand. "How do breathers and ghosts work together to get this thing gone?"

"Well, they have to do it at the site of the original circle. Retrace the original runes, then draw runes with the opposite meanings as a mirror image of the original runes. Like, if you stand on the outside of the circle, you can read the runes properly, right? These would be readable if you are standing on the inside of the circle. The runes are done in chalk, and you need candles, white candles, where the other candles were. Not exactly something we can do; the chalk and candles part. But then, here's where it gets tricky. Where it used blood to seal the circle for the summoning, you have to use our energy, or our blood, to seal it for this ritual. Neither side of the coin can undo this thing without the other. That's another reason why it was banned."

"And there is no evidence of this ritual being written down in a book or diary somewhere?" Cadence asked.

"No, nowhere," Whitfield answered. "I'd be curious to know how they got hold of this. This was verified as being removed from breather hands in 1762. We started purging it in 1714. Um … you … you're bleeding, Ma'am."

"What?" Cadence looked down, and sure enough, she apparently had pulled something, as silvery blood was beginning to blossom on her shirt. "Ah, shit."

Snow jumped to his feet as she rose herself to slip out of her blazer, and she unbuttoned the bottom portion of her shirt. The bandage Ramon had wrapped around her midsection was slowly becoming quite gray.

"What happened?" Whitfield asked as Snow pulled down the bandage a bit to see how bad it was. The NHD agent turned away as he caught sight of the wound.

"The creature tried to make a snack out of me," Cadence replied. She looked decidedly at the ceiling while Snow inspected her wound.

"It bit you!?" He practically squeaked.

"Yeah."

"You're lucky to still be here!"

"Tell me about it."

"Look, Agent Whitfield, who do we have to speak with to get you assigned to help us with the research on this?" Snow asked. He used care as he settled Cadence's bandage back in place. "As you can see, we need the assistance."

"I don't know that they will let me come down, I mean, after what happened with Banks," he said.

"Whitfield, we can't do this without you. Who do I have to beg?" Cade asked. "That is, after I stop bleeding, of course." Snow grabbed her jacket.

"I'll talk to my boss. Tell him what this involves. I'm sure, once they know about the ritual, it will be a priority."

"Go then," Snow said. He began to gesture both Whitfield and Cadence to the door. "We'll be back soon. Just need to get her taken care of."

"Sure, sure," Whitfield said while nodding. He reminded Cadence of a nervous bobblehead. He went off back to his office, and Snow and Cadence headed to their hall of doors, avoiding the alarmed looks of some of the ladies working in the observation bay.

It wasn't long before they stepped into the lobby of Lexington Hills. "I think I have now spent more time here than at my apartment," Cadence commented as she looked around.

It never took long for Ramon to appear. "I didn't expect to see you so soon …" he said, trailing off as she lowered her jacket, which she had folded over her arm in an attempt to hide the bleeding as they had gone through the office. His eyes widened. "You have to be more careful." He held out a hand to her as he gently scolded her. He led her over to the steps. "Sit. I'll be right back."

Snow helped ease her down on the bottom step. "Yes, please do be more careful. This is nothing to play with."

"Yeah, trust me, it doesn't feel too pleasant," she assured him.

"It doesn't look like it does," Snow commented. Ramon reappeared with more gauze and his med kit.

"I apologize in advance," Cadence said as she looked between the two of them. "I'm a pain in the ass patient. Always have been"

"And this would be different than any other time, how?" Snow asked with a smile. Ramon chuckled and took the bandage off. Cadence closed her eyes in an outright refusal to look.

"Are you serious?" Snow asked in mock indignation, thinking that teasing her might be a good way to get her mind off of it. "An inspector who hates the sight of blood?"

"Cop," she corrected him, holding tight to the American title just to be obstinate. "Besides, it's only the sight of my own blood I hate. It's less about the blood and more about the deep puncture wounds and stitches. I figured I might be less of a bad patient if I closed my eyes and pretended I was in Barbados or something." She felt the needle slide into her, replacing the stitches. "Oh God, so much for that."

Cadence spent the next few minutes with her eyes closed and her arm held by Snow to keep it out of the way. She tried hard to play it tough, but an occasional whimper of pain escaped her. "This sucks," she said at length.

"I'm almost done," Ramon reassured her, his voice smooth. "But I'm tempted to put you in a full body cast just to be sure that you stay still."

"I promise not to move around too much, I swear," she replied.

Ramon finished and pulled her shirt back down, having been careful to reveal only the skin he needed in order to help her. "Good. Otherwise, I'll have to start charging you." He grinned a bit at her as he joked, trying to cheer her up.

Cadence's response was cut off by the front door of the hospital opening. Late afternoon sunlight could be seen outside in the overgrown yard. The shadow of a tall, lanky man stood in the door for a moment before moving inside and revealing itself as Aiden.

"Oh, good, his research went faster than ours, I guess," Cadence said as Snow helped ease her up into a sitting position.

"Uh, hey, Ramon," Aiden said hesitantly. He felt a bit foolish to be standing in the middle of the empty and abandoned building, talking to himself. "Tell Cadence Riley, I believe. Please." He looked around uncertainly, then shrugged and turned around, heading out the door and closing it behind him.

"Why does the ghost hunter know my name?" Ramon asked, decidedly unhappy about that little development.

Cadence and Snow exchanged a look, and Cade started to shrug but stopped herself, not wanting to pull anything more. "I told him."

"You talked to him?" Ramon asked incredulously.

"It was necessary, Ramon," Snow assured him. "The group left not only a voice recorder but a video camera in the kitchen. Both devices caught everything. The three of us were expending so much energy during that fight that all three of us were both audible and visible, as was the shadow creature. We had to talk to him to convince him to bury the evidence."

"And he agreed?"

"Apparently," Cadence answered as she gestured to the closed front door. "That was the message he was supposed to deliver to you, letting me know that he was going to do it."

"And what are you doing for him?"

"Looking up someone he knew," Cadence replied and was a bit curious to see how Ramon seemed to relax a little bit at that.

"We should get back to that, actually. And to Whitfield," Snow said.

Cadence nodded, and the two men helped her to her feet. Ramon took both her hands and looked into her eyes. "Please be careful. I like seeing you, but I don't like seeing you hurt."

She didn't quite know how to respond to the expression in his eyes as he spoke. Her brow furrowed for a moment, but she nodded, squeezing his hands lightly with hers before letting go. "I'll be careful. I promise."

Snow led her back through the hall of doors and looked at her for a moment once he had the door to Lexington Hills closed.

"What?" she asked.

"You're going to have to address that soon, you know?"

"Address what?"

"Ramon."

"Oh ... yeah. When exactly did that happen, anyway?"

"I would wager right around the time that you were willing to sacrifice yourself for the safety of the inhabitants at Lexington. I think his general admiration started long ago, however."

"Long ago?" she asked as they slowly made their way back to the office. Neither of them was in any hurry to see how much abuse her newest stitches would take. "I've only been dead a month. How long ago could it have started?"

Snow stopped at the door from the hall back out into the observation bay. "The first night we reported to Lexington, Mr. Suarez confessed to me that he knew you." He held a hand up to stop her as she opened her mouth to speak. "Not personally, of course. Not in a way that you would have known him. He said that you and some friends had come into the asylum when you were a teenager. You didn't stay long, as he managed to scare off you and your friends. But he remembered you."

Cadence stood there, her mind working as she tried to figure this out. "So, of all the people he has seen over the years, he remembered me?"

"It would seem so," Snow said.

"How? I mean, I know he's a ghost, so his social life isn't exactly full of new and exciting people. But how on earth does he remember me when I was sixteen, and how is he able to look at me now and know that it was me? Have you ever heard of this kind of thing happening?"

"What kind of thing?"

"A ghost having feelings for another ghost?"

"Of course! Cadence, just because you don't have a physical form doesn't mean you stop having emotions. I would have thought you would have learned that over the last month. Now, you might want to fix your shirt before you give the observation bay a collective heart attack."

"Right." She nodded and closed her eyes as she imagined a fresh, clean shirt on her instead of the stained one. The blood stain vanished. Snow nodded and took her arm; then the two of them made their way back to the office.

Something gleamed on Cadence's desk, catching the light as they walked back in. The two of them exchanged a look, and Snow shrugged. He sat down at his desk and went back to his laptop as Cadence circled to her desk. There on her desk was the dagger that Agent Banks had loaned her. She smiled and picked it up, turning it over in her hands. She felt better having it with her. She noticed a note on her desk as well.

"Looks like you need this more than the closet does. Whitfield."

"Hey, the kid came through!" She knew Whitfield was older than her, but something in his mannerisms just reminded her of a jumpy, awkward teenager.

"Oh?" Snow asked, then looked up. "Lovely. Now, if he can just come up with the rest of the information on how to get rid of the creature that tried to make a meal out of my partner, I'd feel much better."

"Sourpuss," Cadence said and sat back down. Their office door opened and Cadence quickly hid the blade in her desk drawer. Alistair Croft entered, closing the door behind him.

"Osmund," he said gravely, "what is this I hear about you needing a research agent from NHD?"

"He came up with the information that's pertinent to solving this problem and taking care of the shadow creature. We won't need him for long, just a day or two."

"And I heard your partner was injured?" he asked. He gestured to Cadence but was speaking as if she wasn't in the room, which irked her a little.

"I'm fine," she replied, which got absolutely no response from Croft, irking her even more. She frowned and glanced at Snow, but he was too busy focusing on his former mentor.

"I think perhaps you were right in your initial reaction to this case. I think this is getting too dangerous for you two. I'll designate a new area for you. You're out of this one."

Snow was on his feet in an instant. "What? No, we have this one almost solved. You've got to give us just a few more days."

Croft held up his hand to stop Snow. "It's done. You'll have no need of the NHD agent and no need to get your partner injured."

"Excuse me, but weren't you the one who was all over him to let me be part of this case? You can't just take us off of it."

"I can do as I please, young lady. You may be new, but never forget I am your superior."

"The hell you are," she retorted.

"Cadence!" Snow exclaimed.

"No. You aren't superior to me in any way. If by that term you mean my boss, a good captain knows when to listen to his officers. We have this in the bag. We just need the time to see it through."

Croft's face was darkened with anger and he looked between the two of them, then shook his head. "Desks. Until you can teach your new protégé how to control herself, you'll be confined to desk duty. This is a shame, Snow. I expected more from you." He turned and left.

Snow sank down into his chair, stunned.

"Snow, I …" She stopped when he held up a hand.

"I need a few moments. Excuse me." Snow rose and left the office.

Cadence sighed as the door closed. She hadn't meant to get Snow in trouble with Croft; she really hadn't. She just couldn't stand the way he had come in to their office and started talking. Were things going perfectly? No. But that was no cause for Croft to come in here throwing his weight around, treating Snow like an errant child and Cadence like she wasn't there at all.

She grumbled and got up carefully, moving around to Snow's desk to continue the search for Bethany Saxon. Aiden had come through on his end, and she wasn't about to just give up on trying to come through on hers. The computer had finished its search, and the results were displayed on the screen. She sat down and looked at it, beginning to scroll through names. Apparently, there were a lot of people with the last name of Saxon. She found three instances of a Bethany Saxon, but only one had a death date of a year ago. The data section had designations and a location, but none of it meant anything to her. She needed Snow.

She leaned back in his chair with a disgusted sigh. Things were not going well today. They had found their cultist, and Whitfield had a good idea of how to dismantle the summoning. However, Croft had then come in, taken them from the case, their area, and rendered them useless. But why? Was he just trying to be protective of his old protégé? Was he protective of her? She didn't get it. Why would he have been so supportive of them being on the case in the beginning? Snow had wanted nothing but to take her off the case since she was too new to handle a non-human creature. Then to only turn around and take them off the case when they had started doing so well?

She grunted in frustration and rose, albeit carefully, from Snow's desk. She began to pace the office back and forth, limping badly as she went, eyes going over the pictures of the runes. This reversal ritual could be done; it just took both sides working together to do it. Maybe that's the real reason why it had been taken out of breather circulation. It took too much trust on both sides to put the genie back into the bottle.

They knew about the runes, but not which specific runes were required for the ritual to destroy the creature. They knew how to close the circle and what color the candles needed to be, but not what words, if any, would be needed, or any other specifics for the ritual. She frowned and began pulling the pinned-up notes down since, apparently, they weren't going to need them anymore.

A knock on the door made her pause, and she debated not answering since she wasn't sure she wanted to see how much worse this night was going to get. Finally, she relented when the knock sounded a second time. "Come in," she said.

Agent Whitfield peeked in the door. "Feeling better?" he asked as he entered, closing the door behind him.

"Depends," she said as she moved back to her chair. "But I'm not bleeding anymore, so that's likely a plus."

"Yes, it is. Um, is Officer Snow not here? I had wanted to go over this ritual with you guys."

Cadence was about to tell him not to bother when she stopped. "You got more information on it?"

"Yeah, I explained to my supervisor what you guys were dealing with, and he agreed that I should help you guys out with the research. This thing is dangerous. We need to get it contained or undone fast."

"You got permission to come work with us?" she asked, not quite believing what she was hearing.

"Yeah," he replied, brow furrowing. "I thought that was what you wanted."

"It is. It is. We just didn't think it was going to happen." Her mind was moving a mile a minute. Croft was taking them out of their area and off their case when NHD had apparently already agreed to let Whitfield work with them? It didn't make sense. "Let me call Snow back in here."

She pulled her phone from her pocket and dialed Snow. To her amazement, he picked up. "Snow, you need to get back here."

"Cadence, I'm sorry, there's no need ..." he said, but was cut off.

"Agent Whitfield got permission to work with us from his bosses. He's here to go over what we need to know. Two brains are better than one on this, Ozzie."

There was silence as he considered it, and she hoped to hell he picked up on the same oddities of the situation that she had. Finally, he said, "I'll be right there." He then hung up. She smiled. Obviously, something had clicked for him, too. She pocketed her phone and gestured for Whitfield to take a seat.

"You're doing better then?" he asked as he took the chair in the corner of the office, indicating her midsection. She nodded. "I can't believe it touched you and you survived!"

"It grabbed me in two places," she said. "Wrapped around my middle like you saw, but it got a hold of my leg first."

"And you're walking?"

Cadence shrugged. "Walking might be generous; limping is more like it. But yeah. I guess I got lucky."

"Very," Whitfield said. "Those things can rip appendages off of us like wings off a fly." The door opened and Snow, looking both solemn and perturbed, entered. He offered a nod to Whitfield as he took his seat.

"Is what Officer Riley said correct? That you have dispensation to work with us?"

"Yes, sir. My supervisor agreed that we need to get this thing handled quickly. And since you guys are willing to do the legwork on it, he said that the least we can do is give you a researcher."

Snow thought about it for a moment, then nodded. "Then take notes; Whitfield, this is what we'll need to know." Whitfield pulled his phone from his pocket and apparently hit a record button because he nodded to Snow. "Right, we need to know if there is any specific kind of chalk needed for this ritual. A specific mixture, color, etcetera. How many white candles, and where they go exactly? We'll need the precise runes that need to be put down and any specific way that they need to be drawn. Any specific dagger used in the letting of our energy, or blood. Any chants or gestures that have to be performed, and if there is any specific placing of people or ghosts, including the creature we seek to undo. Do you have all that?"

Whitfield hit "stop" on his recorder and nodded. "Got it, and I'll get right on it. But how are you going to manage it? It's going to take both our kind and the breathers to get this done."

"We've got that handled, I believe. Now hurry on this. I want to get this done before it consumes anyone else."

Whitfield nodded and rose, scurrying from the room. Once the door had closed, Cadence looked over the desks at Snow. "So?" She asked as she waited for him to open up about what was going through his head. He met her gaze, and for a moment, they simply contemplated one another. At length, he finally broke the silence.

"Why on earth would Alistair seem to be so upset about us bothering NHD if they had already agreed to let us borrow Whitfield? Why be so upset and take us out of our area, put us on desk duty? Why all the theatrics?"

"I don't know, but at this point, I'm very sure that's all that was. Maybe he's testing you? To see if you have the balls to keep going without his approval."

"Do you really think that?"

"I don't know, but it is a possibility. It's possible he wants to make sure you can stand alone, without him, both as a mentor and as an officer," she said. "You know him better than I do. And for what it's worth, I'm sorry I lost my temper. I just hated seeing him treat you like that."

Snow smiled wistfully at her. "That's very sweet of you, Cadence. Thank you. Well, I suppose we'll see what he makes of us staying on the case despite his bluster, won't we?"

Cadence smiled and nodded, relieved that he wasn't going to give up simply because his old mentor had yelled at him. "So," she said as she switched their topic of conversation. "I found Bethany, or, at least, a listing for her, but I have no idea what the letters, numbers, and symbols after her name mean."

"Oh! Right!" He opened his laptop up and took a look. "Well … That's almost too bloody convenient."

"What is?"

"She's on our level, a guidance counselor, I suppose you would say."

"Seriously?" Cadence asked. She wondered for a moment if he was messing with her.

"Seriously, indeed," he said. "Come on. If you can manage to hobble across the office, let's see if she has any plans for tonight. And be careful." He reminded her as she started to rise.

They left their office and Snow led Cadence through the observation bay and over to a set of doors marked "Guidance." Once inside, they were met with a very serene white waiting room with soft, gauzy fabrics. At a desk in the middle of the room sat an elderly-looking woman. There were seating arrangements along all of the walls. The old woman at the desk smiled up at them in greeting.

"Yes?" she asked.

"Is Miss Saxon available?" Snow asked.

"Oh no, I'm sorry, she is in with someone right now. But they should be done soon. If you'd like to wait, you can have a seat."

"Thank you," Snow said. He moved over to one of the couches and took a seat. Cadence followed, but did not take a seat. She remained standing, arms crossed over her chest.

"Are you alright?" he asked as he noted the defensive posture.

"Yeah," she responded, a little too quickly.

"Why don't you take a seat?"

"It's all white in here. I don't want to bleed on anything."

Snow arched an eyebrow. "Cadence, the furniture in here can be cleaned just as easily as you cleaned your shirt earlier. You won't be permanently staining or ruining any of the furniture, I assure you."

"It's not that," she said. "I've never been comfortable in all-white places, even when I was alive. It's too … I don't know, too sterile maybe?"

"Reminds you of hospitals?"

"Maybe that's it; I don't know. All I know is that the whiter a room is, the more nervous I get. I've never seen or heard of anything good happening in all-white rooms."

"Oh, I can help with that, dear," the old woman at the desk piped up. She put a hand flat out on her desk, and color spread from there. The colors were soft and muted, blushing pinks and dusty roses. She wasn't a huge fan of pink either, but it was better than white. Cadence relaxed noticeably.

"Thanks," she said to the secretary. It was only a few minutes later that one of the office doors opened and a very pretty young blonde woman emerged from the office alone. She looked quite a bit like an angel or a porcelain doll with her golden hair, blue eyes, ivory skin, and petite build.

"Someone else for me, Mrs. Steinberg?" Bethany asked.

"Yes, dear, those two wanted to speak to you," she said and gestured toward Snow and Cadence, who both rose and made their way over to her.

"Miss Saxon?" Snow asked, ever the expert at asking the obvious.

"Yes." She smiled and waved them back to her office. Much to Cade's relief, Bethany's office was a mix of green and gold. She had a nice wooden desk, comfortable chairs, and a door leading out the back of the office. Once the door they had entered through had closed, Snow offered his hand to the girl.

"I'm Officer Snow, and this is Officer Riley, Miss Saxon."

"Nice to meet you," she said as she shook each hand in turn. "Am I in some sort of trouble?" she asked with a smile.

"Not at all, Miss, not at all. We have, well, rather an odd situation that we were hoping to ask your help on."

"Sure," she said. She gestured to the chairs in front of her desk, an indication that they should sit. They took the offered chairs, Cadence easing down into hers carefully. Snow furrowed his brow, not entirely sure how to start. He looked to Cadence for help.

"Miss Saxon," she began, "we're working on a case where we've had to be a little … unorthodox. We've had to enlist the help of a living being to assist us in taking care of a non-human entity that is currently running rampant and devouring spirits. That person has agreed to help us but asked if we could do something in return for him, to help him."

"Nice of that person to help you, given how dangerous I've heard the non-human spirits can be. But why come to me? What can I do for him?"

"You could visit him?" Cadence said, hoping she was taking this in the right direction.

"I knew this person?" she asked, her smile beginning to falter.

Cadence nodded. "You did, yes. His name is Aiden?"

Bethany's eyes widened and she went still for a moment. "Aiden?" She breathed.

"Yes. Aiden asked if we could find you. Make sure you were alright. I think he might prefer to see you himself, however."

"How can he see me? I'm dead." She looked torn between being devastated at the memory of Aiden and elated at the possibility of a few moments of stolen time with him.

"In his dreams," Cadence replied.

"I'm sorry." Snow interrupted as something occurred to him. "Did no one ever take you to say your goodbyes when you died, Miss Saxon?"

"They said I was only allowed to see two people. I had to see my parents first. So, I never got to say goodbye to anyone else."

"Do you recall who brought you over?" Snow asked. "Usually, it's not limited. The whole procedure is done so that you can say goodbye to those you loved so you can rest easy."

"No, I've never seen the man again. He took me to my parents, then dropped me off here in the waiting room for guidance."

"Well, I'm sorry to hear that. If you want to go, we can take you to Aiden and give you time to say goodbye to him. If you don't want to go, we understand," Snow said.

Bethany thought about it for a moment and then she smiled a bit sadly. "I'd like to go. I would love to be able to talk to him one more time."

"You do realize this is a one-time-only event, right?" Cadence asked, not wanting them to end up being a sort of ghostly dating service.

"Yes, I do, and thank you. Do we go now?"

"Yes, if you don't mind?" Snow asked. He had no idea when Whitfield was going to be able to get back to them about the ritual specifics, but he had a plan. He wanted Cadence to talk to Aiden as well, to set some things in motion.

Bethany nodded, and they all rose and left the office. Snow and Cadence led Bethany out into the observation bay area and across, not to their office but to their hall of doors. She looked duly impressed at the number of doors in there as the two officers led the way down the hall. Snow had installed a door to the parking lot outside of Aiden's building. He unlocked that door and the three of them stepped through.

"Wow. I haven't been here in so long," Bethany commented. "Oh god," she said and laughed, "he still owns that van?"

"Yeah, apparently," Cadence said, smiling as well. Snow and Cadence talked quietly about things that had to be conveyed to Aiden as Bethany took the lead, heading back up to the apartment she had known so well. The apartment itself was dark, being just after midnight. The three ghosts stalked noiselessly through the living room, passing into the bedroom easily.

A noise that sounded half like a sob and half like a laugh came from Bethany. "I'm sorry," she said. "I just never thought I would get to see him in person again." Aiden was splayed out on the bed, on top of the covers, still in his clothes. Bethany moved to his side of the bed and reached down, caressing just over his face.

"Now, Miss Saxon, if you don't mind, I would like Officer Riley to speak with him first. I have a feeling he will be a bit less distracted before he sees you rather than after. And then that gives the two of you plenty of time to say your goodbyes." Bethany nodded, her eyes having welled up with tears.

Cadence looked to Snow and nodded, sitting down on the opposite side of the bed, taking Aiden's loose hand in one of hers and Snow's hand in the other. She closed her eyes.

In his dream, he was pacing around the lobby of Lexington Hills in a Ghostbusters costume. He had the proton backpack and everything. Cadence couldn't help but chuckle as she entered the front doors of the hospital. Aiden turned swiftly, pointing the nozzle of the hose like a weapon at her, then relaxed as he recognized her.

"You."

"Me," she agreed, nodding. "I got your message."

"So I see. You were a detective, huh?"

"I was. Please tell me you didn't go to the precinct."

"No, I just Googled the information you gave me. Sorry about your little brother."

"Thanks. I found Bethany."

Aiden's eyes lit up. "Really? Is she okay?"

"She's fine, and she's here. She's very eager to see you."

"Where?" he asked, looking around. Cadence came over to him and stopped him.

"Three things first. One, you might want to change," she said and grinned. "I'm not sure how well a ghost might take the Ghostbusters get up. I think it's funny, but I've been told that my sense of humor is a little … twisted."

He grinned sheepishly at her. "Sorry. Uh … how do I change? There's no closet …"

"He can change his clothes." She heard Snow's voice project into her mind. "Just like you did with yours, have him settle down and visualize it."

Cadence nodded. "Just calm down, Aiden. You're getting too worked up. You'll wake yourself up. Now, close your eyes, and just imagine what you want to be wearing."

Aiden took a deep breath and closed his eyes. The khaki jumpsuit faded and was replaced with jeans, a button-down shirt, and a blazer. He opened his eyes and looked down, grinning a bit when he saw he had been successful.

"Perfect," Cadence said. "Now, second, were you able to talk to your friend Dan?"

Aiden shook his head. "No. I called him, but got no answer. I even stopped by his place on the way back from Lexington this afternoon. His car was there, but he didn't answer his door. I wasn't about to bust it in looking for him. I figure he's just being a chickenshit and doesn't want to face me after leaving Derrick and Lauren alone with that monster."

"Alright, thanks for trying," Cadence said. "Now, third, we need your help in getting that shadow creature to go away."

"I don't know how to handle that kind of stuff. I'm not into cults and rituals and shit."

"No, but you breathe. You can go to the store and buy a bunch of white candles and bring chalk and draw runes."

"Look, you guys do know I'm not the psychic one in the group, right? That's Lauren."

"Ask him if he thinks Lauren would be willing to help us out as well." She heard Snow's voice in her head once again.

"Would Lauren be willing to help if you asked? Honestly, we may need all of you. You, Lauren, Derrick, and Dan."

Aiden paused, frowning for a moment. "I'll help, and I'll ask. I want Derrick there, too, anyway, for something you aren't going to like, but what the hell."

"What do you mean?"

"I want to record this."

"We've already had to ask you to bury the evidence you got last time."

"And I have no problem burying this, too. I don't want it to show the world. I want it for me, for my own edification."

"I don't understand."

"You know how some people collect movie memorabilia or teapots or clocks?"

Cadence nodded. "Yeah."

"I understand where he is going with this; it'll be fine," Snow said in her mind.

"I just want to collect the evidence. It's just something I need to do."

"Alright," she said, not entirely happy, but willing to go with it if Snow said it was okay. "Bring Dan, Lauren, Derrick, and whatever recording devices you like. Also, chalk and white candles. We'll meet you tomorrow evening at Lexington Hills."

She paused and looked around. "This isn't very romantic." She let out a pulse of energy and the scene changed to a forest clearing with a blanket on the mossy forest floor. Sunlight fell through the treetops, leaving dappled shadows on the blanket. Birds were chirping and a stream could be heard nearby. Green and gold, just like Bethany's office. She nodded to herself. "Much better. Now, wait here. Bethany will be along in a moment."

She opened her eyes and rose from the bed, moving aside and gesturing for Bethany to take a seat. The blond sat down and did as she had seen Cadence do, slipping one of her hands into Snow's and the other into Aiden's. She closed her eyes and went still, a soft smile on her face.

CHAPTER 14

And Today's Surprise Cameo is...

Cadence idly wondered if she was going to get any more sleep ever again. She was tired and hadn't really had much rest at all since being mauled by the shadow creature. But when they got back to their office, Agent Whitfield was already there, pacing back and forth.

"Agent Whitfield," Snow greeted, and pushed his own weariness aside. "How wonderful to see you again."

"Good to see you, too. Are you sure you have the breather side of this equation taken care of?" he asked nervously.

"I believe so; why?" Snow asked as he slipped into his chair as Cadence edged around to hers.

"Well, it's tricky. It takes five to summon the thing, but six to unsummon it. We'll need three breathers and three spirits."

"Actually, I think we can manage that," Snow said.

"You're working with that many breathers?" Whitfield asked.

"Not in a way that violates too many of our rules, you can rest assured."

"Yeah, believe me, Ozzie here doesn't break rules," Cadence said, grinning.

"Ozzie?" Whitfield asked.

"Ignore her," Osmund said. He rolled his eyes at Cadence.

"I exist solely to annoy him, and that's one way to do it real fast," she said with a self-satisfied smile.

"Uh, okay," Whitfield said, frowning. "I have all of the runes we'll need and all of the information you requested. But there's one more problem."

"Just one?" Cadence asked as she leaned back in her chair. "That's almost refreshing."

"The creature has to be inside the circle before you close it."

"Ah." Snow frowned. "That is an interesting problem."

"Once the circle is closed, it can't hurt anyone. The circle acts as a shield or a prison. It can't reach through the circle to get at anybody, breathing or not."

"But it can hurt a hell of a lot of people on its way to the circle," Cadence commented sourly.

"Yes," Agent Whitfield agreed. "And there's also the fact that it isn't going to want to go back into the circle. How are you going to lead it there?"

"Can I not volunteer to be bait again on this one, please?" Cadence asked.

"We'll think about how best to accomplish baiting the trap. But for right now, I think we could make use of a few hours of rest. I know I could, so I'm certain my injured partner can as well. Will you meet us here tomorrow evening?" Snow asked the agent.

"I'll bring all of the information we'll need," Whitfield said with a nod.

"Perfect," Snow declared.

Whitfield nodded and turned to head out of the office, but just as he reached the door, Bethany appeared and knocked on the open door. The NHD agent excused himself and left the office.

"Ah, Miss Saxon," Snow greeted her. "How are you?"

"I'm fine, thank you. And thanks again for what you did. It meant a lot to me." She was wringing her hands and fidgeting slightly, which caught Cadence's attention.

"But you didn't come over to thank us again, did you?" she asked.

"No, no. I just received someone in my office for guidance. Well ..." She faltered, "I think maybe you should come over."

That caused both of the officers to furrow their brows and rise to their feet. They followed Bethany out of their office and across the observation bay. Mrs. Steinberg smiled happily at them as they entered the waiting room, and Bethany led them straight into her office. There, in one of the chairs, was the hefty form of Dan.

Both Osmund and Cadence's jaws dropped. "Dan?!?!?" Cadence blurted out.

He came to his feet swiftly and turned around. He looked alarmed and bewildered. "I don't know you. Do I?" he asked.

"What happened?" Snow asked. "How …?" He looked at Bethany and shrugged.

"Heart attack," she said quietly. "In reaction to fear."

"There was something there!" Dan said loudly. "There was something in my apartment! I know it sounds crazy, but it was there, throwing things around!"

"Sir, please calm down," Snow said.

"How do you know my name?"

"We watched you summon the thing that scared you to death," Cadence replied curtly. Part of her was happy that the shadow creature had gotten to Dan. It served as a sort of cosmic justice. But another part of her was pissed that another body, a corporeal one this time, had been added to the body count.

Dan's jaw dropped in response to Cadence's statement, and Snow shook his head at her. "Really, Riley, you should try tact sometimes."

"I'm done with tact in regards to this. Now, I don't mind leaving the room if you two want to coddle him, but I am not about to." She had gone into bad cop mode, and Snow recognized it, as well as the veiled request for the two of them to confer outside the office.

He offered an apologetic smile to Bethany and Dan and moved to escort Cadence to the waiting room. As they left the office, Mrs. Steinberg flooded the room in scarlet and gold to make it less white for Cadence, which drew a tight smile from the officer.

"Get him to volunteer," Cadence whispered to Snow.

"What?"

"Bait," she said. "He can be bait. What's more poetic? He summoned it; he can help get rid of it."

"I'll see what I can do. In the meantime, you go home; get some rest. I don't need you low on energy come tonight. For god's sake, be careful and don't pull any more stitches."

Cadence nodded. "Not on my top ten list of things to do, trust me. I'm serious. I don't care if you have to cuff him and drag him kicking and screaming. Three spirits are no more because of that douchebag in there. It's the least he can fucking do."

"And if it consumes him, too?"

"He should have thought about that before he summoned the damned thing."

"You're being unreasonable."

"No, I'm fucking pissed, Snow," she replied, her voice quiet and tight and controlled. "There's a difference. And I'm pretty sure the NHD will back me up on this since they lost an agent because of him, too."

"Look, I'm going to talk to him, find out how he got the ritual in the first place, and we'll go from there. I'll try to get him to see reason and to be a part of the solution to the problem he has created. However, I am not going to forcibly sentence him to non-existence because he made a mistake."

"Mistake, my ass." She grumbled.

"That's enough. Go home. Get some rest. I need you on your game tonight. I'll see you later."

Cadence frowned, but nodded. She waved a half-hearted goodbye to Mrs. Steinberg and left the office, heading for her apartment.

Somehow Aiden had been added to her list of people she watched over. She had gone home, and to let some of her anger cool down, she had started flipping through channels on her television. She checked in on Andy, her cat, and others. The addition surprised her, but the more she thought about it, the more it made sense. She did consider him something of a friend now. However, the thought of making friends with a breather after your own death still struck her as odd.

She had taken a few minutes to watch over Andy and the others, and sleep took her unawares. She was so exhausted from the last couple of days she fell asleep on the couch, with the television still on, remote in hand. The shrill ring of her phone woke her with a start.

"Hello?" she said, her voice sounding sleepy as she answered it.

"Cadence, it's me." Snow's voice came through the device. "Sorry to wake you, but can you meet me in the office?"

"Sure," she said. She sat up and ran a hand through her hair. "What's up?"

"We'll need to have a chat with our cultist. Shortly after you left, he claimed that he was tired as well. Miss Saxon had a temporary room assigned to him, and we're meeting with him this afternoon. Miss Saxon will be there as well, as will Agent Whitfield."

"Should I wear a party dress?" Cadence asked sarcastically as she rose to her feet.

"Only if you're bringing Ramon," he countered.

"Ooh, score one for the stuffy English guy." she grinned at his retort. "Give me a few to freshen up, and I'll be right there."

"Fell asleep in your clothes?" he asked.

"Did you really think I was going to make it all the way to my bed?"

"No. In fact, I'm pleasantly surprised you made it in your front door. I was afraid I would find you passed out in the hall."

"Thanks for the vote of confidence," she chuckled, rolling her eyes. They hung up and Cadence went to her bedroom. She was adjusting to the idea that your appearance depended solely on your mental image of yourself, but she had been in these clothes for a couple of days, and she wanted to get changed.

She opened a drawer and was greeted by the sight of fresh clothes. Going to the wardrobe, she found the same. Clean clothes, all things she would have had in her own closet back home. She had done this before, in the few weeks she had been living on this side of life, but it still was new enough to be something of a surprise to her. She selected a pair of black jeans and a pale green blouse, over which she put a black jacket. She ran a brush through her dark gold hair and nodded at herself in the mirror at the results. She still looked like herself, though with a few more bandages; her leg, arm, and middle were still securely wrapped. She also still looked tired. She sighed and shrugged, as there wasn't much more she could do to improve the reflection in the mirror. She grabbed her phone from the coffee table on the way out, flipping off her television.

In moments, she was opening the door of the office she shared with Snow. "Hey," she greeted him, nodding. "Where is everyone?" She crossed to her desk and opened the drawer. The knife Whitfield had left for her was still there, and she pulled it out, slipping it into the inner pocket of her blazer.

"Conference room," he said. He rose and grabbed a file folder from his desk. "I'll take you there."

"We have conference rooms?"

"Really, Cadence," he said as he guided her back out of the office. "You shouldn't be so shocked at the things we have."

"So says the man who has had nearly fifty years to get used to it all." She pointed out.

He chuckled and led her through a back hall and opened a door. There, seated around an oval table, were Bethany, Dan, and Agent Whitfield. Dan looked a little worse for wear, this time, a bit more haggard than he had. Cadence wondered if perhaps his conscience was eating at him. She hoped it was.

"Thank you all for joining us," Snow said as he and Cadence sat down. "We're here to discuss the ritual that let out the shadow creature that has been plaguing Lexington Hills and that has recently added Daniel Kurtz to its growing list of the dead." He tossed the file folder he had brought with him down on the table.

"I didn't realize what it was going to do. Honest," Dan said.

"What did you think it was going to do, Mr. Kurtz?" Snow asked

"I … I don't know. I thought it was some kind of ritual for wealth or fame or something. I just … something needed to change."

Bethany frowned at Dan. "I would think after what happened to me, you would have learned to not go looking for change in a kind of cult ritual. What made you go looking for a cult, anyway?"

Dan looked at Bethany, puzzled. "Beth … We were all really sorry about what happened to you, but what does that have to do with a cult?"

Bethany gawked at him for a moment. "You … Wait … What do you know about what happened?"

Still looking confused about why this was an issue, Dan answered. "You were kidnapped as you left work. They found your body in an abandoned warehouse the next day."

"Oh," she replied. She frowned and looked troubled now as she stared down at the table. Snow frowned. This seemed to be going from bad to worse.

"It wasn't that?" Dan asked hesitantly.

"No … it wasn't. I was kidnapped, yes. But by a cult, and I was killed as a sacrifice for a ritual."

Dan shot to his feet. "There was no evidence of any kind of ritual, not that the cops reported to us, anyway."

"Are you saying I don't know what happened to me?" Bethany asked indignantly, coming to her feet as well.

"Miss Saxon, Mr. Kurtz," Snow cut in sharply. "Please, sit down. Arguing about each other's manner of death is fruitless. For now, we shall take it on face value that whoever did commit the murder of Miss Saxon went to lengths to clean up any evidence of it being ritualistic in nature. Based on comments Aiden has made, he, too, believed it was a kidnapping. So, Mr. Kurtz, we come down to asking you how you got your hands on a ritual that has been out of circulation in the living world for almost three hundred years."

Bethany and Dan sat down slowly, neither speaking to each other just yet about their argument. "It was given to me," Dan said quietly.

"Given to you by whom?" Cadence asked.

"By the leader of the cult."

"Wait," Cadence said as she leaned forward a bit in her chair. "You aren't the leader of the cultists?"

"No. You said you saw me summon it. Were you there?"

"Yes," Snow replied. "We were monitoring your activities in the hospital that night. We were also there for your previous visit with your ghost-hunting friends."

"Do you haunt the hospital?" Dan asked.

"No, but we monitor haunted places when people come to investigate or disturb those locations. However, what we do isn't important, Mr. Kurtz. What you did and how you knew to do it is what we are here to discuss," Snow replied, trying to put the conversation firmly back on track.

"Well, the five of us who went into Lexington Hills to do that ritual were initiates. This was what we had to do to get into the cult."

"So, you had to summon a shadow creature for the leader of the cult to gain entry into the cult?" Cadence asked. "Doesn't that seem a little backward? I mean, having the ones who aren't a part of your sect do something so secretive and so powerful and so dangerous to prove that they belong to the sect?"

"Look, lady," Dan shot back, "I don't know, okay? They told me what to do, and I did it."

"Where did you meet these cultists?" Agent Whitfield asked as he took over the questioning while recording the whole thing on his phone.

"Lauren's shop," he answered with a sigh.

"Lauren is his ex-wife," Bethany explained. "And part of the ghost hunting group."

"If she is your ex, why were you at her shop?" Cadence asked.

"It's not like we don't talk," Dan replied defensively. "The divorce was amicable."

"Dan," Bethany said, "we all knew you didn't want the divorce."

"No," he said, "but it was still amicable. We remained friends. But you're right. I love her. I wanted her back."

"Was there someone else in her life?" Cadence asked.

"I don't think so," Dan said. "I went to the shop to talk to her. I wanted to ask her out on a date and see if we could start over, but she refused. We argued about it. When I left, there was this guy hanging around outside of her shop. He said he had heard the argument, and if I wanted help winning her back, he knew how."

"Was this man you spoke with the leader of the cult?"

"No, I think he was just a member, maybe a recruiter."

"Did you ever meet the leader?" Whitfield asked.

"He was in the van that night," Dan answered. Cadence and Snow exchanged a look. They hadn't even thought to go outside to check for others. They had simply assumed those who came in were all there were.

"Did you get his name?" Whitfield asked.

"They just called him Wolf."

"My, how original," Cadence said with a roll of her eyes.

Dan shrugged. "Original or not, it's the only name I got from him."

"So, this Wolf person gave you the ritual?" Whitfield asked. He was trying to keep them on track.

"We each were given one of the runes to draw. None of us knew the whole thing. I was shown my rune and told where the candles had to go. I wrote it down in a notebook so I wouldn't forget it. One of the others was told to carve the circle into the floor. I was given the cat, told to kill it and pass it around as it was bleeding."

"Seems like you knew the most about this ritual," Cadence said, which drew a glare from Dan.

"Do you always keep a knife in your boot?" Snow asked.

"Yes, I do. It's especially handy in investigations in getting doors open or cutting things out of the way."

"Convenient," Cadence said sourly.

"Did this Wolf tell you how he knew this ritual, or did he tell you what the ritual would bring?"

"No, he never told us what was going to happen. He just said that we would know if we had done it right. And he never said anything about how he knew the ritual. Look, I'm sorry. I was stupid. I was really stupid. I thought this would be something that could help me get back in with Lauren, or maybe do something that would give me money so that I could prove I deserved her." He stopped and sighed. "Guess I just ended up proving the opposite."

Whitfield frowned, as he had been hoping to get more concrete evidence as to how the ritual had gotten out. "You know nothing more about it?" he asked.

"No. But I've thought about what you said," he added, looking directly at Cadence. "And I do want to help. It's my fault this is happening. If I can help stop it, I will." Cadence frowned. He had turned noble. She didn't want him to be noble; she wanted to be angry at him. It was much harder to be angry at him when he was all conscientious and nice.

"Good, thank you for volunteering," Snow said.

"Why Lexington Hills?" Cadence asked suddenly. She wondered if the place had any kind of weird significance or if it had been a coincidence.

"I'd wanted to investigate it for a long time, but we never did get there. Then one night … I don't know … I guess I just got it into my head to go there, to finally do it. When Wolf asked about a place to do the ritual, I suggested it. We went in to investigate, and I was there to also kind of scout it out for the sect. After what had happened with the ritual, I didn't really want to go back to do another investigation, but Lauren and Aiden, even Derrick, they didn't want to give up on the place. They wanted to go back and finish the investigation. So we went. It was waiting there for me."

"That would be when you tucked tail and ran. That would be when you left all three of your friends and all of the other haunting spirits there in harm's way. Right?" Cadence pointed out sharply as she tried to hold on to her righteous indignation at the man.

Dan hung his head. "I'm no hero, and I'm not proud of it. I just panicked. All I could think of was just getting the hell out of there. But it kept following me back to my place. It wouldn't leave me alone."

"That's because the rune you drew was the primary rune in its summoning. You were the one who made the sacrifice whose blood sealed the circle. You were the one who broke the circle, releasing it. Any one of those things could make it want to go after you. Put all three together and … haunting you was pretty much a sealed deal," Whitfield stated.

"Will it go after the others now?" Dan asked.

"We don't really know," Whitfield said. "It's a creature of chaos. That makes it a little hard to predict."

"Given your involvement in the summoning and that you broke the circle, we were able to predict it would go after you," Snow explained. "Though we didn't know our supposed head cultist and the leader of the ghost hunting group were one and the same. Not until the night of your second investigation at Lexington."

"When it attacked me," Dan nodded.

Cadence blinked. "It didn't attack you. It yelled at you. It attacked others. And no, we figured it out when you whipped the knife out of your boot to jimmy the lock, just like the cat killer had done on the night of the ritual. Same knife plus same boot equals the same person."

"Did any of the others get hurt that night? Lauren, is Lauren okay?"

"She's fine; so are Aiden and Derrick," Snow replied. "She's the one the creature went after," he said as he pointed to Cadence.

Dan's gaze moved to Cadence. "That explains why you're so angry with me. I'm glad you're okay."

"Okay? I have something like seventy or eighty stitches because of that thing. That's not okay. And even less okay are Carl and Maggie and Agent Banks. The creature consumed them. That's like a final death. No more haunting, no more existing, just gone. That, Dan, is why I am angry with you. Because you couldn't man up and accept that your ex-wife just was not that into you anymore, you did something so spectacularly stupid that it's costing lives."

"Riley," Snow said in his usual "you're being unreasonable" tone. "Mr. Kurtz has already admitted to the poor judgment that brought him here and he has already said he is willing to assist us in cleaning up the mess he made."

"I just want to make sure he knows what and who were lost because of him."

Dan shrank back into his chair, a stark look of guilt on his face. "I know it's too late, and I know it doesn't mean much, but I am sorry."

Cadence huffed and sat back in her seat, wincing slightly as she felt a pull from her stitches. Whitfield, who had been watching her, arched an eyebrow. She shook her head, indicating it was nothing to worry about.

"Alright, here is what we are going to do then," Snow said. "Agent Whitfield has everything we need to know and do tonight to undo the summoning that brought that creature into being. Mr. Kurtz, Agent Whitfield, Officer Riley, and I will go to Lexington Hills and meet with the monitor there, Mr. Suarez. Miss Saxon, I thank you for your help in this matter, but you won't be required at the location tonight. We will prepare for our part in this ritual. Now, it has been said that Lauren is a psychic?" he asked as he looked between Bethany and Dan. He already knew she was, but he wanted to make sure everything was in order.

"Yes, she is," Dan replied after clearing his throat.

"Good, then we should be able to easily communicate with her to teach them what to do on their end of things,"

Snow said. "Hopefully, we will be able to have the world short one shadow creature by dawn."

Everyone nodded and rose from the table. Cadence pulled Whitfield to one side as the others left. "Hey, I wanted to thank you for the knife. I have it with me. It was a nice surprise," she smiled.

"Like I said in the note, you need it more than the arsenal does right now. I just wish I'd let you keep it all along. You might not be in such bad shape."

Cade shrugged and smiled. "I have it now, when it is going to count."

Snow peeked back into the conference room. "Is everything alright?"

"Yep, just dandy." She smiled and walked out of the room.

CHAPTER 15

Rules? What Rules?

It was dark when they entered the lobby of Lexington Hills. Ramon was waiting for them. He smiled when he saw them, visibly relaxing some.

"Good, you're here," he said.

"Is something wrong?" Snow asked, instantly on alert.

"No, just everyone here is on edge, given the last few nights." He looked at Cadence and smiled a bit more. "Managed to stay together this time?"

"More or less," she said with a smile.

Ramon's eyes went over to the others. He nodded to Agent Whitfield, then stopped on Dan. "Um … isn't that …?"

"The leader of the ghost hunting group, yes," Snow answered. "He also was the cultist who killed the cat and summoned the shadow creature."

"But why is he … here … like that?"

"The creature got him," Cadence said. "Which means I don't have to be bait," she said cheerily, which drew a reproachful look from Snow.

"Well, it does." She shrugged, her voice sounding more like a scolded teenager than an adult.

"And this is Agent Whitfield. He's a research attaché from the NHD. He's managed to find the ritual we need to destroy the creature for us. Gentlemen, this is Ramon Suarez. He's the monitor of Lexington Hills."

"Monitor?" Dan asked.

"Kind of the head ghost," Cadence explained. "He keeps the other ghosts in line and calls us in when ghost-hunting groups or cultists come around."

Agent Whitfield and Snow took Ramon over to where the ritual circle was, leaving Cadence to guard Dan, making sure he didn't have an attack of cowardice and try to flee. They stood together in awkward silence for a moment before Dan finally broke it.

"So, if we're ghosts, how come you needed stitches?" he asked.

"This creature you summoned consumes the energy of spirits. I guess when it takes your energy, but not enough to kill you, they have to stitch what you have back together, like when you cut yourself too deep."

"Yeah, but stitches?" he asked. "It just seems so … mundane."

"I don't know." She shrugged. "They keep telling me that a lot of this afterlife stuff has to do with mental images and projections. Maybe it's just the best thing our minds can comprehend."

"You sound like you're still kind of new at this, too."

"About a month," she said.

"Oh shit, I thought you looked familiar. You're that cop! The one who got killed getting the Somerset Strangler."

"Yeah," Cadence said with a nod. She had a sinking feeling she was going to be saddled with that moniker forever, that she would forever be the cop who got killed in pursuit of the Somerset Strangler.

"Yeah, you were in the papers. Sorry to hear about that. But it seems like you've found a good place on this side, right?"

"I'm still doing what I did before … only weirder," she said, and chuckled.

Snow waved the two of them over as lights were visible outside. Aiden's van was pulling into the yard. Cadence and Dan joined Ramon, Snow, and Whitfield at the ritual circle as Lauren, Aiden, and Derrick entered with their usual cases of equipment.

"I still don't understand," Derrick was saying as they entered. "Why are we doing this without Dan?"

"Dude doesn't want to pick up his phone; that's his problem," Aiden grumbled.

Dan groaned. "Oh God, no one's found me yet. No one knows I'm dead."

"Don't worry," Snow said. He clapped the larger man on the shoulder. "We'll give them a nod in your direction."

Derrick and Lauren went back out to get the rest of the equipment, and Aiden paused, looking around. "I hope you're here, Cadence."

Snow looked at Cadence and nodded. "When they get settled, I'll need you to be the one to contact Miss Lauren."

She looked taken aback by that. "What? Me? Why? Other than Dan, I have the least amount of experience."

"And yet, despite all that, you are the one that Aiden has spoken to before. You are the one he trusts. The only other to speak to them could be Dan, and I think that would do more harm than good in the effort of keeping things on track tonight."

"Good point," Cadence agreed.

"They are going to need you to tell them how to draw the runes," Whitfield said. "When you are in contact with Lauren, just show her the image as I have it drawn. I'll give them to you in order and how it all should look. Once we get everything drawn and all the candles lit, we will wait for it to come to us."

Cadence nodded in understanding. The ghosts watched as Derrick and Lauren brought in the rest of the equipment. Aiden began setting up the camcorders on tripods facing the circle. He then set out a couple of digital audio recorders as well. Lauren set down a shopping bag, from which chalk and candles could be seen.

"Aiden," she asked. "Why are we doing this? What is this all about?"

Aiden looked around. "Now would be a good time to prove that I'm not crazy, guys."

Snow looked at Ramon and nodded. Ramon gathered his energy and stepped forward, making sure to stay out of the line of the cameras.

"Woah!" Derrick exclaimed, pointing as a faint image of Ramon's face could be seen in mid-air. Lauren gasped in shock and Aiden smiled, reassured by the face he had seen quick glimpses of in their tapes.

"Guys, relax," he said. "That's Ramon. He works here."

"Works here?" Derrick asked incredulously.

"Well, he was an orderly here when he was alive." He looked at their shocked faces and shrugged. "What? Once I knew a little bit, I went on a research binge."

"How did you know some of the history? I thought the research thing was my gig here?" Derrick asked.

"So, are you two best friends now?" Lauren asked.

"No, but we need to help him," Aiden answered Lauren and let Derrick's question go unanswered. He didn't feel like explaining how he had learned about Ramon.

"What do you mean?" Lauren asked. "How did you know a little bit to go on this research binge?"

"See this circle?" Aiden asked. He pointed to it and ignored Lauren's question. "This released something bad. We're here to undo it."

"How do you know how to undo it?" Derrick asked.

"I don't," Aiden replied. "But we'll be getting instructions."

At that moment, Cadence reached out and touched Lauren's arm. She shivered a moment then, looked to the side where Cadence was standing. "Is … is that Ramon?"

"Lauren, you need to do your psychic thing here. They need to use you to tell us what to do," Aiden instructed.

"Hold on, just a minute here," Derrick protested. "Are we forgetting that something here scratched me? That Dan said he felt like he brought something bad home with him from this place? Or the fact that last time we were here, something threw a door at us? I don't think

Lauren opening herself up to what's in here is such a good idea."

"Relax," Aiden urged. "I'm pretty positive I know who is going to talk to Lauren."

Despite Derrick's protests, Lauren closed her eyes, trying to attune herself to what was around her that she couldn't see. "There's more than one spirit here," she said.

Cade stepped closer to the psychic. "My name is Cadence." She introduced herself to Lauren. "You can ask Aiden; I've come to him in dreams before."

Lauren canted her head. "Aiden? Does the name Cadence mean anything to you?"

Aiden couldn't help the grin. "Yes! She did it!"

Agent Whitfield walked over to Cadence with a drawing of the ritual area and pointed to where the candles were to go. "Lauren," Cadence continued. "I need you to imagine a blank sheet of paper. Then let me draw on it for you, to show you where you need to place the candles for this."

Lauren did as she was bid and envisioned in her mind a giant blank sheet of paper. She caught her breath as the page began filling in with a drawing, perfectly resembling the one she couldn't see that Whitfield was holding. When Cadence was certain that the image she was looking at was the same as the image in the psychic's mind, she touched Lauren's shoulder. "Make the area look like that picture in your head. Don't light the candles yet; just set them up." When she released Lauren's shoulder, the woman's eyes opened.

She looked in awe at Aiden. "This is incredible. I know what to do." She went to the shopping bag and grabbed the bundles of white candles they had bought.

She handed some to Aiden and some to Derrick, instructing them on where to put them. "Don't light them yet, though," she warned.

Snow, Whitfield, Cadence and Ramon smiled at each other as they watched the candles get set up. "This is going to work," Cadence said.

"Don't jinx us, please." Whitfield shot back.

Once the candles were set up, Cadence went back to Lauren. She laid her hand on Lauren's arm again. Lauren shivered from the cold and then closed her eyes as she opened her mind up to Cadence again.

"Okay, same as before," she told the psychic. "Imagine a blank piece of paper. I'm going to show you a rune. When I let go, I want you to go stand inside the center of the circle and face that rune. Then I'll be back to tell you what to do. Oh, and take a piece of chalk with you."

Cadence showed her the rune the Whitfield held up to her, which was the last of the runes that had been drawn. They had to work backward, drawing the runes in reverse order of importance. Cadence released Lauren when she was sure that the psychic had it clearly in mind. The woman walked over and stood in the center like she had been told. Once she stood where she needed to, Cadence reconnected with her and showed her the rune she had to draw and how it looked in relation to the original rune it was countering.

Lauren took a deep breath when Cadence let go, and she hunkered down, drawing the first rune. Derrick sat nearby on the floor, watching uneasily. Aiden watched it all with a smile, happy that everything he had dreamed hadn't just been a dream and that he wasn't crazy.

Whitfield, Cadence, and Lauren repeated this step with the next three runes. Once they began showing the fourth rune to Lauren, Dan looked sharply out toward the back.

"Uh oh," he intoned quietly to Snow and Ramon, not wanting to break the concentration of the others.

"What?" Snow asked sharply under his breath.

"It knows," Dan replied.

"It … It knows? How does it know? What does it know?" asked Ramon, suddenly very worried. A sharp glance from Snow reminded him that he needed to stay quiet to not disturb the work of the others.

"I don't know why … I can just feel it. It knows what we're doing here. It's pissed, and it's coming."

"Here?" Snow clarified.

"Yeah," Dan responded.

"Now?" Snow asked uneasily.

Dan gave Snow a look and nodded again.

"I'll go lock everyone down," Ramon said and disappeared.

Snow gave an uneasy look to where Cadence was now showing Lauren the fifth and final rune. He frowned and marched over to where they were.

"Whitfield, what's after the runes?" he asked quietly.

"Light the candles, then show them where to stand."

"Just have her show Lauren where to stand. I'll get the candles lit."

Whitfield looked unsure, but nodded. "Okay."

Snow walked to one side of the circle and closed his eyes. He gathered his energy up, pulling from the battery of the audio recorder next to him. He wasn't as good at communicating with those still breathing as Cadence was, nor was the recipient of his message a psychic, but he did his best.

"Light the candles," he yelled into Derrick's ear. The young man jumped to his feet, fumbling instantly in his pocket for the lighter he had brought with him.

"Holy crap!" he exclaimed. "Trying to give me a heart attack?" he yelled to the ceiling.

"Ignore them," Whitfield said as Cadence and Lauren both broke their concentration with the commotion. The fifth and final rune was done.

"Wait," Cadence said to the NHD agent. "Five runes, five points to the star; where does the sixth person on this stand?"

"You and Lauren will stand together at the main rune. Flesh and spirit together with one will."

Dan made his way closer to the circle as Ramon reappeared back in the lobby. From outside, an all too familiar howling scream sounded.

"Oh shit," Cadence said, her eyes going wide. "Show me, Whitfield. Quick!" She grabbed onto Lauren's arm and showed her where everyone needed to be, as Whitfield showed her.

"Now comes the tricky part, Lauren," she said to the woman, trying to be calm despite being keenly aware of the creature's approach. "This is going to require a lot of trust on both our parts, but we have to do this fast. You and I have to stand together. Occupy the same space. Use our will as one to get this creature unmade."

"I'm not sure I'm comfortable with that," she said in reply.

"Lauren, to be honest, I'm not so wild about the idea myself. But I'm being told this is what we have to do.

And we have to do it fast because this thing is coming back here, and it doesn't sound like it's interested in a tea party."

"This is the thing that scared Dan away?" she asked.

"Yes."

She set her mouth in a narrow line. "Fine." She told Aiden and Derrick where to stand, and Ramon and Snow took up the other points. Agent Whitfield directed Dan to the center.

"Bethany was telling me that you get to say goodbye to people when you die," Dan said as he shuffled into the center. "It's kind of looking like I won't get to." He looked at Cadence. "Would you tell them goodbye for me, and that I'm sorry?"

"If that's what you want, yes," Cadence agreed, her heart breaking a little for the guy. "But here's hoping you'll still be okay enough to do it yourself." The back doors crashed open under the force of the creature and its wrath. Another hair-raising scream was sent up from it.

"Now," Whitfield urged as he shrank back towards the front doors, not wanting to be anywhere near this creature's radar.

Cadence took an unneeded breath and stepped into Lauren. Her vision swam, and she was inundated with sensation. The pounding of Lauren's heartbeat, the itchy feeling of the tag of her shirt, the rasp of breath as it was drawn in too quickly, and the sound of the creature as it approached. She could feel Lauren's uncertainty, just as Lauren could feel her anxiousness.

Lauren opened her eyes and saw everything as if the images were superimposed upon themselves. She saw the room as it was, but she could see the silvery shadows of the room as it once was through the ages. She saw the very solid forms of her friends, and she saw the silvery ghostly shapes of the spirits. She saw Snow and Ramon standing on the edge of the circle, just as Derrick and Aiden were. Because of Cadence's presence, she knew who they were. Then she caught sight of the portly man in the middle, and her jaw dropped.

"Dan?" she asked, and the heartbreak in that one word made Cadence feel like crying. Lauren had loved Dan very much. Cadence could see that in her mind, just like Lauren had seen who Snow and Ramon were in hers. Lauren had just wanted more from life, whereas Dan had always wanted to take the easy way in everything. That had ultimately been what drove them apart.

Dan turned sharply as he heard his former wife say his name. "You can see me?" Dan asked Lauren. She nodded, emotion tightening her throat to where she couldn't say anything. "God, Lauren, I'm sorry. I was stupid. I did something so incredibly stupid. I didn't want you to find out like this."

His tearful apology was interrupted by the shadow creature as it pulled the last remaining door between the lobby and the dining hall down. It howled an unintelligible challenge in anger at them and charged. Derrick and Aiden both made faces at the terrible smell the creature brought with it as the wind kicked up in the room. Cadence pulled her knife from her blazer pocket and reached out, taking Lauren's hand with it and grabbing Dan's arm. As on board as Cadence had been with making Dan the bait, she now found herself hesitant. It had been easier to be blindly angry at him for the mess his bad decision had made, but now? While she knew it was necessary, she didn't really want to anymore.

"I'm sorry, Dan," Cadence said softly, and she meant it. She sliced open his arm with the knife the same way Snow had cut her when she had been the bait.

"No!" Lauren screamed in protest as she began to understand what was happening, but Cadence held on firmly.

"Lauren, you kick me out, and we won't be able to send this thing back to where it came from, and Dan's sacrifice will be for nothing," she said.

The creature howled again, a note of hunger in its echoing voice. Shadow tentacles reached out for Dan, but Dan shrank to the back of the circle, as far back as he could go, and still be inside it, both out of fear and a desire to make it come as far into the circle as he could. He was well aware of what was at stake and that they had to draw the creature into the circle. His blood was dripping from his arm, falling onto where the blood of the cat had been, following the rivulet that he and his group had carved into the tile floor. He wasn't going to be a coward this time; he wasn't going to run.

"Come and get me, you bastard," Dan said, his voice a growl.

The floor was shaking, and the walls cracked in a few places as the building reacted to the violent anger of the creature. Snow watched with bated breath as the blood from Dan's arm began to make its way around the circle. If the circle sealed before the creature was in it, this was all for nothing, and with Dan safely behind the shield of the circle, Cadence would be the next best meal.

The beast hesitated, as if it sensed a trap. Dan waved his bleeding arm around, throwing droplets of his blood everywhere. "Come on!" he yelled as Lauren cried.

The wind had whipped up in the room, and debris was starting to fly, candles going out and knocking over. The terrible stench of the creature filled the room. A loose plank of rotted wood flew across the room, and Derrick had to duck to avoid being knocked senseless by it. Aiden wasn't sure what was going on with Lauren, but he knew he would find out. He had a bad feeling about Dan, however, since Lauren mentioned him.

A drop of Dan's blood fell square on the shadow creature, and it could resist temptation no longer. It lunged at Dan, moving within the circle and picking him up and instantly ripping him in half, as it had Maggie and Agent Banks. It was as if Dan was a jelly donut and the creature was after the gooey center.

Lauren closed her eyes, unable to watch yet unable to keep herself from hearing the sounds as the creature consumed the spirit of her ex-husband. She and Cadence picked up the chant that Whitfield was yelling over the din of the creature. The spirit blood circle completed and the shield of energy sprang up into life. Snow and Ramon echoed Whitfield's words while Aiden and Derrick repeated what Lauren and Cadence said as they spoke together.

The creature seemed to smash itself against the walls of the shield, howling in fury, Dan's blood dripping from its every tentacle and mouth. Dan was no more; no shred of him left, save that of a decomposing corpse alone in his old apartment. The creature that had just consumed him writhed and howled in agony inside the circle. The wind inside the lobby of Lexington Hills grew violent, tossing candles across the room, along with other debris accumulated from several decades of abandonment.

The wind seemed to tear through the energy shield of the circle and take a bit of the creature each time it gusted. Derrick had to steady himself once when a particularly strong gust hit, but all the time, they kept chanting non-stop. A candle was tossed across the room by the wind, and it hit Aiden in the shoulder as Cadence took momentary control of Lauren, who was too lost in her anguish over Dan to see another loose board flying across the lobby toward her head. Finally, the wind eased to a breeze, then to nothing. The shadow creature, which had been very visible to all of them once the shield sprang up, was no more—in its place was simply a cleaner smell, like the smell of spring.

Cadence stepped out of Lauren and the living woman's knees buckled; she collapsed to the floor. "Dan." She covered her face with her hands and sobbed. Aiden and Derrick moved to her. Cadence felt weak and completely drained as she staggered over to Snow, Ramon, and Whitfield.

"What's wrong, Lauren?" Derrick asked.

"Dan's dead," Aiden said grimly. It suddenly made sense as to why he hadn't been able to get the man on the phone.

Lauren nodded, unable to stop the flow of tears. "He was here. He said … he said he was sorry … that he had … done something stupid," she explained in between sobs. "Then it came and it … it ate him!"

Aiden kneeled down and hugged Lauren gently. "It'll be okay," he said as he rocked her. "It'll be okay."

Cadence watched all of this with a heavy heart. Sure, at first, she had wanted nothing more than to see Dan pay for what he had done. Now she realized it was a mistake made by a very gullible guy who was thinking with his heart, not his brain. Maybe he hadn't deserved what he got in the end. Cadence rubbed her face wearily and sighed, feeling like dirt for having been so vocal about Dan being bait.

Snow and Ramon shared a look before Snow very pointedly turned to speak to Whitfield. Ramon reached out to Cadence and took her good arm. "Are you okay?" he asked gently.

"Yeah, just … wishing I'd been nicer to him."

"I can understand why you weren't," he said. "At least, this time, it wasn't you that got torn to shreds."

Cadence laughed bitterly. "Yeah, I didn't get torn to shreds because I was the one who kept pushing for him to be bait. Forgive me if the finality of his death doesn't have me leaping for joy. Somehow being in one piece now, relatively so at any rate, doesn't feel as good as I thought it would."

"Sorry," he said. "I wish it could have gone differently." He didn't like seeing her so torn up over this, but he could understand where the feelings were coming from.

"Me, too," she sighed. "I thought maybe we would have a second to pull him out of there."

Ramon wrapped his arms around her in a hug, just as Aiden was doing with Lauren. For her part, Cadence hugged him back, glad for the gesture of comfort.

Snow cleared his throat and offered the two an apologetic smile. "Sorry to disturb you, but Whitfield thinks it might be a good idea to wrap things up here. You should talk to her, Cadence."

"I'm not sure she'll want to talk to me. She did just see me wield the knife that got his blood everywhere," Cadence replied.

"Make her listen. Then we'll have to go to Aiden tonight, too. And then there's the paperwork," Snow added.

"God forbid we forget the paperwork," Cadence said with a sigh and a roll of her eyes.

She detached herself from Ramon and moved over to Lauren, where she sat on the debris-strewn floor with Aiden. Derrick was quietly beginning the job of packing up. Cadence reached out and touched Lauren on the arm.

"No more," Lauren whimpered, wrenching her arm away. "I don't want to see anymore or hear anymore. Just leave me alone," she said dejectedly.

Cadence frowned, but it was Aiden who spoke. "If they need to talk to you, let them. That's why we got into doing this, wasn't it? To help lost souls, to prove that they are out there and that we can communicate? To prove that sometimes they need help, too? You have a gift, Lauren. Granted, what happened here tonight was awful. No one denies that. But if they need to talk to you, let them." His voice was gentle and understanding and seemed to get through to her. Cadence tentatively reached out to touch her again, and this time, Lauren didn't reject the cold chill on her skin.

"I'm so very sorry for what happened tonight with Dan," Cadence said. "But we thank you for everything you did to help us. That shadow creature is what was haunting Dan, not some random spirit from here. It is what killed him; it scared him badly enough to have a heart attack. He and some others summoned it, and then they accidentally set it free from the circle. They didn't know what they were doing. But he was a true hero tonight. He laid down whatever he might have had in the afterlife to keep everyone else safe from the monster he had let loose. We couldn't have stopped that thing without him or you. You, Aiden, Derrick, you were all integral to this. Thank you."

Lauren angrily wiped tears from her face with her free hand. "You're welcome," she said begrudgingly.

"He loved you, Lauren," Cadence said. She wasn't sure at this point if she was doing more harm than good, but she felt it was important to tell Lauren that. Cadence released the woman's arm as there was nothing more she could think of to say. She hoped in time that Lauren would see that it was the creature that killed Dan, not them. But she knew that right now, his ex-wife was going to be angry and lashing out at everything. Cadence rose slowly and made her way back over to Snow, Ramon, and Agent Whitfield.

"I need to get going. I have a bit more paperwork to do than you two," Agent Whitfield said. He looked happy, but a little shaken.

"This was your first field assignment, huh?" Cadence asked.

"Yeah," he admitted, giving them an embarrassed smile.

"Well, you did great," she said. "We couldn't have done this without you. We wouldn't have known how."

"Cadence, you can get back to the office on your own now, yes?" Snow asked. He looked tired and worn out. "I'll go ahead with Agent Whitfield back to the office."

Cadence gave him a suspicious look, but nodded. "Sure, no problem. I want to check in on Ruby, anyway." Snow smiled and turned, gesturing for Agent Whitfield to follow him.

"I'll take you up to see Ruby," Ramon said quietly. Derrick continued packing up, and Lauren had gotten ahold of herself enough that she and Aiden had started helping. Cadence figured they didn't need supervision to pack up and go. She nodded to Ramon, and whether due to weariness or some other unknown factor, they turned and took the stairs up instead of teleporting.

"You go talk to her. I'll go let the others know that everything is okay now," Ramon said.

Cadence nodded and turned, making her way down the hall and knocking on the door frame.

"Miss Libby," the old woman greeted her. "You sure have brought a lot of ruckus with you these last few weeks."

Cadence offered a smile to the old woman as she entered the room and pulled a chair over to sit by her. "Sorry about that, Miss Jones. We took care of it, though, so there will be no more ruckuses to disturb you," she said.

"Well, that remains to be seen," Ruby said. "No more ruckus from that thing. But given time, something else may come."

"True, that's very true. You've been okay through all of this?" Cadence asked.

"You're sweet to check, not that anyone else cares."

"That's not true, Miss Jones." Cade admonished gently. "Ramon checks on you; you know that."

Ruby frowned. "Now, don't you let that good for nothing go fooling you, Miss Libby."

"I won't," Cadence said with a soft chuckle.

"Some of the spirits here don't know what's been going on. Most of them don't deserve the protection, sorry sons of bitches that they are. But for all of us, thank you. That thing would have picked through us all at some point."

Cadence smiled and nodded, then paused. "Miss Jones, can I ask you a question?"

"You can ask anything you like, Libby. I may not answer if I don't like the question, is all."

Cadence chuckled. "Okay, fair enough. If you're aware, why do you play at not being aware? Of your death, I mean. More than once now, you've talked about knowing you are a spirit, knowing others aren't aware of it. Why?"

Ruby gave the young woman a sly grin. "It's simple. I don't want that asshole Ramon's job."

Cadence shook her head, laughing, and rose from the chair. "I guess that's a fair answer. Have a good night, Miss Jones."

"You, too, Libby."

Cadence left the room and saw Ramon waiting for her by the door to the room he had stitched her up in. She made her way silently through the deserted and decrepit halls to him and into the room.

"I want to check your wounds," he explained. "You got some sleep before all of this excitement tonight, right?"

"Yeah, Snow pretty much grounded me until I got some sleep."

Ramon nodded. "Good, I'm glad. Take off the jacket." Cade slipped off her jacket as instructed and gingerly hopped up on the bed, where he patted it. He pushed up her sleeve and carefully removed the bandage. There was a long cut, but it didn't look as deep as she remembered, and Cadence couldn't see any stitches.

"I don't recall being that fast of a healer," she said.

"You don't heal like a breather anymore," he said. "It's all based on energy. You got some sleep, which helped replenish your energy. Hence, you healed up a bit. Your arm isn't going to need a bandage anymore. Let me see the leg."

Cadence dutifully pulled up her pants leg, revealing where the creature's tentacle had wrapped around to hold her. He unwound the bandages, and Cadence winced in spite of herself. The leg wasn't a simple scab like the arm was, and she had never actually seen the damage done to it. The stitches were still there, and in between, some parts had scabbed while some still seemed open and juicy.

"Oh, God." She moaned and turned her head to look anywhere but at her leg. "This is why I try not to look."

"You need more rest," he said, his mouth set in a stern line of concentration as he wrapped a clean bandage around her leg. Once that was all secure, he pulled her pant leg gently back down. "Okay, I need you to lie down and lift up your shirt a bit."

Part of Cadence wanted to tease him for handing her a straight line like that, but he caught the grin on her face and looked embarrassed. "I need to check the wounds, Cade," he explained needlessly.

"I know," she said and chuckled as she laid back on the gurney. "It's just where I come from as a female cop who hangs out with a bunch of guys every day, you just get used to having your mind in the gutter."

He laughed a bit; the smile seeming to light up his face and dark eyes. "I'll keep that in mind," he replied as he lifted her shirt up just enough to do what he needed. As he pulled off the bandages, even he winced. "This one is going to be the worst, since it's where you bend all the time. At least the stitches held tonight."

"How long before this one is all healed up?" she asked.

"Depends on how well you rest, but I'd say you won't be able to tell you were hurt at all within a week. You know, unless you go throwing yourself in front of hungry shadow creatures again before that." He smiled but remained focused on his work as he cleaned and re-bandaged her stomach and sides. It stung like hell, but she managed to keep herself still as he worked.

"Now, the tricky part," he continued. "Your back. You'll need to sit up and lean forward, but carefully so that you don't damage the front and sides." Cadence did as she was told and tried not to wiggle at the light touch of his fingers on her back.

"This is looking good back here." He did put another bandage on it, despite how good he said it looked. He lowered her shirt when he was done and walked back around.

"So, doc, what's the bill?" she asked with a grin.

He surprised her by actually taking a moment to think about that. She had expected him to wave the question away as he had before. "A conversation," he replied. He held up a forestalling hand as she opened her mouth. "Not tonight. I think we all need to rest after everything that happened the last few nights. But sometime soon, you owe me some time. Come by when there isn't a slavering monster beating down our doors. Come by, and we'll just talk."

Cadence looked at him uncertainly for a moment. "Ramon," she said as she frowned. Her mind raced as she tried to think of what to say and how to say it. Finally, she smiled a little and nodded. He didn't ask for a date. he didn't ask for a kiss. He just wanted a conversation. She could do that. "I'd be happy to," she finally said.

He grinned and offered her his hand to help her to her feet. She rose carefully, and he escorted her from the room. "Come back tomorrow night, so I can check the wounds again, okay?"

"You got it, doc," she said as she grinned.

CHAPTER 16

Putting Things to Bed

Aiden was fast asleep in his bed when Snow and Cadence walked in. Cade took her seat on the bed carefully, then looked up to Snow. "One of these days, you're going to have to teach me how to do this myself."

He smiled and nodded. "One day, I will, but not tonight. I think we've all had enough of a learning curve these past few weeks." He took her hand as she took Aiden's.

Cadence found herself by the merry-go-round in an amusement park. She saw Aiden on the ride, looking somewhat terrified, like he wanted to get off, but it was going too fast for him to jump. She walked over to the unattended control box and hit the button to bring the ride to a stop. Aiden hopped off as soon as it had slowed enough, and he went stumbling dizzily to the railing around the ride as Cadence made her way over to him.

"I had a feeling you might show up tonight. And thanks," he said, gesturing to the ride behind him. "Nice to know I have someone to save me from my nightmares."

"This isn't a regular thing; I don't just hang around to swoop in and save you from your dreams," she said. "But you're welcome."

"So, you're just going to pop in randomly?"

"I guess," she said. "I don't know. Ghosts and the living don't normally work together like we did. Our partnership is uncharted territory."

"What are you going to do if it isn't a normal dream?" he asked after a moment's thought, looking uneasy. "Like a sexy dream?"

"I can change your dreamscape, remember? I took you from the lobby at Lexington Hills to a forest."

"Oh, right. Thanks, by the way, for bringing Bethany to me to say goodbye. I hated saying it, but it was good."

"You're welcome. And thanks to you for everything you and your friends did tonight. We could not have done it without everyone's help. I'm so sorry about how things ended."

"Yeah," he said, frowning. "We called the cops, and they found Dan in his apartment. Lauren's still pretty upset."

"I can imagine. I'm sorry that we couldn't save him and that the night couldn't have gone differently."

"It sucks, but I get it," he shrugged. "I haven't even watched the tapes from tonight, but don't worry. I'll bury them."

"We appreciate it."

"So, are you riding off into the sunset now?" Aiden asked.

"Pretty much," she nodded. "I'm sure I'll see you again. Especially if you guys keep investigating haunted sites," she said.

"Do me a favor?"

"If I can," she replied.

"If you guys are hanging around, let me know?"

"I'll do my best, but it has to be within my rules when you have recording devices out. If we're in your apartment, however, put something on a shelf or a table that I can knock off to let you know we're there."

"You have a deal, detective," he said.

"Enjoy your amusement park." She waved to him, then opened her eyes, fading from his dream and into the bedroom once more. It took them only moments to teleport back to their office. They opened the door to find Alistair Croft sitting at Snow's desk.

Snow tensed. They had violated Croft's directive, worked with the NHD, solved the case, and had absolutely nothing to do with the desk duty he had ordered them to perform. Croft rose from the chair, looking sternly at both of them, his presence seeming to fill the room like a dark roiling storm cloud. But then suddenly, it was like light broke through the clouds and Croft smiled.

"Osmund, my boy, I knew you could do it!" he said as he came over to clap a floored Snow on the shoulder.

"You … You're not angry?" Snow managed to stammer, shocked by the sudden switch of mood.

"Angry? No! I did what I had to do to push you, to test your resolve. I must say, the two of you make one hell of a team." He nodded to Cadence. "The spitfire is a good compliment to your caution, Osmund."

Cade frowned slightly. She wasn't sure, maybe it was just the after-effects of everything that had happened, but the vibe coming from Croft was strange. Maybe he was pissed that they hadn't listened but couldn't argue since they got results. Maybe he was jealous of the rapport that she and Snow had developed. Maybe she was just imagining things because she had been through hell the last few days.

Snow smiled nervously. "Well, I'm glad you think so. She's a hell of a partner."

"She seems to be at that. Well, I just stopped by to congratulate you two on your accomplishment. Especially given it was your first real assignment together, not just a training case."

"I work better without training wheels," Cade said as she squeezed past the large man's figure to get to her desk.

"Right you are, right you are," Croft said as he moved so she could get by easier. "Yes, well, I know you have reports to file. I'll not keep you from it." He clapped Snow on the shoulder once more and turned, leaving the room and closing the door behind him. Both of them took their chairs and sank wearily into them.

"I feel like I could sleep for a week," she said.

"Me, too," Snow said. "I'd forgotten how draining it was to try to manifest and talk to them," he said as he referred to his shouting at Derrick to light the candles.

"We got it done, despite everything," she said. "No more beastie."

"True." He said and opened his drawer, pulling out the files of paperwork and tossing one across to Cadence.

"I still hate paperwork," Cadence said with a sigh.

Snow paused for a moment, then smiled a bit at her. "Why don't we leave it for tomorrow?"

She looked up at him, surprised, and then smiled back. "Wow, putting off paperwork? Procrastinating? I like the way you think, Ozzie."

"Then you'll love this. I think you've earned something, a prize of sorts, for getting through this. Are you up to visiting one last destination tonight?"

"I think I can manage," she replied, curious about what he had in mind.

He took her hand and that now familiar sensation of teleporting washed through her. When she opened her eyes, they stood in front of a large three-story Victorian home that had a chain-link fence around it, along with several warning and trespassing signs. The place had obviously been abandoned for several years; however, the street around it was anything but deserted. Streetlights shone on the sidewalk, and other houses on the street were well maintained and had lights on in them. There were even people out walking, talking, and laughing. This house, however, was dark and boarded up.

It didn't matter how it had deteriorated over the years or how much time had passed since she had been there. Cadence knew the place well, and her jaw dropped as she looked at Snow.

He gave her a kind smile and nodded as he gestured for her to go. "I think this reunion is well earned and long overdue."

Cade smiled and turned, heading into her brother's college dorm.

CADENCE AND SNOW WILL RETURN IN
DEAD VESSEL

"**W**hy was Mike Caulfield's ghost in the dorm today?"

"Well, that's why we're going to the man's home. To see if he's died," Snow said, curious as to why he had to explain this at all.

"And if he hasn't?"

"Honestly, Cadence, he must have. The man we dealt with today was no residual haunting or psychic trauma impression. This visit is simply to dot all the I's and cross all of the T's."

The house had Christmas lights on in front. Icicle lights hung from the eaves of the front porch, lights were in the bushes, and there were some white wire and light figures of reindeer in the yard. The lights were on in the living room.

"Awfully awake and festive for a dead man," Cade said dryly.

"He could have passed last night, and no one has found him yet," Snow suggested.

The door opened, and the Michael Caulfield from the newspaper picture stepped out onto the porch in robe and slippers. He went to the electric outlet on the porch and bent down, unplugging the outside lights. He then went back inside and the living room lights went off, too.

"Yep, he's obviously very dead. No one has found him. Nothing to worry about at all," Cade said in a dry, sarcastic tone, her eyes glued to the house.

"While sometimes I hate being right, I think I'm finding I hate it more when you are."

Author Bio

Growing up in a haunted house and having a father who loved horror set the stage for Amanda's creative life. This Urban Fantasy author has been writing since her teen years, blending horror, fantasy, and the paranormal. Amanda balances a day job, her writing, her family, and helps her husband run a board game group and YouTube channel, Tabletop Misfits. Local to Southwest Florida and a total geek, you can often find her conventions, either as a vendor or an attendee.

Book Club Questions

1. Aside from ghosts, what do you think is the theme of the story?

2. What is Cadence's biggest flaw? Snow's?

3. Was it worth it to break the non-communication rule?

4. What do you think the repercussions of Cadence and Snow breaking the rules could be?

5. Do you foresee the spirits working with the ghost hunters again? Why or why not?

6. What are your thoughts about Croft? Good guy, bad guy, or too early to tell?

7. How do you think the spell got into human hands? Who leaked it?

8. The title of Book 2 is Dead Vessel; how do you think that might play in to what you have already seen here?

9. Do Snow and Cadence make a good team, or do you think they would be better off partnered with others?

10. Lauren saw what Cadence did to Dan. Do you think she will eventually forgive her?

11. Aside from Snow and Cadence, who would you like to see develop as part of the normal team?

ROBERT J. LEWIS
Shadow Guardian and the Three Bears

VALERIE WILLIS
Cedric: The Demonic Knight
Romasanta: Father of Werewolves
The Oracle: Keeper of the Gaea's Gate
Artemis: Eye of Gaea
King Incubus: A New Reign

FANTASY

D. LAMBERT
To Walk into the Sands
Rydan
Celebrant
Northlander
Esparan
King
Traitor
His Last Name
The Inbetween
Hannah's Heart

DANIELLE ORSINO
Locked Out of Heaven
Thine Eyes of Mercy
From the Ashes
Kingdom Come
Fire, Ice, Acid, & Heart
A Fae is Done

LOU KEMP
The Violins Played Before Junstan
Music Shall Untune the Sky

R.J. YOUNG
Challenges of Tawa

VALERIE WILLIS
Cedric: The Demonic Knight
Romasanta: Father of Werewolves
The Oracle: Keeper of the Gaea's Gate
Artemis: Eye of Gaea
King Incubus: A New Reign

J.M. PAQUETTE
Klauden's Ring
Solyn's Body

DISCOVER MORE AT
4HorsemenPublications.com